# Family Myths

### Tamara Merrill

**AUGUSTUS FAMILY TRILOGY**
**BOOK THREE**

 KONSTELLATION
PRESS

Published by Konstellation Press, San Diego, CA. USA

ISBN: 978-0-9987482-2-1

eBook ISBN: 978-0-9905183-3-4

Cover Art by Teresa Espaniola

Images used under license from Shutterstock.com
Girl: sniegiro mariia/Shutterstock.com
Golden Gate Bridge:Radoslaw Lecyk/Shutterstock.com

Edited by EditorHelen/fiver.com

## Other Books by Tamara Merrill

Family Lies, Augustus Family Trilogy, Book 1

Family Matters, Augustus Family Trilogy, Book 2

Thank you to everyone who accompanied me on the long journey to publication of the AUGUSTUS FAMILY TRILOGY.

A special thank you to all four of the writing groups I've enjoyed working with during this process. Your support, encouragement, and tactful criticism help me grow as a writer.

And last but not least, thank you to the characters in these books. You've talked to me, been in my dreams, and some of you have become my friends. Now go away, so I can move on to another story.

To Buz

who was there at the beginning

# Table of Contents

**Epilogue**

# Prologue

The web of lies that had been created to protect the Augustus family secrets was directly responsible for Elizabeth's disappearance, but it was also responsible for the family's success and position in the community. The lies told to protect the family name were generations old, and through the years, the truth has been lost as the lies are now assumed to be the truth.

# Chapter One

Michael Augustus stepped through the door of the plane and paused at the top of the metal stairs. The hazy smog that filled the air did nothing to block the heat of the California sun. He took a deep breath and squared his shoulders. Shrugging off his jacket, he walked down the stairs and across the tarmac toward the group gathered just inside the terminal waiting to meet the arriving passengers. He spotted the private detective.

Ron Schwartz stood a head taller than anyone else, and despite his casual attire, there was an air of command about him that showed his military training. Michael lifted a hand in greeting and Ron acknowledged him with a nod. They fell into step, and Ron asked, "Any luggage?"

"Just this," Michael lifted his carry bag.

"Need anything before we hit the road? Ventura's about an hour drive." Michael shook his head, and they walked toward the parking lot together. They spoke only of the flight and the difference in weather. Both men tacitly agreed to wait for privacy before talking about Elizabeth.

Ron indicated his battered Chevy convertible with a wave of his hand and the men settled in. "I'm leaving the top up so we can talk unless you'd rather have it down."

"No, it's fine. What do you have this time, Mr. Schwartz?"

Michael Augustus had spent the cross country flight thinking of nothing but his family's search for his missing sister. Three years ago when his father, John Augustus had been informed of her disappearance from San Francisco State College, they'd known that she was angry and troubled, but no one thought she would vanish completely, that no police department or private detective would be able to find a trace of her.

As a teenager, Elizabeth had rebelled against everything. When she was told that John and Sylvia Augustus (her adoptive parents) had known her birth mother but had no idea who her father was, she railed against her privileged adoptive family for the lack of information. She wanted to know why Sylvia refused to act as her mother and lived in Paris. Even though she had admitted that Sylvia wasn't interested in being a mother to her birth son, she demanded different answers.

By her senior year of high school, she had begun hanging out with a group of older friends in the city, wearing nothing but black, and started to talk about "opening up her inner self and living authentically without material possessions." Michael had tried to reason with her, but she declared that unlike her family, her friends were "real" and that they cared more about her. She'd said that she was tired of him "always butting in" and that she wanted to "drop out and drop in". At last their father, John Augustus, allowed her to travel across the country for college and she had disappeared.

Michael refused to accept that she might be gone for good. He knew in his heart that she loved him as much as he loved her. He'd been her protector and her champion from the very moment of her birth, and he was certain that their strong connection would bring them back together again.

The day they'd learned of her disappearance, his Uncle Sam had insisted to his father that it was time to reveal to Michael the truth about his affair with Valerie Smithson. John had reluctantly agreed and admitted that he was, in fact, Elizabeth's birth father and that Michael's mother – Sylvia – had always known.

In addition to the secret of Elizabeth's parentage, he'd confessed that he was not Michael's biological father. And that he had no idea who Michael's father might be, explaining that Sylvia had taken this name to her grave.

Even now, Michael feels unsure about these secrets. He remained angry that John had never had the courage to admit to Elizabeth that he was her father, but he felt grateful that John had protected him from his alcoholic mother. John's promise to keep both secrets had meant that Michael had been allowed to live with John and Elizabeth instead of being relegated to boarding school and summer camps.

"Call me Ron," the PI's voice jerked him out of his memories. "There's a girl calling herself Lizzy Augustine that is about twenty-one, although she claims to be twenty-five. She's living in a commune in Ventura. I've got some pictures in that folder on the floor." Michael reached down and flipped it open as the PI continued his report. "I heard about her in Santa Cruz and came down here to take a look. She said she dropped out of school in San Francisco and has been living kind of rough ever since. When I first approached her, she didn't want to talk about the past, but since I've been hanging around the bar where she works, she's opened up a bit. She told me about dropping out, and that she came to California from the east coast. She's refused to talk about her family."

Michael flipped through the pictures again. "I guess there's a resemblance and the name makes sense. But Elizabeth never had light hair."

"Well, I can assure you this girl isn't a natural blond. Try to envision her with dark hair and a classier outfit."

"Maybe," Michael stared at the pictures again.

"Three years living rough can change a person."

*Three years changes everything,* Michael thought. *I wonder if Elizabeth will hate me when she finds out I joined the family business as soon as I got my MBA?* It didn't feel like a cop out to him, but he was sure Elizabeth would see it that way.

Three years had certainly changed his father. Each previous time Ron had called with a possible sighting, his father and uncle had swung into action. John was always excited and sure that this time the girl would be his daughter. Usually, he would quickly brief his cousin Sam on AmCo business, contact Michael at college to tell him about the sighting. John had then traveled, as quickly as he could, to see for himself the town or the person who reported the sighting. He'd been to Bend, Oregon, to Ocean Shores, Washington, to Yreka, Napa, Marin and Paradise, California.

But this time, with a new sighting and an actual girl to meet, John had shifted through the snapshots, only minutes after their arrival by special delivery, and declared. "I don't think this can be Elizabeth."

Michael and Sam had each taken the pictures; the PI proffered, and studied them carefully. "Ron thinks it might be," Sam had said. "She's about the right age."

"There must be a million girls that age in California. We paid the PI to find the right girl, to find my daughter." He'd shaken his head and returned the photos to the envelope. "I always thought Elizabeth looked like her mother, but I can't see any resemblance between this girl and Valerie."

"Dad," Michael had turned and stared out the window of his office attempting to compose himself. "I know you're discouraged, but if the detective thinks there is a chance, you have to go." The lights of the city were just winking on. The river caught the reflection of the setting sun, and for a moment, he'd allowed himself to feel the deep pain of losing his sister. He'd forced a smile and turned back to his father.

John had disagreed. "Someone has to go, Michael. But not me, I want it to be you. You've finished school, and you'll only need to be away a few days. I want you to find Elizabeth and bring her home. I want a chance to make things right."

Michael realized that Ron was saying something and forced himself to concentrate on the present, "What?" he asked.

"Just saying, that I'm sure that Lizzy isn't this girl's real name."

"Will she be working or do you have an address?

"I know where she lives. I thought we'd go straight there unless you'd like to get a look at her first. I figure surprise is a good idea – we don't want her to run."

Michael considered for a moment and then said, "If it's Elizabeth, I don't want to give her a chance to disappear before I have a chance to talk to her and if it's not – well, then it doesn't matter – so let's surprise her at home. Does she have a roommate?"

"Yeah, a bunch of them. She's living with a guy. They aren't married, and she has no kids."

"Kids?" Michael's shock showed in his voice, and Ron chuckled.

"A girl on her own for a couple of years," Ron grinned. "Any thing's possible."

"Does she sound like she's from the east coast?"

"Not really. But you don't either. Most kids that go to fancy schools just sound alike."

Michael wondered if that was an insult, but he thought it might be true, so he didn't rise to the bait and instead asked another question. "If it is Elizabeth, do you think she'll be glad to see me?"

Ron looked over at Michael and realized he was serious, "Not sure, kid. In this kind of situation, you get all kinds of reactions. Unless your Dad hasn't been honest with me, she doesn't have much reason to be mad. But on the other hand, she ran away, and it's been over two years since she communicated in any way – so I'd say – your sister wants to stay lost. And, if that's true, there's no way to guess what she'll do when she sees you. Like it or not, she's legally an adult now, and she can disappear if she wants to."

Michael looked down at the girl's picture, seeing Elizabeth as he remembered her. He'd been four years old the night of her birth, but he vividly remembered the bombs falling, the violent shaking of the earth and then the miracle of the tiny baby girl. It was also the first time he'd seen and heard Valerie's ghost. When the ghost told him the baby's name and gave her into his care, he had taken the message to heart, and he still believed that he was meant to protect and support his little sister. He flipped the folder closed and turned to Ron. "Is there anything else I should know before we get to the house?"

Ron turned the convertible off Highway 101 and onto California Street. Michael sat up straighter and took a deep breath. As they turned again on Main Street, Ron pointed at a building that was painted in bright, swirling colors and featured a mermaid with long red hair perched on a rock amid the swirls. "That's where she works, *The Siren's Song*. It's not a bad place, mostly a bunch of hippies. Not too rough."

Michael's head swiveled as they drove past. "Wow," he said softly.

Ron grinned, "Not like home, huh? This town's pretty easy on the "weirdo" kids, kind of a live and let live place. There's a bunch of them renting this place together. No one is older than twenty-five. It's a pretty open lifestyle if you know what I mean. Free love, drugs and all that shit." Michael stayed silent, not sure what to say, as Ron continued, "Just want to warn you, I'm not sure what we'll find. It's that gray house up there with the big porch. I'm going to drive past, so you can get a look at it before we go in."

Michael's eyes swept across the ragged lawn and took in the boy and girl sitting on the steps.

They were smoking and talking and even though the boy's hair was long, way past his shoulders, they looked pretty normal. The door stood open, and he caught a glimpse of movement from inside. An assortment of old furniture cluttered the porch and a big dog of some sort sprawled in the shade. "It doesn't look too bad," he said relief apparent in his voice. "That wasn't the girl on the porch, was it?"

"Nope, not sure which one she is. I think about fifteen maybe twenty kids are living here. Most of them are some kind of runaway or drop out. It seems to me Lizzy is one of the few that keeps a regular job. You ready?"

Michael nodded, and Ron swung the car around and cruised to a stop. They exited the car and crossed the street. Ron took the lead, "Hey, man," he said. "Lizzy around?"

The couple on the porch didn't move, but the man lived a hand and waved toward the door as he said, "Maybe, go on in."

Taking that as permission Ron knocked on the open door frame, but walked on into the house without pausing, and called, "Hey, Lizzy."

"In the kitchen," a girl yelled back, and they followed the sound of her voice. Ron stepped aside so that as the girl turned, she saw Michael first. "Hey," she smiled warmly.

There was no sign of recognition in her eyes and Michael's disappointment caused him to blurt out "You're not my sister."

"Sorry, man. I've got a brother, but I'll have to admit you're not him." She grinned. "Guess you were expecting someone else." Ron stepped into the kitchen, and she shook her head at Ron, "I should have guessed you were a PI, you asked way too many questions last time I saw you. But now that you guys are here tell me who you're looking for and I'll see if I can help."

# Chapter Two

Serena lay back on the grass outside the DeYoung Museum and stretched her arms over her head. She listened to the stillness and sighed deeply. If she were asked, she'd swear that everything was fine, but it wasn't. *I'm bored. I'm tired. I'm hungry. And I want to scream,* she thought. She pulled her arms back to her chest, clenched her hands into fists and sat up. Golden Gate Park might be her favorite place in San Francisco. There always seemed to be something to do and people to watch, but today she was working and bored.

This was definitely not the life she'd planned when she left school and struck out on her own. She looked at her watch. *I need to find Arabella.* If they didn't come back to the house on time, Maurice would ask too many questions, questions she had no intention of answering. *Someday soon,* she admitted to herself, *I'm going to have to leave here.* The Spencers might call her job a live-in companion for their daughter, but she called herself a glorified chaperone and a maid. Arabella would soon turn eighteen, and there'd be no more need for her presence.

She stood up and stretched. Looking around, she spotted Arabella and waved. "Time to go," she called.

The girl waved back and then reached down to pull a young man to his feet. They wrapped their arms around each other in a passionate embrace. Serena walked slowly toward them, hoping the farewell would be complete before she was close enough to be sure exactly whose hands were where.

The two separated slowly, kissed again, and when Arabella started to walk away from her date, Serena caught up with her and fell into step.

"Isn't he the cutest thing you have ever seen?" Arabella grinned at Serena. "And he's the best kisser I've ever known."

Serena wondered how many guys Arabella had kissed, but she only smiled and replied, "That was Mario, right? Where did you meet him?"

"Does it matter? Are you planning to tell Daddy?"

"Of course not, you know I promised that as long as you weren't doing anything more than hand holding and kissing, I wouldn't say a word." Arabella smiled a smug little smile and Serena knew her suspicions were probably right and that she was only pretending to herself that nothing more was going on, but as long as it didn't happen while she was with Arabella, it was none of her business.

"Tell me about the exhibit at the DeYoung," Arabella commanded, "in case Daddy wants to know what we did all afternoon."

The Spencers always ate dinner together, and Serena was expected to be at the table. However, she knew her place and didn't participate in the conversation unless someone asked her a direct question. She didn't really mind. It gave her a chance to observe the family and allowed her to make up stories about them.

Tonight the family conversation involved a discussion of an upcoming charity event, and she found herself smiling as she listened to Maurice supervising what "his women" should wear and to whom they should speak. She glanced at Arabella, who gazed at her father with what appeared to be adoration, but Serena saw how tightly Arabella's fingers clutched her linen napkin.

Mrs. Spencer – Henny to her friends but Mrs. Spencer to Serena – pushed her food around her plate, not eating anything at all. Serena knew Mrs. Spencer heard every word her husband said and would buy exactly the dresses he described, but it would be a battle to get Arabella to wear anything that her father called "sweet and girly."

Serena was delighted that she was not a member of this family. She'd thought her own family to be over bearing and controlling but compared to Maurice Spencer, her father was a real pussy cat. *It's funny how different, things look when there are three thousand miles between myself and my family,* she thought.

"I'm not going to wear anything that makes me look like Jackie Kennedy," Arabella blurted. "Let Mama do that. I'm too young."

"For once you are right," Maurice agreed. "You're only seventeen. You'll wear something sweet and soft, maybe pink. I think you look beautiful in pink."

Serena thought of the tight capri pants and the sleeveless shirt, tied at her waist that Arabella had worn to the park today. *It was a good thing Maurice hadn't seen that. He hated woman in pants.*

"I suppose you'd like Mama and me to wear Mother-Daughter dresses."

"Don't be silly, Arabella. It's not a tea," Mrs. Spencer snapped.

"Your mother will help you find something appropriate." Maurice folded his napkin and stood up. "If you ladies will excuse me, I have a meeting tonight."

They stayed at the table pretending to eat until they heard the front door open and close. Mrs. Spencer pushed her chair back and rose, "I'm going to my room. Please keep the noise down."

"Good night, Mother." Serena wondered how Mrs. Spencer could miss the sarcasm in her daughter's voice but if she noticed she didn't react and simply left the room without looking back. "Well," Arabella looked at Serena, "I guess I better get out of here so that I won't make any noise. The Kingston Trio is performing at the *hungry i* tonight. Want to go with me?"

Serena knew Arabella didn't want her to come along, but it was her responsibility to keep Arabella out of trouble, "You have to be twenty-one to go there."

"Doesn't matter, you're over twenty-one, and Mario works there. If anyone asks he'll vouch for me."

"I don't think it's a good idea. Your dad wouldn't want you to go to a night club."

"What he doesn't know won't hurt him." She grinned. "I'll just sneak out later if you don't come along." Serena knew that she would, and Arabella saw her waiver. "It'll be okay. I promise not to drink alcohol, and you might even have fun." Against her better judgment Serena agreed to go.

Serena sat at the table by herself in the back corner of the long room and toyed with her glass of Coca-Cola. *I should have brought a book,* she thought. Instead, with nothing to do and with Arabella off somewhere with Mario, she studied the other occupants of the nightclub and waited for the performance to begin. Over at the bar, a group of well-dressed young men were laughing and talking. They reminded her of her brother and his friends. She brushed the thought aside. It had been three years since she'd seen any member of her family and she'd learned that the easiest way to deal with memories was to simply refuse to think about them. She spun her glass again and scanned the room for Arabella.

"Hey, beautiful," a voice slurred at her, and she looked up to see a drunk swaying next to the table. "Wanna dance?"

"There's no music," she said, trying to be polite.

"Doesn't matter. Let me buy you a drink."

"I'm not interested."

"Sure you are. A pretty girl like you shouldn't be sitting here alone." He started to pull out the opposite chair, and she quickly reached across the tiny table, grabbed the chair, and held it in place.

"No. Really I'm waiting for someone."

"I'll wait with you."

"No, you won't, buddy." One of the men she'd noticed at the bar spoke firmly. "The lady said she's not interested."

The drunk seemed to realize that her defender appeared serious. Trying to preserve his dignity, he straightened his jacket, and spoke again, "You remind me of my third wife. She was a tease, too."

"Okay, buddy. That's enough. Move along." Her defender spoke confidently, and the drunk ceased his pursuit and stumbled away.

"Thank you," Serena smiled up at the man. "I could have handled him, but I appreciate the thought."

"I'm sure you could have, but I noticed you here by yourself, and I took advantage of the situation to come over and introduce myself. Logan Walker." He held out his hand, and Serena automatically extended hers.

"Serena. And I'm just waiting for someone."

"Wow! Who's this?" Arabella slid into a chair and grinned up at the young man. "I'm gone for a minute, and you pick up a good looking guy. Nice work, Serena."

"I'm Logan." He grinned. "But I think I was being banished not picked up."

"That's no surprise. Serena doesn't know how to have fun. Sit down, Logan Walker, and tell us about yourself." Logan took Arabella at her word and sat. "I'm Arabella Spencer, and this is Serena Miller. If you buy me a drink, I'll tell you all about myself."

Logan lifted his hand to signal a waitress.

"Nothing but cola, Arabella is not twenty-one, and I'm working." Serena glared at Arabella as she continued, "And you look like you've already had something to drink, Bella. What would your father say?"

"My big, bad daddy would be very mad at you, Serena."

Logan looked back and forth between the two young women. "Okay, I've obviously stumbled into a hornet's nest, but now I really want to know your story."

Mario saw Arabella talking to another man and arrived at the table with a beer. He pulled up the fourth chair. "I'm Mario," he introduced himself to Logan. "Get yourself a drink, man. This ought to be good. I've been wondering what the real story on this girl is." He hugged Arabella. "Tell us everything, babe."

"Everything? I don't think so." Arabella giggled. "No girl is willing to tell everything." Music surged and the *hungry i* announcer, Alvah Bessie, stepped in front of the red brick wall to introduce the opening act. "Oops, too late, guess my story will have to wait."

As the lights dimmed Serena thought she saw Arabella take a long drink from Mario's beer but she wasn't certain and instead of saying anything she let it slide. After all, she'd done the same thing when she was younger than eighteen.

Serena looked around the North Beach, basement nightclub. The room was often called a "cavernous entertainment room," and she could see why. Each of the three hundred seats, at the long bar and surrounding the three sided stage, were mostly filled with a clean cut, college-aged crowd. Since owner, Enrico Banducci, didn't allow drink service during the performance, the waitresses were hurrying to place ordered drinks in front of the patrons. Quickly the buzz in the room subsided. Comedienne Phyllis Diller took the stage, her wild hair flying in all directions, and she launched into a story about her husband, Fang.

Serena's laughter bubbled up and out, and she realized she hadn't laughed so fully in a long time. Logan's laughter matched her own, and they grinned at each other. Mario sat with his arm draped over Arabella, their chairs pulled tightly together. Serena was happy to see that they were also enjoying the performance and not making out.

Phyllis Diller concluded her act by introducing the Kingston Trio and reminding them that "the only reason they were famous tonight was because she'd had to take care of Fang and they'd been invited to fill in for her at *The Purple Onion*."

The trio bantered with her a bit and then struck the opening chords for *Tom Dooley*. The crowd roared, Phyllis waved goodbye and the next hour was completely magical as the trio sang one folk song after another concluding with *Scotch and Soda*. The last notes drifted away. Logan leaned closer and said, "Wow!"

"Exactly," Serena agreed. "I'm so glad Arabella talked me into coming tonight."

"Me, too." Logan smiled. "Now, may I buy you another soda?"

"Not tonight. It's time for us to head home."

"Don't be silly, Serena." Arabella interrupted. "We have plenty of time."

"And," Mario said, "Arabella promised to tell us all about herself."

Logan raised his hand to signal a waitress and Arabella reached for Mario's glass. Serena started to speak, but Arabella withdrew her hand and quickly said, "Don't worry, Serena. I'll have a Coke, please." She smiled sweetly at the waitress and then at Mario. "Come on, Serena. Let's freshen up."

The two young woman rose from the table, and Serena followed Arabella across the room. As they waited in line, Arabella teased, "That Logan is so cute and I think he likes you."

"Don't be ridiculous. We haven't said two words to each other."

"You need to learn to relax and have fun, Serena."

*Right,* Serena thought. *That's exactly what I don't need to do.* "We are having one soda, and then we are leaving. Okay?"

"Yes, Mam!" Arabella entered a cubicle. "I'll meet you back at the table."

When it was her turn, Serena stepped into her cubicle and closed the door. For a long minute, she leaned her head against the cool metal wall. "Relaxing and enjoying myself is exactly how I got here," she whispered.

When Serena rejoined the group, Logan rose to his feet and held her chair. She sat and murmured, "Thank you."

"Okay," Arabella took a breath and started, "here's our story. My daddy is Maurice Spencer."

Mario sat up straighter and took a gulp of his beer. "The famous Maurice Spencer?"

Arabella nodded. Logan looked blank. Serena kept her eyes on the table not sure how this story would go. "Yes, he's pretty famous." Logan's growing confusion showed on his face. Arabella continued, "He makes movies. Well, not exactly makes movies. He lends money to people so that they can make movies." Logan shrugged. "Doesn't matter," Arabella continued. "I'm his only daughter, and he's very protective of me. He's always worried that someone will kidnap me, so Serena is my body guard."

Logan and Mario both started to laugh. "Right, babe," Mario said. "She looks really tough."

"Looks can be deceiving," Logan said. "Serena said she was working so I guess that..." he smiled at Arabella, "that since you are someone semi-famous - she's some kind of reporter and she followed you to the *hungry i* - so that she could feature you in a tabloid story about your first night out on the town without your parents."

"I've been in a night club lots of times," Arabella protested. "But think what you like, I've told you our story, and I'm sticking to it. What's your story, Logan Walker?"

Logan looked directly at Serena as he answered, "I'm from Pennsylvania. I'm a sailor. I'm stationed on the USS Princeton. We are in port here in San Francisco for a few days."

"Shit, man!" Mario was visibly impressed. "I thought you were some college kid trying to pick up on my girl."

"He's not interested in me, Mario." Arabella grinned at Serena. "I think you should show this lonesome sailor the town, Serena." Serena shook her head. "Oh, come on. It'll be fun. You went to college here. I bet you know lots of great places to go."

*I know lots of places all right but none that I ever want to visit again.* "I'm sure, Mr. Walker has friends of his own," she said primly.

"Mr. Walker," Arabella mocked. "How la-di-da. If Serena won't show you the town, I will."

"I think I'd love to see the town with you, Serena." Logan turned to look directly into her eyes.

Serena met his gaze and couldn't stop herself from smiling. *He's certainly good looking,* she admitted to herself. She looked away, down at her hands, and then back to Logan. "How long will you be in San Francisco?" she asked.

"Just until Tuesday. I'm free on Sunday afternoon."

"So are you, Serena." Arabella interrupted. "It's a date, Logan. Do you have a car or should Serena pick you up?"

Serena laughed. "Okay. I surrender. I don't drive but I'm sure Mr. Spencer would allow his driver to pick you up."

"That won't be necessary. The ship's docked at Hunters Point. I can catch a shuttle, and we can meet in the city."

"We live in the Marina." Arabella couldn't refrain from helping with the arrangements. "Meet at The Palace of Fine Arts. It's so romantic."

"That's actually a good idea," Serena agreed. "Not because it's romantic, but it is beautiful, and we can walk from there to Cow Hollow and then through some of the neighborhoods, maybe even up to Golden Gate Park."

"I'd love that. I haven't seen any of the real San Francisco yet, just the Naval Shipyard and Fishermen's Wharf. Is one o'clock too early?"

"No. It would be perfect. But now we really do need to leave."

Logan flagged down a taxi and held the door for Serena as they discreetly looked away from Arabella's passionate goodbye to Mario. "Until Sunday then," Logan said closing the door.

Arabella slipped in on the opposite side and grabbed Serena's hand. "So? What do you think?"

"I think he didn't have any choice but agree to an afternoon of sightseeing with me."

Arabella giggled. "He wanted to ask you out, and I just gave him a little push because I knew you'd never go out on a 'real' date. And I know that you like him. I saw you blush!"

Serena allowed herself to relax. "He is very nice, and it will be fun to show the city to someone."

"Just don't bore him with all that history stuff."

"Some people like to know about that 'history stuff."

"Not on a first date."

"It's not a date," Serena protested.

"Oh yes, it is. You better just relax and enjoy it. What are you going to wear? Maybe you should borrow something sexy from me. You'd look really good in those St. Laurent slacks I bought at I. Magnin last week."

"I am not wearing hip-riding slacks out in public. I'm sure I'll find something in my own closet that will suffice for a walk around the city."

"With your small waist, you'd probably look better in my hip-riders than I do. But suit yourself."

On Sunday, Serena found herself remembering the taxi conversation as she searched for something to wear. It didn't seem possible that only three years ago she been ready and willing to flaunt every convention and take on the world. Now she was hiding behind a false name, in a nothing job, pretending to have an education that she'd never completed, with no clear plan for the future.

She settled on loose fitting gray slacks and a pale pink sweater set and dressed quickly, refusing to remember herself as the rebellious girl who wore nothing but black. She piled her long hair into a beehive, allowing the back to hang free. A few curling tendrils framed her face and made her eyes look huge. She found herself smiling. *It is not a date,* she reminded herself. But it would be fun to be out and about in the city.

Quickly she ran down the stairs and into the crisp, sunny fall day. The Marina District was busy with tourists strolling and admiring the beautiful homes; most of them hoping to catch a glimpse of a famous resident or two. Unlike many of the mansions on this street, the large Spanish style Spencer home was not connected to its neighbors but stood alone at the corner of Jefferson and Baker Streets. Just across the street from the lagoon. As she hurried away, hoping to avoid Arabella, an ocean breeze from the bay lifted her curls, and she caught a whiff of salt air.

The raucous calls of the sea gulls caused her to look up and focus on the deteriorating roof of The Palace of Fine Arts. It was a shame that the city had allowed the once magnificent building, built for the 1915 Panama-Pacific Exposition, to become so run down. The Palace was nothing but a deteriorating ruin, but none the less, Arabella was right, it did have a romantic quality. She glanced at her watch. It was one o'clock straight up. She quickened her steps and circled the lagoon, hurrying toward the crumbling dome.

Serena saw Logan a second before he turned, caught a glimpse of her, and smiled. She smiled in return, and he rushed forward and caught her hand. "You look very beautiful."

"And so do you!" Serena exclaimed. "I didn't expect a uniform."

"It's a regulation. We're required to leave the base in uniform, and we represent the military when we are interacting with civilians. Hence," he waved his hand across his chest, "the uniform."

"You didn't have on a uniform at the club."

"No, I didn't," Logan agreed. "But today is different. I was on leave then. Now I'm not."

"I don't know anything about the Navy."

"No problem. Today is all about getting to know each other, and the Navy is only one part of who I am. Tell me about this beautiful place."

Serena was pleased to tell the facts and legends she had collected about her adopted city. Talking to Logan was easy. He seemed interested in everything, asking questions and taking pictures with a small camera. "I can tell you love this city," Logan said. "Did you grow up here?"

"No," Serena shook her head and answered carefully, "I came here for college, and I stayed."

"Where did you grow up?"

"Nowhere special." Serena deftly, changed the subject. "How about you? I know you said you were from Pennsylvania but where exactly, and do you have brothers and sisters?"

'I'm from Monongahela." Serena laughed at the sound, and Logan grinned at her before he continued, "It's a small city, very small, close to

Pittsburgh. My dad is the high school principal and my mom took care of my brothers and me."

"Brothers?"

"There were four of us. I'm the youngest. They are all married and have kids."

"That sounds nice. I always wanted to have lots of brothers and sisters."

"Only those of you who grow up without them want them. Are you an only child?"

"No. I have an older brother, Michael. But I haven't seen him for a long time."

"Why not?"

Serena realized she'd said more than she wanted to and shrugged, "Oh you know... people grow apart."

Logan took her hand and squeezed it gently. "I'm sure you'll get back together, my Mom always says that, in the end, family is the only thing that truly matters."

*Not likely*, Serena thought and quickly pointed out the eight-sided Octagon House with its centered cupola. "The story is that it was built in this shape because scientists believed that if you lived in an octagon, you'd live a healthy and happy life. I don't know if that's true, but I think it looks like a giant's spinning top."

Logan chuckled. "I can see that."

With the conversation safely turned away from family, Serena relaxed and suggested lunch. They strolled along Union Street and settled at a sidewalk cafe for sandwiches and coffee.

# Chapter Three

It was cold at the lake house on Christmas Eve. A fire burned in the large ornate fireplace. As was their custom, the Augustus clan was gathering together. Sam and John sat, sipping hot buttered rum, and waiting for their various children to arrive. "Do you think that Elizabeth misses us?" John asked stretching his long legs towards the grate.

Sam considered his cousin. He wasn't sure how to respond to John's question. *If Elizabeth missed her family, there was no reason why she couldn't get in touch with them. She would be welcomed back by everyone.* He settled on the polite, expected answer, "I'm sure she does. Wherever she is tonight, she'll be thinking of family. Everyone thinks of family during the holidays. Perhaps this is the year you'll hear from her." He smiled at his cousin. "What time will Michael and Anne get here? Helen is hoping they will announce their engagement soon."

"They are a lovely couple," Helen agreed as she gracefully sank down on the sofa next to her husband. "Sam and I often talk about how kind Michael and Anne were to Sarah." For a moment, the three were silent each remembering Sarah and the sad months that followed the death of Sam and Helen's youngest daughter. Helen dabbed at her eyes and said brightly, "It would be lovely to be planning a wedding. I'm sure Elizabeth won't let Michael marry without her. Those two were always as close as two peas in a pod."

John hoped that she was right but how would Elizabeth know if a wedding was in the planning stages. Helen seemed to read his mind. "I'm sure no matter where she's living; she keeps up with the family gossip. Even without that awful Chatsworth woman and her nasty column, the press likes to report on our family. Just this morning there was a picture in the paper of Minette and Henry at a party in London."

"It's strange to be having Christmas without them. She was a bit sad about not seeing all the children."

"Speaking of children, they should all be here soon," Helen smiled at Sam. "Even Christopher has leave from the Air Force this year. He and Beth are driving up together. Peter and Evelyn will arrive late because their three children are in the Christmas Pageant but Jennifer and Geoff and the twins should be here in time for dinner."

Sam kissed his wife's cheek. "The mother of five and the grandmother of five, and you are as beautiful as the day I met you." He raised his glass in a toast. John smiled at their happiness. *It is at times like this that I miss Valerie the most,* he thought. *Our time together was so very short. If she had lived, life would have been so different. I would have been happier.*

Within a few hours, the big old house that Sam and Helen had lovingly restored, rang with laughter and holiday cheer. The cousins – all three generations – had grown up together; attending the same schools and spending holidays and vacations in the company of one another. Whenever they were together, the noise level rose rapidly. The conversation flew from one topic to another as they brought each other up-to-date and laughed together at old stories.

When the five grandchildren had been put to bed, the adults came back together in the living room. Christopher looked around at his family and raised his glass, "To Sarah."

"To Sarah," they responded and were silent for a moment.

"And to Elizabeth," Christopher continued.

"To Elizabeth," they chorused.

For a moment the only sound was the crackling fire. A record dropped on the turntable. The room filled with the voice of Bing Crosby singing *White Christmas.* Feeling watched, Michael turned and saw Valerie standing in the doorway. She smiled sadly, shook her head and faded away.

Anne took Michael's hand and squeezed it gently. "Are you okay? You look like you've seen a ghost." Hearing her words, Christopher caught Michael's eye and raised a questioning eyebrow.

Michael kissed Anne's cheek. "I'm fine, honey. Let me get you a fresh drink." He moved toward the cocktail cart. Christopher followed him.

With their backs turned toward the family, Christopher whispered. "It was Valerie wasn't it?" Michael nodded. Chris continued, "I didn't think you still saw her."

"At first when Elizabeth disappeared I saw her mother's ghost all the time but tonight was the first time she has appeared in a long time. Did you see her?"

"No. I just saw your reaction. Did she speak?"

Michael shook his head. "She just looked very sad." He lifted his glass and took a long drink. "I think she wanted to tell me something, but she just disappeared."

# Chapter Four

Serena woke late to the haunting sound of a fog horn. The last three Christmases had been dreadful. Most of the time, living her new life was fun, even exciting. But on Christmas she always found herself wondering what was happening at the lake house. Today she'd be with Logan, and she wouldn't be missing a thing. She stretched and smiled. This would be a merry Christmas.

Serena bathed and dressed quickly, pulling on her hose, straightening her seams, and slipping into her black pencil skirt and the bulky white mohair sweater that Arabella had given her last night. She slid her feet into Capizios, brushed her hair into a French twist and hurried downstairs just in time to answer the door.

"Hello, Beautiful," Logan smiled down at her. Serena lifted her face for a quick kiss.

"Hey, Lovebirds," Arabella called from the living room. "Where are you going so early on Christmas Day?"

"Just for a walk," Serena called back. She quickly stepped outside and pulled the door shut behind her.

"Aren't you coming to church with me?" Logan seemed confused.

"Of course," Serena took his hand, and they started down the path together. "I just wanted to get away without having to explain our plans to Arabella."

They walked the block to Marina Boulevard, swinging their clasped hands and enjoying the crisp breeze off the bay. Logan hailed a cab and directed the driver to Saints Peter and Paul. Serena hoped this wasn't a mistake. When Logan had suggested she attend mass with him on Christmas, she agreed without thinking it through. Her family had been members of an Episcopal Church but seldom participated in Sunday services. The private schools she'd attended had required weekly Chapel attendance. Her family hadn't been what anyone would call religious; it was more just something you did. *Oh well*, she shrugged, *in for a penny in for a franc*. It was too late to back out now. She grinned.

"What's so funny?" Logan smiled down at her.

"I was just thinking of something my grandmother used to say."

"Tell me about her. You haven't said much about your family."

"There really isn't much to tell. My grandmother was born in France, and her second husband is from England, so sometimes, she says things that are a bit mixed up."

Logan waited, and Serena searched her mind for an example that would be more appropriate than what she'd really been thinking. "Oh you know, just using the wrong word. She's lived in the states for a long time, but sometimes things just slip out. My brother and I used to try to get her to make mistakes, but she was usually way too smart for us."

"Did she live with you?"

"For a while. Then when my father came home from the war, she moved back to her own house. We still saw her almost every day."

"What about your mother?" Logan continued to probe.

Serena dropped his hand and pretended to search her purse for a head covering as the cab pulled over in front of the twin spires. Exiting the cab, she looked up at the beautiful rose window and changed the subject. "Look at all the poinsettias. Aren't they lovely?"

The inside the church was as beautiful as it was outside. Every statue was graced with pine boughs and more poinsettias. The sharp tang of the pine mingled with the incense and the candle wax.

The congregation, dressed in their best, smiled and greeted one another as they filed in, genuflected and took seats on the welcoming, heavily carved, pews. The organ soared, and the familiar strains of *A Child Is Born* filled the sanctuary with music.

Serena watched as the families, young and old, reverently followed the mass, responding, kneeling and praying together. Logan's deep voice twined with the others, and Serena felt at peace.

She remained in her seat when Logan rose and went forward for communion. She wondered how religious he was and if it mattered to him that she wasn't. She watched him return and kneel and then felt relief when he sat again and reached for her hand. *What am I doing?*

They exited the church. Serena felt her momentary unease lift. It was a perfect San Francisco day. The sun was shining, the breeze blew gently, and the entire city was sparkling with holiday cheer. Everyone seemed to be smiling at them. Logan pulled her hand through his bent elbow and held her close. He whispered in her ear, "I think they know I'm in love with you."

Serena stopped walking and stared at Logan. He grinned at her, "I love you, Serena Miller."

She knew she should walk away, but her heart was pounding. Logan was so close looking so happy. Instead of telling him the truth she said, "I love you, too."

# Chapter Five

The days between Christmas and New Year's Eve flew past. The Spencer's always gave a large party, and both Serena and Arabella were caught up in the whirl of preparations.

On the thirty-first, Serena joined Arabella at the beauty parlor to get their hair and nails done. They chatted about the upcoming party. Arabella confessed that she had invited Mario to attend and was worried that her parents wouldn't approve of him. Serena agreed but tried to be supportive by saying that she was sure it would be fine. After all, Henny Spencer would never let an unpleasant episode mar a social event. "I know that's true," Arabella agreed. "But..."

"But what?" Serena encouraged her to confide her fears.

"Mario is beautiful, but he calls me Babe."

Serena laughed. "Is that all? I thought you liked it."

"I do. But Daddy and Mommy will think it's low class and..."

"And?"

"And," Arabella took a deep breath and finished in a rush, "he rented a tuxedo for tonight and Daddy will know because a rented tuxedo never fits right and I don't think he has the correct shoes."

Serena almost laughed aloud, but she could see that Arabella was serious and she knew that, for Maurice Spencer, the keeping up of appearances was very important. "I'm sure it will be just fine. There are over 100 guests tonight, and Mario will blend in."

"No, he won't! I asked him to come early so that he could meet Daddy before the party starts." Serena's eyes widened. "I know it wasn't a good idea, but I thought it was, and now it's too late to take back the invitation. And ...." Serena nodded encouraging her to continue. "And, Daddy invited Mark Wainwright to be my date."

Serena sat down and tried to think what to say. She managed a shake of her head. "How long have you known that?"

"Since Christmas."

"Then why did you invite Mario?"

Arabella shrugged. "He was so sweet the day after Christmas. He gave me that little elf charm for my bracelet and when he asked me for a date on New Year's I just forgot about Mark and I asked him to the party."

"You either need to tell Mark that you have another date or call Mario and tell him. They can't both show up tonight expecting to be your date."

"I can't call Mario. He'll be so mad that he'll never speak to me again and I can't tell Mark because Daddy will be furious." She looked pleadingly at Serena. "Can't you call Mario and tell him I'm too sick to attend the party?" Serena shook her head. "Please," Arabella pleaded. "It's too late to do anything else."

Reluctantly, before they left the beauty parlor, Serena gave in. Arabella asked to use the phone, dialed Mario's number and handed the phone to Serena. Arabella pressed her head close to the receiver in order to hear both sides of the conversation. Serena stumbled a bit as she recounted Arabella's excuse.

Mario exploded. "What the fuck? What am I supposed to do now? I already rented this monkey suit."

Serena waited until he regained his composure. "It is New Year's Eve, and the whole city will be dressed up and celebrating. I'm sure Arabella won't mind if you go out with your friends tonight." Arabella glared at her and vehemently shook her head "no."

Mario seemed to consider for just a moment. "Yeah," he said. "I guess I'll do that. It'd be a shame to waste my rent money. I gotta say, I look pretty damn good in that monkey suit. You tell Bella to get well quick, and I'll give her a call tomorrow."

Arabella was furious. "What were you thinking? If he goes out tonight in a tuxedo, all the other girls are going to flirt with him."

"I'm sure it will be fine. You certainly didn't expect him to stay home alone on New Year's Eve, did you?" Serena knew that was exactly what Arabella expected and wasn't surprised when Arabella began to sputter a protest.

"Come on," Serena said. "We need to get home."

⁓

"It's almost midnight," Logan warned Serena. They stepped through the open French doors into the cool night air. A crescent moon hung low in the night sky and cast a romantic spell on the garden. Logan pulled her close. The strains of Ray Charles' big hit, *I Can't Stop Loving You*, drifted around them, floating on the night air. They swayed to the music, and Logan whispered in her ear. "When I hear this song, I'll always think of you." Serena lifted her face and welcomed his kiss. They pulled apart to chant the countdown to midnight with the rest of the guests. *Auld Lang Syne* began. They kissed again and held each other close.

Serena relaxed and allowed herself to drop her guard and savor the moment. It was a perfect evening. For the first time since she'd accomplished her disappearance, she allowed herself to believe that perhaps things would work out, that she could stop pretending and just be herself again. Logan kissed her, tucked a loose curl of hair behind her ear and spoke softly, "I need to tell you something."

Instantly, Serena stiffened and pulled back. "Hey, it's nothing bad. The ship is leaving on Friday, and we'll be gone for four months." Serena stood still barely breathing. Logan continued, "I know we've only known each other a few months, but I want to marry you." Serena started to speak.

Logan pressed his finger to her lips. "Don't answer now. I want you to think about it and write to me. When we return from this deployment, you and I can make plans." Serena nodded. She was stunned. Logan smiled, "You know I love you, right? I can't imagine anyone else I'd want to spend the rest of my life with. You're smart, funny, honest, kind and very beautiful."

*No, I'm not*, Serena screamed in her head. *I'm not who you think I am. I'm a fraud, a liar, a terrible person.* She reached for Logan and held him close. "I love you, too," she whispered.

Serena paced the floor. It was almost 5 AM, and she hadn't been able to sleep. Over and over she reasoned with herself. It should be easy to just tell Logan the truth. It really wasn't that bad. She'd changed her name and lied to get an id with a fake birth date. She hadn't really finished college, and for three years she'd hidden from her family. But she hadn't broken any laws. She wasn't doing anything that bad. She'd actually stopped living a wild lifestyle almost as soon as she'd started.

Sure, the first year on her own, she'd done some things she wasn't proud of, but nothing that bad; just too much alcohol, drugs, and sex. Nothing that all the kids she'd been hanging with hadn't been doing. She supposed her family was looking for her, but she didn't want to be found. She wasn't ready to go home yet. She wanted to prove something first. She wanted to find her "real father," and she wanted her "real father" to want her. She wanted to be happy.

She needed a plan. For the first time in a long while, she wished she could talk to her brother Michael. He'd always helped her even when he thought she was wrong. But, she admitted to herself, that wouldn't work. Michael was way too sensible.

He'd just tell her to come home and appreciate the family that she knew. That she should quit looking for someone who had probably died in the war. Someone who; if he did happen to be alive, had never shown any inclination of wanting to find her. At last exhausted, she laid her head on the pillow and fell into a deep sleep.

Serena sat drinking a cup of coffee, enjoying the peace and quiet, and thinking about Logan. The Spencers had all slept in after the late night and the morning had been hers to savor. But now she could hear them stirring. She was no closer to knowing how or what to tell Logan this morning then she'd been last night. Fortunately, he'd said he didn't want any answer until after the deployment, so she had a little time. She heard the loud thud of the paper arriving at the door, set her cup on the saucer, and went to retrieve *The Chronicle.*

Serena placed the paper on the table and looked at the front page. She smiled. The Spencer party was pictured. It was a great photograph of Mr. Spencer, Arabella, and Mark talking to Governor Pat Brown. The young couple was holding hands and appeared to be laughing at something the governor was telling them. *Mrs. Spencer will be delighted to see this,* she thought and poured herself another cup of coffee. She carried the coffee to her room before anyone else appeared.

Serena had just finished dressing when her door burst open, and a disheveled Arabella rushed in waving the paper. "Look at this. This is terrible." She pushed the paper at Serena.

"I saw it," Serena said calmly. "It's a great picture. Your mother will be very pleased."

"It's not a great picture. It's an awful picture."

Serena took the proffered paper and looked again to determine what she had missed. Seeing nothing bizarre, she waited for the explanation. "What if Mario sees this?" Arabella demanded. "You told him I was sick."

"That was your idea. Not mine," Serena reminded her. "I can see why this will be embarrassing. If he sees it. But maybe he won't see it."

Arabella brightened. "Maybe. He probably doesn't look at the paper. I never do." She smiled. "I bet you're right. If Mother hadn't shown it to me, I wouldn't have seen it." She perched on Serena's bed and grinned. "Wasn't the party a blast? Mark is a righteous dancer."

Henny Spencer appeared in the doorway, and both girls stopped smiling. Henny glared at her daughter. "Please do not use that awful slang. You have a visitor. He's waiting in the living room."

Arabella sprung to her feet. "Cool. I knew Mark would want to see me again."

"It's not Mark. It's someone claiming to be your boyfriend." Arabella gasped. Henny frowned and continued. "He's a very rude young man. He demanded to see you. Your father is with your visitor. He wants you to come down and explain yourself."

Seeing Arabella hesitate, Henny said coldly, "Now." Arabella looked at Serena, hoping for support but her mother intercepted the look. "Just you, Arabella, I'm sure your father will want to talk to Serena later."

Arabella crept down the stairs as slowly as possible trying to think of an explanation for Mario's claim. She could hear the raised voice of her father and the low rumble of Mario's answer. She squared her shoulders, lifted her chin, and entered the living room. Her father's back was to the door. She smiled radiantly at Mario and gave him a wink.

He didn't smile back. "Good Morning, sweetheart," Mario sneered. "How are you feeling this morning?"

Maurice swung around. Before Arabella could answer Mario's taunt, Maurice demanded, "Who is this young man? Why does he think he is your boyfriend?"

Arabella reached for her father. "Daddy, this is my friend Mario. I'm sure he's introduced himself." Maurice stepped away from her touch. "He's just a friend, Daddy. Not my boyfriend. I don't know why he's here."

Wanting to believe his daughter, Maurice turned to Mario and waited for his response.

Mario opened the paper he held rolled in his fist and confronted Arabella. "After I rented that damn tux and got a haircut, you told me you were too sick to attend the party last night. But it looks to me like you were only too sick to attend with me." He shook the paper angrily. "I guess I'm not your boyfriend anymore, Bitch."

"Don't you dare talk to my daughter that way," Maurice threatened.

Mario didn't flinch. He moved his gaze from Arabella to her father. "You need to watch your daughter." Mario started to walk away and then spun back to face Arabella. "I better not see you or your "nanny" at the club again." He ripped the front door open and gave it a resounding slam as he exited.

Maurice pointed at a chair. "Sit," he said. "How and where did you meet that creature? And what club is he talking about?"

From her bedroom, Serena could hear the raised voices, and she knew that Maurice would want to talk to her. It had been a mistake to allow Arabella to meet with Mario in the daytime and to cover for her dates in the evening. *Better go face the music,* she thought.

Serena and Arabella sat side by side on the sofa. Henny perched on the edge of a chair, and Maurice paced the floor. No one spoke. Serena felt Arabella relax next to her. *Perhaps things would work out.* Maurice stopped and glared at her.

"What were you thinking?" he demanded. "I hired you to be sure this kind of thing didn't happen. Not to help make it happen, and certainly not to accompany my underage daughter to night clubs. I thought you had common sense."

Serena gulped. Arabella pulled away slightly. *No support there.* She started to speak, but Maurice continued "I want you out of this house today. Now. The sooner, the better."

Serena nodded. She didn't protest. She knew that Maurice would never accept an apology or believe that his headstrong daughter was the problem. "And, as for you," he pointed at Arabella.

"You are not going anywhere without your mother by your side."

This time Arabella nodded. It could have been much worse. She knew it would be easy to get around her mother. *Henny won't give up her social life. Within a day or two, my life will be back to normal. Without Mario, maybe, but I bet they'll let me date Mark Wentworth.* "I'm really sorry, Daddy." Arabella reached up and hugged her father. This time he let her touch him.

"I know, honey." He kissed the top of her head. "I should have kept a closer watch on where you two were going and what kind of people Serena was introducing you to. Next time you need to tell me when someone suggests that you do things, or takes you to places, you know I'd find inappropriate. People always try to take advantage of pretty young girls, especially wealthy girls."

Serena worked slowly and methodically, trying to formulate a plan as she carefully folded her clothing and filled the luggage she'd received four years ago as a high school graduation present. She needed to find a cheap place to live and a new job. Her savings wouldn't last long.

Arabella knocked and came in without an invitation. "I'm sorry, Serena. I didn't think Daddy would fire you."   Serena knew that the apology wasn't really heartfelt.   She didn't speak but kept sorting and folding. "Don't be mad at me," Arabella coaxed. "We can still be friends."

*Not likely.* Serena began to pack her makeup and accessories into the small train case that matched her suitcases.   "I'll need to leave these suitcases here until I can find a room.  Do you think that will be a problem?"

"Of course not. Daddy's just mad.  I'm sure you don't really need to leave right now."

"I think I do," Serena said calmly. *I need to get out of here before Maurice decides to take a closer look at the references I gave him.* "It will only be a few hours. I'll call you before I come to pick them up." She closed and locked the train case. Dropped the tiny key into her pocket and looked around.  It had been a good place to hide for few months, but now she needed to disappear again. "When Logan calls, tell him I've moved."

# Chapter Six

Serena gazed out the window. She knew she'd been lucky to find a bed at the Chinatown YWCA. It didn't feel good, but it would have to do until she found another job and a place to live. She ignored the bustle of the busy street and the ripe smell of the Chinese market. The chatter of her roommates was simply noise. Serena was completely absorbed in thinking about her plight.

When she'd left college without telling anyone where she was going, she'd believed that it was the right thing, the only thing, to do. But now, here she was, sharing a twelve dollar a night room with three girls from Ohio. Unlike her, they had plans and jobs. They were moving into an apartment together. And while that wasn't what she wanted, she was jealous. She told herself that she wanted to be a free spirit, to live free, to be her real self. But, she admitted to herself, *what I really need is a job and some security. Then I can be myself.* Without skills or references, she wasn't sure how to accomplish that goal.

Serena turned from the window and focused on her roommates. They were buzzing with the excitement of having found a place they could afford. Serena forced herself to smile at them. "I'm so happy for you guys," she said. "How long have you been in California?"

"We moved out here in September," one of them answered. Serena didn't know which; she hadn't been paying attention when they introduced themselves. She didn't care; she was just looking for information.

"So, where do you work?" Serena asked casually.

"I'm an RN at Saint Luke's, Sally is a clerk at Walker Scott's, and Donna is a secretary at a law firm."

Serena was impressed. "I just moved here," she lied, "and I need to find a job quickly. Got any ideas?"

"What kind of work do you want?"

"Right now I just need a job. I've done a little bit of everything. I had to pay my way through college, so I've been working at whatever would fit into my free hours." Serena realized that that story didn't really work since it was January, and she quickly added, "I graduated last June and had a decent job for an insurance company, but I broke up with my boyfriend, and I wanted a new start, so I moved out here."

The three young women nodded. "Man-trouble is the worst. But don't worry. There's a lot of jobs available in San Francisco. In fact, I think we need a couple of file clerks where I work," Donna offered. "I'm not sure what they pay, but I could get you an interview."

"Wow. That would be super. Are you sure? You don't even know me."

"Women on their own have to stick together." Donna smiled broadly. "We're going to get Chinese food to celebrate finding an apartment. Want to come with us?"

Serena grabbed a jacket and joined the others. She listened as they chattered but was careful to say as little as possible about herself. The idea of landing an office job was appealing, and she didn't want to miss out on the interview opportunity.

Donna was as good as her word, she quickly set up the interview. Serena chose her clothes with care, she wanted to look professional. Her pencil skirt and cardigan set were much like the clothes Donna wore to work each day. Serena brushed her hair back into a clip and wore only lipstick. As she walked the few blocks from the YWCA to the law firm on Clay Street, Serena rehearsed her story. She'd never worked in an office before, but it certainly couldn't be too hard to file things. She knew the ABC's and she could read; what more could it entail? She decided to claim experience working for an uncle while she was in school. She pushed the heavy glass door open and presented herself to the receptionist.

"Here you go, honey." The receptionist handed Serena a clipboard with a form attached. "Just fill this out and when you're ready Mrs. Albrecht will see you." She winked broadly. "Don't look so scared. If you can walk and talk, she'll give you a job. I happen to know that they need three new girls fast."

"Why?" Serena was surprised to hear a slight quiver in her voice. She cleared her throat and asked again, "Why do they need to hire three?"

"There's been a change in management recently, and the file room is a mess. They have to get it cleaned up and working right, or heads are going to roll. If you need a job, this is your lucky day."

Serena filled in the application. She would stick to her story that she was new in town and looking for both a job and a place to live. She chose to use Andrew Miller for her uncle's name and made him an insurance broker, just in case Donna had mentioned that she used to work for an insurance company. Counting backward, she gave herself five years of part time experience working in his office, from age fifteen to nineteen. Then to make it real, she added a couple of student jobs during her "college years" and signed her name.

The receptionist checked the form and squealed, "Oh, you're from New York. I always wanted to go there."

"Manhattan, actually, and believe me the weather is much better here." Serena smiled at her excitement. "I always wanted to live in California, and now I'm here."

"I'm Mandy." The receptionist wiggled like a happy puppy. "I hope you get the job. I'll keep my fingers crossed for you."

Mandy had been right. Mrs. Albrecht, the office manager, barely glanced at the application. They needed three clerks, and they needed them fast. Serena was a college graduate, she looked over qualified, but she was available to start immediately, and so the job was hers. The $1.50 per hour she'd earn would be enough to rent a tiny apartment in the city. Serena knew she couldn't afford to live by the college or in the Marina, but that was for the best. The last thing she wanted to do was run into anyone who knew her. Walking back to the YWCA after her interview, she took the long way and watched for rental signs. She needed a place of her own, no roommates.

Above almost every commercial space, she could see apartments but few rental signs. Turning down Taylor Street, Serena's eye was caught by the building at 520. Its turn-of-the-century bay windows sparkled in the sun. Looking up, she saw an elderly woman setting a birdcage on the wide sill of an open window. The woman waved to her and Serena waved back.

That's a sign, she thought and, sure enough, posted on the door was an advertisement for a furnished studio apartment, utilities included for $49.50. It sounded like exactly what she needed. Serena rang the buzzer for the manager's apartment and prepared to tell her story again.

# Chapter Seven

On April first, Serena followed Logan's instructions and called the number for Ships Movement. She waited as the recorded voice read, in alphabetical order, the details for the Naval vessels current arrivals and departures.

When she'd said goodbye to Logan in January, she'd been uncertain of what her future held. Now with a good job and an apartment of her own, she was looking forward to seeing him. For the past three months, Logan's letters had been very supportive and loving, and she had responded in kind. She hadn't mentioned his marriage proposal, and neither had he, but Serena knew that he would want an answer when he returned. If she loved him, and she thought she might, it should be easy to say yes.

The voice finally reached the USS Princeton. She focused her attention and jotted "3 PM Friday - Hunter's Point" on her desk pad, hung up the phone, hooked her hair behind her ears and returned to her work with a smile.

Finding the job as a file clerk had turned out well. The work was easy, and she knew that the office manager and the attorneys liked her. It wasn't her dream job, but it was certainly much easier to work with a bunch of files than it had been to live with the Spencers. Serena spent her free time, and weekends, wandering the nearby streets of Chinatown and Haight Asbury finding inexpensive treasures that she used to personalize and fix up her studio apartment. She admitted to herself that she was a bit lonely sometimes, but it was wonderful to answer to no one.

As Serena walked home through the April sunshine, she pondered what she was calling the "Logan Question." She had three days to make a decision. He'd explained that the unmarried men usually accept duty the first night in home ports so that the married men could be with their families. So, she thought, I might have four days. But even if he didn't get to leave the ship the first night, she'd soon need to respond to his proposal.

Friday afternoon, standing on the pier surrounded by excited women and children, Serena waited for the Princeton to dock. Everyone seemed to be wearing a combination of red, white, and blue and she was glad that she'd chosen her navy suit, a crisp white blouse and her navy and white spectator pumps. Small boys dressed in Cracker Jack uniforms darted in and out of the crowd waving flags and chasing one another. The women all seemed to be about her age or even younger but it looked like everyone had at least one child. Many seemed to have two, or three, or more. There were small babies everywhere. *But,* Serena noted, *everyone looked happy.*

"Who are you here to meet?" a voice with a decided New Orleans twang asked.

Serena turned. The young woman standing next to her was breathtaking. Her dark auburn hair fell to her shoulders in a smooth wave. Her green eyes sparkled and the red dress she was wearing hugged her curves. Serena was dumbstruck for a moment, and then she grinned. "Logan Walker. Who are you meeting?"

"Steve Martinelli, Master Chief, whatever that means. We only met three days before this damn ship went out to sea and I hope I can recognize him."

Serena laughed. "Don't worry. In that dress, he'll find you."

"I love to wear red. My mama said I couldn't because of my hair, so now that I'm on my own I wear it all the time. I'm Mary Lou McGuiness."

"Serena Miller. And I think you look spectacular."

"I think we might be the only two women waiting for this ship that have no children." Mary Lou grinned again, and Serena laughed.

"I was just thinking the same thing. Do you have any idea how this works? I've never met a ship before."

A tiny woman with a baby in her arms turned toward them and said, "I didn't mean to eavesdrop but..." she shrugged. "I'm Pamela Brighton. My husband is the XO on the Princeton. When the ship rounds that curve," she pointed, "you'll see the men manning the rails. The wives and kids will go crazy. The ship will tie up, and the guys will stream off, enlisted first and then officers. Just watch for your guys and start waving like crazy when you see them."

"What's manning the rails?" Mary Lou asked.

Pamela laughed. "You really are new at this. The ship's crew stands at ease, shoulder to shoulder along the deck, facing out toward the shore. It always makes me cry a little."

Mary Lou nodded. "Okay. One more question, what's an XO?"

"Executive Officer." She blushed. "Gary is second in command on the ship."

"That sounds important." Mary Lou tossed her hair back and continued, "I guess if I'm going to marry my guy I'll need to learn all this stuff. Steve already told me he's going to stay in the Navy for thirty years."

Serena looked at the women around her. The excitement was palpable, but now that she thought about it, she could feel more than that. Everyone was talking and telling stories, complimenting one another, commenting on babies and laughing at the antics of the children. *It was like a club,* she thought, *an inclusive club.* She wondered how many of them had secrets. How many were not really who they appeared to be. Or was she the only one?

A shout went up, and her attention was drawn to the approaching ship. Women straightened their stocking seams, smoothed their hair and gathered their children close as they began to wave and shout to the sailors manning the rails.

The ship pulled alongside the pier and lines were tossed to sailors waiting on shore. Now the men on board were shouting and waving to the excited crowd. The noise was deafening. Everyone was eager to be heard and seen. Finally, the gangplank stretched across the gap and sailors poured off.

Mary Lou grabbed Serena's arm and shouted, "There he is. That's my Steve." She tugged Serena forward. "Come on, let's go meet our guys." Mary Lou's excitement was contagious. Serena allowed herself to be swept along in the tide of families surging toward the disembarking sailors. All around her couples were laughing and crying. She watched Mary Lou be engulfed in a bear hug and saw Pamela reach up to greet a tall, handsome man. She noted what a beautiful couple they made and then turned at the sound of her own name to find Logan grinning down at her. He swept her into his ardent embrace.

Breaking apart, Logan kept his arm tightly around Serena. He looked her over carefully and smiled broadly. "You look great. Come on." He turned her without removing his arm, "I want you to meet my XO."

Serena offered her hand to Commander Brighton and smiled at Pamela. "Thanks again for your help," she said and explained to Logan, "Pamela told us 'newbies" what to expect."

"It was a pleasure to meet you, Miss Miller." Serena started to protest that he should call her Serena but the commander continued. "We need to get back on board. I'll see you tomorrow, Pamela."

Logan quickly gave Serena a kiss and a squeeze. "I'll be off about 8AM, and I'll be at your place by 9:30. We'll have breakfast and make our plans."

Without a backward glance, the men moved up the gangplank, smartly saluted the deck officer, and disappeared through an opening. Serena stared after them. Pamela shifted the baby and touched

Serena's arm. "Navy first," she said. "You'll get used to it. Come on. Let's go get a drink, and I'll tell you my story, and you can tell me yours. The O Club is right over there. Just leave your car, and no one will bother it."

"I came in a cab." The two fell into step. The family groups were dispelling rapidly. Pamela acknowledged a few hellos as they crossed the pier, but she stayed mostly silent until they reached a large black Buick.

"Hop in. I'll drop the baby at home and then we'll go enjoy our last night of freedom."

"I thought you said the O Club was on base."

Pamela smiled sadly. "It is. Everything is on base."

# Chapter Eight

Michael and Anne strolled together, holding hands and talking. The cool spring air was filled with the smell of new grass and blooming trees. They were deep in a conversation that had gone on for months. "I'm really worried this time," Michael said. "Dad hasn't been to work for over two weeks, and neither Sam nor I can get him to talk."

"He's sad, Michael." Anne squeezed his hand. "You know he feels Elizabeth's disappearance was his fault and it hasn't gotten easier for him over the years."

"I tried to get him to talk to a doctor, but he just got angry and told me it was none of my business."

"He's going to join the rest of the family at Sam and Helen's for Easter, isn't he?"

Michael nodded.

"I like your Dad, Michael, I'll try to get him to talk to me, okay?"

"Thanks, honey. Maybe he will talk to you, not about forgetting Elizabeth, but about moving forward. None of us will ever stop looking for her or missing her."

Anne stayed silent. She had some decisions of her own that she needed to make. She and Michael had started dating when she was sixteen, and now, nine years later, they were still just dating. Her friends were planning weddings, or were married with children, and she wanted to do the same. She was tired of being a bridesmaid and never the bride. *Talk about needing to move forward,* she thought and shook her head slightly.

"What's wrong?" Michael asked.

"Nothing." Anne pointed at a window display. "Look at that hat. I don't know anyone that would wear that thing."

Michael laughed. "You'd look great in that bikini though." He pointed at another display.

*And I might buy it,* Anne thought, *if we were going on a honeymoon.*

Holidays at Sam and Helen's lake home had become a family tradition. No invitations were needed, and everyone knew they were welcome to bring guests. Helen loved hosting family and friends. She had always decorated the entire house, and served delicious food. Now that there were grandchildren, she made an even greater effort. Michael and Anne drove up the curved drive and the rambling stone house came into view. Michael slowed the car to a crawl, and Anne laughed aloud. "Are those real rabbits?" she asked.

"I think those would be Easter Bunnies." Michael shook his head in wonder as they slowly drove past the frolicking children and their new pets. They parked along the edge of the drive and greeted the gathered adult family members. "Aunt Helen, you've out-done yourself this time."

Peter Augustus threw his arm over his mother's shoulders, "I love you, Mom, but we live in the city in a no pet building."

"I know," Helen acknowledged his complaint. "But it's not as bad as it looks. I borrowed the bunnies from the petting zoo, and I told the children that they are just visiting because it's Easter."

Sam laughed at his son. "You know your Mom thinks of everything and just look how happy your city children are."

Laughing and chatting, they moved to the wide porch and settled in, ready to catch up on what had happened in each life since the last family gathering. Sam poured a refill of coffee for Michael and asked, "Where's your Dad? I figured he'd drive up with you and Anne."

"Nope, he said he wanted to drive himself because he might want to stay over."

Sam nodded. "Good. We don't see enough of him lately. A few days in the country eating Helen's fine cooking, might be just what he needs."

"I hope so, Sam."

The church bells woke Serena on Easter Sunday. She lay in bed; her head cushioned on Logan's shoulder, watching a butterfly make lazy loops outside her window.

Logan stirred and smiled sleepily. "Good Morning, Beautiful." He kissed her temple. "What are you frowning about so early in the morning?"

"I wasn't frowning," Serena protested. "I was just watching a butterfly and thinking about things."

"Things like marrying me?"

Serena distracted him with a kiss. "Things like breakfast," she said kissing him again. "Rise and shine, I'm hungry."

Logan groaned good-naturedly and pushed back the covers. "You can change the subject, but you can't avoid the question. I want to marry you, Serena Miller. And I want to marry you soon."

Serena laughed and headed for the bathroom, pulling her robe on as she went. "Make some coffee, please." She pulled the door shut behind her and sank down on the lid of the stool, overwhelmed by her thoughts. During the two weeks that Logan had been back in San Francisco, they'd had so much fun. *He's easy to be with, loving, kind, generous, smart, and good-looking, exactly what I'd want in a husband, if I wanted a husband,* she thought.

Serena and Logan had spent every minute together that she wasn't at work and he wasn't on the ship. He slept at her apartment, and the sex was great, but marriage was impossible

Even if she'd thought it might the right thing to do, her evening with Pamela Brighton at the O Club, the night the ship docked, and then a party at the Captain's home had convinced her that Navy life wouldn't work for her. Pamela had shown her that the life of a Navy wife was determined first by the Navy and then by the demands of her husband's particular job and everything else came after that. At the party, she'd watched and listened as the women were judged entirely on who they were married to, or dating, and what rank that person held. She'd been looking forward to seeing Mary Lou McGuiness again and meeting her guy, but when she'd asked if they were expected, the Captain's wife had looked down her nose at Serena and explained that enlisted men were not invited to this type of event, ever.

She could smell the coffee brewing and knew she couldn't linger in the bathroom any longer.

Pulling a quick brush through her hair and straightening her shoulders, she pushed the door open and joined Logan. He was too much fun to stop seeing, but she'd have to find a way to postpone marrying him. *Maybe an engagement would be okay.*

Logan had opened the tall, wide window that overlooked Taylor Street and the bright, warm sun lit every corner of her tiny apartment. He handed her a cup of coffee and perched on the window sill. "I love this apartment." He smiled at her, "But it's very small, and we'll need a much bigger place after we are married." Serena took a drink to avoid answering. "Of course, we can move to housing and then you'll have the other wives to keep you company when I'm gone."

"What about my job? The base is too far from where I work," Serena protested, forgetting for a moment that she'd promised herself to stay out of conversations about marriage.

"Oh, you won't want to work. The Navy will keep you busy, and you'll want to stay home with the kids."

"But I like my job, and I'm not even sure I want to have children."

"Don't be silly. Of course, you want children. Don't you think we'll make beautiful babies?" Logan grinned at her and Serena allowed herself to smile in return.

"Yes, but that's not the point. I don't think I'd be a very good mother."

"You would. I know you would. You're smart, funny and sweet. You must have had a great mom. All you have to do is do exactly what she did."

Serena's hand shook, and she had to set her coffee down quickly to avoid spilling. *Exactly why I don't want children,* she thought. *I'm not honest, and I certainly don't want to be anything like Sylvia.* Logan looked concerned. "Are you okay," he asked.

"Just hungry. Let's walk over to David's Deli and have lox and eggs for breakfast."

"It's Easter Sunday. My mom would be scandalized if I eat Jewish food and skip church. I want to take communion but you go ahead and have a piece of toast or something, and I'll take you out for brunch after mass."

Serena stared at him, her eyes wide. "Doesn't your church disapprove of premarital sex?"

"It does, but I went to confession yesterday, and I believe that God understands about young people in love."

*Perhaps Logan isn't so perfect after all,* she thought. "You go. I'll wait here and read the paper until you get back."

A few minutes later, Logan reappeared fresh from the shower but dressed in casual clothes. Serena raised her eyebrows, and he smiled sheepishly, "You're right," he said, "I'm not sorry that we are in love and that I like making love with you. I'll skip church. Get dressed, and we'll go to the deli."

Serena started to apologize for questioning his belief but stopped. *I refuse to be one of those women who do whatever their man wants,* she reminded herself.

꧁ೋ꧂

Quiet descended on the lake house as the last car drove away. Sam and John sat on the wide front porch watching Helen round up the rabbits. They laughed at her antics. Sam said, "It's good to have you here, John. Helen misses having a full house." John nodded but remained silent.

Having succeeded at penning the rabbits, Helen joined them. "Come on, you two, it's getting chilly out here. Let's go inside and have a glass of brandy." The cousins followed her into the cozy living room and settled in. The silence stretched comfortably between them as they sipped their drinks and watched the sun set over the lake. Helen settled into a chair and picked up her knitting.

"This is nice," John finally spoke, "very nice. I hope you two know how lucky you are to have each other."

Helen laughed and then smiled fondly at Sam, "We do, John. Sam and I have been blessed but so have you. Michael is a wonderful young man, and you just have to believe that Elizabeth will come home someday soon. You need to let yourself be happy." Sam stayed silent, knowing that his wife was better at this kind of conversation than he could ever be. "When Sarah was born with such a terrible birth defect, I thought the world would end, but it didn't. She was with us for twenty amazing years, and despite the heartbreak, I wouldn't give up even one of those memories. You shouldn't stop believing that Elizabeth loves you enough to come home either."

John's voice broke as he spoke, "It's not the same thing, Helen. I drove her away. I'm guilty."

"You don't think I felt guilty, John? Of course, I did. I still do. I was Sarah's mother. I know that something happened to her even before her birth; something I did led to her premature delivery. I used to hate myself for causing her pain, and I would still do anything if I could change the circumstances. But

I can't. You did nothing but love Elizabeth in the way that you thought best. She chose to leave, and she can choose to come back."

"I should have told her that I was her father, her real father, not just her adopted father."

"Perhaps, but it really doesn't matter now. You need to forgive yourself and allow yourself to live. Michael needs you and, frankly, we all miss the man you were. Don't you think Valerie would have wanted you to remarry and live a full and happy life?"

"Valerie and I were never married."

"Perhaps not in the eyes of the law but you were in love, you had a child that you both wanted, and if the war hadn't intervened, you would have raised Elizabeth together and, most likely, raised Michael, too."

"Sylvia never would have allowed that."

"Sylvia did allow that, John. She went to Paris and left Michael with you. Stop thinking about what might have been and start creating your future. You're a young man. It's time to start living again."

"I'm fifty."

"Yes," Sam entered the conversation, "and your grandfather died at ninety-five. You're only half way there. You still have half your life to live, and we want you to be happy."

"I can't be happy until we find Elizabeth."

"Yes, you can. You'll always miss her and search for her and hope for her return, but you can be happy." Helen said. "I'll never stop being sad that we lost Sarah, but I am happy. I can enjoy the rest of the family, I can live my life, and I want you to have that, too." She took a deep breath and smiled warmly at John, "We love you. Michael loves you. Please try."

John twirled his glass and looked out the window. Sam and Helen waited until he turned, tears filling his eyes. "I'll try," he said. "I think I need help, but I'm ready to try."

"Anything you need, Cuz. We're here for you."

"Michael suggested I talk to a therapist and Anne seems to agree. What do you think? Will it hurt the company if it gets out that I'm crazy?"

"John!" Sam almost chuckled. "If nothing else, I hope we've learned the Augustus family lies are not important to anyone but the Augustus family. It's time we all live the truth and let the arrows fall where they may. There is no shame in seeking help from a doctor when you need it."

"But…people will talk."

"So what? They've always talked about our family. Maybe it would be good to give them the truth to gossip about.   Remember that awful Chatsworth woman and her gossip column?"

John smiled and grinned at his cousin, "Oh God.  Granddad hated it when we were mentioned, and we always were."

# Chapter Nine

Life had fallen into a rhythm for Serena and Logan. The other tenants in their building assumed they were married, and Serena didn't dissuade them. Mostly, they kept to themselves. Serena went to work Monday through Friday. Logan had duty every three days, which meant he was gone every third night. It was kind of boring, Serena admitted to herself, but not in a bad way.

On July twenty sixth, the weather reached a record breaking ninety-six degrees. Serena slipped into the ladies room and removed her hose before leaving the office. She put her sandals back on, wiggled her toes, enjoying the freedom, and left the building. Her summer dress swished against her bare legs. Out on the street, instead of walking the few block back to her hot apartment, Serena swung herself up onto a trolley headed for Fisherman's Wharf. She returned the smile of a young man who was admiring her legs, tipped her head back and let the wind play with her hair. She sighed.

"You're looking mighty fine, Missy."

Serena opened her eyes and grinned at Mary Lou McGuiness. "So, are you!" Serena took in the cascade of red hair, the pure white sun dress, and the broad brimmed straw hat but mostly, she saw the broad smile. "I wondered about you. Did you get married?"

"Not yet, silly. But we will be before the ship leaves port again. How about you? How's your handsome sailor?" Mary Lou noted the shadow cross Serena's face and quickly finished. "Let's get a long, cool drink by the water and talk about life."

The trolley came to a stop at the wharf, and Mary Lou jumped off. Serena followed. "Come on," Mary Lou said grabbing her hand. "There's a great new place back here called Tarantino's."

Sitting at a small table on the wharf, under a striped umbrella, and sipping tall cool cocktails, Serena allowed herself to relax as she listened to Mary Lou chatter away. It had been a long time since Serena had had a girlfriend, but, even now, she knew she needed to keep her guard up. She was living with too many secrets to really let anyone into her life. "Goodness, Mary Lou, didn't you just move here? How in the world do you know so much about the Navy and the people on the Princeton?"

Mary Lou grinned at Serena. "Steve's a chief, not a la-di-da officer. He loves his men, and we see them and their families all the time. They call him for advice on everything, and," she shrugged, "I'm kind of bossy, so I get involved."

Serena laughed. "I'd say friendly not bossy."

"You don't know me very well. Trust me. I'm bossy. Last week there was this kid that thought he wanted to marry a fifteen year old girl. You better believe I set him straight in a hurry." She dropped her voice, "See that sailor at the end of the bar?" Serena nodded. "His wife just had a baby. Stay here. I'm going to remind him that he needs to be at home with her, not drinking in a bar."

Serena watched as Mary Lou spoke to the sailor and gave him a hug. The sailor obediently left the bar, and Mary Lou sauntered back to the table, smirking at Serena's surprised look. "See, I'm bossy."

They laughed together, and Serena asked, "What did you say?"

"The words aren't important. It's all in your tone. I have five brothers, and I learned early how to make them do what I want. My mama always said, 'A southern woman knows how to get exactly what she wants and smile while she's doing it.'"

"And what do you want, Miss Mary Lou?" Serena teased.

Mary Lou's smile faded, and Serena was afraid she'd asked a rude question. Mary Lou took a sip from her cocktail and answered, "I used to want to be rich and famous, maybe a movie star or something, but now I want to marry Steve and be the best Navy wife in the whole damn US Navy. Maybe have a whole bunch of kids." She dipped her glass and drained it. "How about you, kid. What do you want?" When Serena didn't answer, Mary Lou continued, "Not sure you're ready to marry, huh?"

"I'm only twenty-one. I just haven't thought much about marriage yet. I have things I want to do. I don't think I'm ready to get married."

"Well, then don't let anyone talk you into it. What kind of things do you want to do?"

"Travel, I guess. I'm a war orphan from England, and I want to find out who I am."

"That's a tough one. But I get it. In the south, we love our families."

"My adopted mom was from Charleston," she paused and said slowly, "I don't think she liked being a mother. She didn't live with us." Serena finished her cocktail and didn't continue.

Mary Lou studied her empty glass and waved at the waiter for another round. "Travel sounds like a good idea to me, too. I'm hoping Steve gets stationed somewhere in Europe before he retires."

"Retires? How old is he?"

"He's thirty-one, and I'm twenty-seven so he's got at least eight years left in the Navy. But I really think he wants to stay as long as they'll let him and we both think it would be great to see the world and raise our children as Navy Brats."

"Have you guys talked about all that?"

"Sure, we're getting married soon, and in the military, the guys are gone a lot, so we need to know as much about each other as possible, as quickly as possible. And, I like to talk!" she clinked her glass against Serena's. "Look, here come Adam and Jessie. Do you know them?"

Serena turned and looked at the couple Mary Lou was waving toward. She shook her head and watched as the young couple approached the table. Mary Lou hugged them and urged them to sit down. When everyone was settled, she introduced them to Serena as a petty officer first class and his wife. At Serena's blank look, Mary Lou chuckled, "You really don't know anything about the Navy, do you? Adam is the LPO, leading petty officer, who works with Steve." Serena shook her head as if to clear it. "Don't worry Sweetie, you'll catch on if you marry your sailor."

Jessie patted her hand. "It's a whole new life and language. Who are you dating?"

"Logan Walker," Serena said, sipping her cocktail.

"Lieutenant Walker?" Adam asked. Serena nodded. Adam mumbled, "Pleased to meet you, Mam."

"Just Serena will do fine," Serena smiled at him. "We aren't married yet."

"Yes, Mam." Adam took a gulp of his beer, visibly shaken.

Mary Lou laughed her infectious laugh and changed the subject to weekend plans. After one beer the young couple excused themselves and hurried away. "What was that all about?" Serena asked.

"Enlisted men don't really socialize with the officers or their wives. You'll get used to it." Mary Lou shook her head. "I hope we didn't ruin their dinner plans."

"Tell me about your wedding, when and where and what are you wearing?" Serena said changing the conversation back into more comfortable channels. She only half listened as she thought about what it would mean to be a "Navy Wife" or even a "Navy Girlfriend" and when Mary Lou paused to catch her breath, Serena said, "It all sounds lovely, but I guess I'd better get home. Logan will be there soon, and I need a cool bath."

Mary Lou checked her watch, "Yikes! It's 6:15. I'm supposed to meet Steve at 6:30." She waved for their check, and the two young women quickly said goodbye, promising each other that they'd get together again soon.

# Chapter Ten

Michael and Anne checked the social pages to ensure that their engagement announcement was included. Anne was almost humming with excitement as she carefully clipped the picture and column. Michael couldn't help but laugh at her, but his own heart was heavy as he asked, "Do you think Elizabeth will see this?"

"Once a New Yorker always a New Yorker." Anne smiled, at him. "I'm sure she still sees the Times if she's anywhere in the United States."

"I hope so." Michael shook his head. "I wish we could find her."

"I know you do, darling. But you and your dad have tried everything. When she is ready, she'll come home."

"Maybe she thinks we're angry or," he hesitated, "maybe she can't."

Anne hugged him close and said. "Your family would have been notified if anything bad had happened."

"I try to tell myself that," Michael admitted, "but I don't know if it's true. We are pretty sure that she changed her name and she could be living anywhere in the world. Grandmother Minette says she knows Elizabeth is still alive and well, and that we just need to believe it. But sometimes it's so hard."

They'd had this same conversation many times in the four years since Elizabeth's disappearance, and Anne still didn't know how to handle his sadness. It seemed to her that Elizabeth was just being selfish, or playing a game of some sort, but she had never admitted that to anyone. She loved Michael and wanted to be his wife. After being a couple since high school, she was ready for marriage. "Remember when you told me about talking to Valerie's ghost? Perhaps you could contact her, and she'd know where Elizabeth is hiding."

"Don't you think I've already tried that?" he asked impatiently. "I seldom see Valerie anymore, and when I do, she just fades away and doesn't talk."

"But if she's around maybe a psychic could contact her."

"I've done that, too," Michael admitted. "Several times but nothing comes of it. Maybe if I knew the right psychic, a real psychic, they could, but they all just give me some vapid words about how everything will be as it should be and that a woman is watching over me. None of them have any idea where Elizabeth really is or how to find her."

There was something about the hint of fall in the air on Sunday that made Serena remember the East Coast. It wasn't often that she missed her family. Today was one of those days. The *San Francisco Examiner* was great, and it covered all the national news, but she wanted to feel like a true New Yorker. She decided to go to the market and on the way home stop at the newsstand and pick up the Sunday edition of the *New York Times*. If Logan questioned her choice, she could tell him that she wanted to read the Book Review section. Logan, however, was delighted with her choice and they spent Sunday afternoon reading bits and pieces of the paper to each other and discussing the huge rally in Washington DC where Martin Luther King had delivered a stirring speech on civil rights.

It wasn't until evening when Logan had gone in to take a shower that Serena turned to the society pages. At once, Michael's picture jumped out at her, and she almost cried out. He and Anne looked so happy in the formal portrait. Serena's eyes filled with tears as she cut the engagement announcement out of the paper and hid it under the liner of her underwear drawer. She wondered when and where the wedding would take place. If it were a big affair, maybe she could attend without anyone seeing her. It would be lovely to see Michael and Minette again. And, she admitted, she'd like to see her adopted father, too. She brushed the tears from her eyes and put the paper aside; she didn't want Logan to wonder why she was upset by the society pages from a city on the other side of the continent.

The next Friday, Logan returned from a week at sea with an invitation to Chief Martinelli and Mary Lou McGuiness wedding. He handed it to Serena and said, "I don't know why he invited us but since he did, we need to attend this. We won't have to stay long."

"What are you so grumpy about?" Serena read the invitation. "It'll be fun. I'm sure we were invited because Mary Lou is my friend. She's pretty much the only person I know in this city."

"I didn't realize that you two were that close," Logan said.

"I'm not sure you'd say we're close, but I like her. I've enjoyed the time we've spent together and the conversations. I think it's lovely that we've been invited."

Logan drummed his fingers against the counter-top. He gazed out the window avoiding

Serena's eyes. "Have you been spending much time together?"

Surprised by his tone, Serena answered carefully, "We've had lunch a few times and last week we met for dinner and drinks. I told her I'd help her shop for her wedding dress. Why?"

"I'd rather you weren't seen around town with her."

"Excuse me?" Serena could feel her anger rising, and she attempted to divert it with a laugh. "I don't choose your friends, and I don't think you should choose mine."

"I'm sure she's perfectly nice. It's just that I'm an officer on Steve's ship." Serena cocked her eyebrow and waited for the rest of his statement. "It doesn't look right for you to fraternize with the enlisted wives."

"Fraternize?" Serena's scorn was apparent. "Exactly what does that mean?"

"The military code states that in order to maintain good order and discipline fraternization between officers and enlisted should be kept on a professional basis."

"How archaic. Do you really buy into that?"

"I'm a naval officer, Serena." He caught her hand and pulled her toward him. "I'm proud of that.

The military code is not a problem. It is a guide line that I'm honored to follow. And as the wife of a military man, you will need to respect and follow the code and the traditions of the Navy."

"Logan," Serena pulled her hand away, "I'm not sure exactly what that means, but it sounds horrible. No one, including you, can tell me who I can be friends with or anything else."

Logan stayed very still for a moment. Serena watched the emotions play across his face until he reached again, for her hand, and spoke slowly. "It's not a bad thing, Serena. It's a matter of discipline. If I am "one of the boys," when I need to give an order, it is much more difficult for them to follow that order without question."

"Well, I'm not giving any orders to "your boys," and I won't take orders from you or the damn Navy." Serena tossed her head and pulled away. "I like Mary Lou, and I'll be friends with her or anyone else I choose."

Despite Logan's edict, Serena called Mary Lou on Monday and suggested that they get busy on the dress shopping. Since the wedding was only weeks away, they agreed that a ready-made dress was best and that Macy's would be a good place to start looking. As they walked across Union Square toward the rococo facade, Mary Lou excitedly told Serena her plans.

She and Steve were both Catholics and not members of any San Francisco parish, so they'd chosen to be married on Treasure Island by the Navy Chaplin. "Steve knows him from some other ship they served on. He's squeezing us in." Mary Lou bubbled. "Usually, we'd have to wait but ..." She shrugged. "We really want to be married before they deploy."

"Deploy?" Serena asked, unsure of exactly what she meant.

"Hasn't Logan told you? The ship is leaving in September for a Pacific Cruise; they'll be gone at least a year."

Serena stopped and caught Mary Lou's arm pulling her to stop, too. "A year? Logan said that they were leaving on a Pacific Cruise, but I certainly didn't understand he'd be gone a year." Mary Lou wasn't sure how to respond so she stayed silent and allowed Serena to continue. "A year, a whole year? I guess I knew that was possible but why would you get married now when Steve is leaving?"

Mary Lou laughed and shook her head, "Why? Because I love him. I'm twenty-seven years old, and I'm ready to settle down and have a bunch of kids. With any luck, I'll be pregnant before the ship leaves."

Serena stared at her. "But if he's gone for a year, you'd have the baby by yourself."

Mary Lou laughed and tucked her arm through Serena's pulling her forward. "I have a Mama and five brothers, honey. Believe me, I won't be alone."

# Chapter Eleven

Shopping with Mary Lou for her dress and meeting with her to hear about the wedding had caused six weeks fly by. Logan was working long hours, as the ship readied for deployment, and when he was home in the evening, they talked about anything other than the Navy or the wedding. They carefully avoided talking about how much time she spent with Mary Lou.

On Labor Day, Serena woke slowly and stretched luxuriantly; she gazed around her small apartment. The bright sunshine caused the lace curtains she'd hung across the bay window, to cast interesting shadow patterns on the wall. It was lovely to have a Monday off work. She turned her head to look at the alarm clock, it was only eight. She had plenty of time.

Sleeping with her hair twisted up on the pink foam hair rollers was uncomfortable, but worth it. Serena pulled the rollers out of her hair. She brushed and back combed until she'd created a high bouffant with the ends turned up in a perfect flip. She lined her eyes with kohl, in the cat-eyed style Liz Taylor had made popular in Cleopatra and outlined her lips in red. After pulling on slacks and a sweater, she checked her look in the mirror, and sprayed her hair liberally with Aqua Net. During the week, she had to wear a skirt or dress and conservative makeup. It was fun to go a little crazy on the weekend.

She grabbed her bag and opened the door. Then gasped and almost screamed. Logan, key in hand, was reaching for the door. He grinned at her. "Sorry, I didn't mean to scare you. Where are you headed?"

"I didn't think you'd be home this morning. I'm meeting Mary Lou and her family at David's Deli for breakfast. Why don't you join us?" She held her breath hoping he wouldn't say yes.

"No thanks." She let out her breath. "I've been up all night. I'll just take a nap." Logan slid past her and into the apartment. "Have fun." He closed the door. Serena hesitated. He hadn't kissed her or even hugged her. He was probably upset. If she wanted to keep the peace, she should go in and soothe his hurt. She shrugged. *Later,* she thought, *I'll be nice later.*

Saturday morning at the deli was always busy. Serena wove through the crowd waiting on the sidewalk, keeping an eye out for Mary Lou's bright hair. She stepped inside and immediately heard her name called. "Serena, over here." She turned toward Mary Lou's voice, and her face broke out into a wide grin.

There was no doubt that this was Mary Lou's family. The back corner of the deli was filled with red hair and happy faces. Serena hurried toward them and was immediately engulfed by a tall, statuesque women who hugged her close and said drawled, "It's so good to meet you, honey." She pushed Serena away slightly and looked her up and down. "You're just as pretty as a picture."

With her arm still around Serena, she spun toward the others in the booth, "I'm Mary Lou's mama, and this is her daddy and brothers." All six red headed men rose to their feet and smiled at her.

Serena was overwhelmed. She stammered "I'm delighted to meet you" to them all as Mary Lou rushed to her rescue.

"I told my Mama and Daddy all about you and how much help you've been." She took Serena's hand and moved forward to the table, and to the standing men.

Before she could say more, Mr. McGuiness stepped forward and reached to give her a hug. Serena stiffened, and he paused and then smiled warmly as he took her hand instead. "Don't mind us. We are a hugging family, and we feel like we know you. My princess has done nothing but rave about you for the last couple of months."

Serena smiled back into his warm gaze. "Thank you," she murmured not sure how to respond. A "hugging family" was an entirely new concept to her, and she wasn't sure she knew what that meant. Again, Mary Lou saved her by beginning to introduce her to the red headed young men. "These are my brothers, Mason and his wife Angelica, Tommy and his wife Sara, David, Brian, my baby brother Eddie, and..." she spun Serena around toward the next table, "these four little darlings are my nieces and nephews. My grandparents aren't here yet but they will be here on Wednesday, and you'll meet them then."

Serena was overwhelmed. Without thinking, she said, "Wow!" They all laughed. Serena blushed.

"Don't worry, honey," Mrs. McGuiness said, patting her on the shoulder. "Sometimes I'm a little overwhelmed by all of them, too." She slid into a chair at the table. "Sit down and let's get to know each other" indicating the chair next to hers.

"Oh, oh, you're in for it now," Brian said. "Mama, leave the poor girl alone. She's not from the south, so you don't know her people."

"I wasn't going to question her."

"Yes, you were. You always do."

Serena squirmed. She hadn't considered that she would need to explain her parentage. Quickly she decided that a bit of the truth would be the best way to handle this. She turned to face the older woman and began, "Mrs. McGuiness."

"Call me Mama or Gilda. Otherwise, I think you are talking to my mother-in-law. And while we are talking about it, call my husband Daddy or Scott. All the children's friends call us Mama and Daddy, but I realize that you don't know us so, Gilda and Scott will be fine." She waited for Serena's nod. "Now, tell us about yourself.'

*I've never experienced a family like this*, she admitted to herself, *even Uncle Sam and Aunt Helen hadn't been this approachable.* She took a deep breath and said carefully, "There really isn't very much to tell. I'm a war orphan, so I never knew my mother or father. I was sponsored by a nice family on the East Coast. They made sure that I got an education. After college, I decided to stay in California." Serena could feel Mary Lou watching her, and she knew she had to say something about Logan. "I don't have a family, but I have a good job, and I'm dating a very nice man."

"Damm," Brian said. "I was hoping you were unattached."

The tension was broken as everyone laughed. The conversation turned to the wedding plans. Serena allowed herself to relax a bit and joined in the laughter as they told old stories and teased one another. This was the kind of family she'd always wanted.

Walking back to the apartment, Serena thought about the way Mary Lou had watched her. She knew that the next time they were alone, she'd have to answer her questions. Maybe being this close to friends and family wasn't a good idea. She knew she wasn't going to marry Logan and she needed to tell him and then tell Mary Lou. She squared her shoulders as she approached the house.

But the apartment was empty. A page torn from the phone pad was propped up against the sugar bowl.

# I had to return to the ship. I'll back in time for the wedding on Saturday. Enjoy your week. Logan

Serena reread the paper. No salutation, no statement of love at the end, Logan must be mad at her. She crumbled the note and tossed it in the garbage. *Actually,* she admitted to herself, *she was glad he'd gone.* It had been fun this morning, and now she wouldn't have to explain anything to Logan, and she could join the McGuiness family on their tour of Fisherman's Wharf. She grabbed a jacket and scarf and hurried out, hoping to catch them before they boarded the trolley.

Saturday dawned bright, crisp and clear. It wasn't fall weather like Serena had grown up enjoying, but there was definitely something happening that felt like a season change. She made herself a cup of coffee and sat in the bay window watching the street below. With Logan busy, she spent every evening this week enjoying the clubs with Mary Lou and her family. Brian was so sweet, and, she admitted to herself, so good looking.

Last night, they'd all met for cocktails and dinner at the Top of the Mark, and when the rest of the family had called it a night, she and Brian had stayed and continued to dance and talk until the room closed at 2 AM. She smiled as she remembered their walk back to her apartment. A thick fog had rolled in and the sound of a fog horn, somewhere in the bay, echoed eerily across Union Square. They'd paused under the statue of Victory, and she's told him the story of how the beautiful model, six foot tall Alma de Bretteville, had become Mrs. Adolph Spreckels and how because she called him her sugar daddy, that term had become common phrase.

Brian had laughed, and for a moment she thought he was going to kiss her but instead he'd said, "You really love this city don't you?" And Serena had been reminded of Logan saying almost the same thing on their first date.

With Mary Lou's wedding only hours away, Serena watched for Logan to appear and when he did, she raised her hand in greeting and went to the door to welcome him.

"Are you still mad at me?" she asked.

"No," Logan admitted. He pulled her into a warm hug and kissed her. "But…after this wedding is over; we really need to talk." He kissed her again. Serena relaxed against his chest and avoided eye contact. "But, now let's just enjoy this day. I missed you this week."

"I missed you, too," Serena murmured.

"You look beautiful," Logan said.

Serena watched him in the mirror as he lifted her hair and kissed the nape of her neck. She wondered what it would be like to kiss Brian. She tilted her head slightly and met Logan's eyes in the mirror, "You look beautiful, too. There is something about a man in uniform." Logan grinned, and she tipped her head up, so her lips met his. "If we are going to grab a cab to Treasure Island, we'd better get going. I don't want to be late."

Serena and Logan reached the chapel and waited to be seated. Brian, who was an usher, approached them. He grinned at Serena, then turned to Logan and thrust out his hand, "You must be the reclusive Logan, I was beginning to believe you were a figment of Serena's imagination." As they shook hands, Serena explained that Brian was Mary Lou's brother and that they'd all had dinner together last night. Brian cocked an eyebrow quizzically, but only looked Logan up and down and asked, "Bride's side or Groom's side."

"Groom's, please," Logan said firmly. Serena took Brian's arm, and he escorted them to a pew, Logan one step behind. Serena slid in. She looked over her shoulder at Logan and saw Brian grin and wink. Serena almost laughed, but she caught it in time, looked down and pulled at her glove.

"You look happy," Logan whispered. "Soon we'll be the ones getting married." He gathered her hand in his and looked around the chapel. "This is a pretty chapel. Maybe we should get married here. The military priests are very helpful; even if we are not members of this parish, they'll usually marry Catholics."

"I'm not Catholic," Serena withdrew her hand and used it to adjust her hat.

Before Logan could pursue this line of conversation, the priest entered, followed by Steve and his Groomsmen and the wedding mass began. Mary Lou floated down the aisle on her father's arm. Steve beamed. Serena actually felt a bit teary at their happiness. *Maybe I will marry Logan; perhaps it is a good idea.* She thought about Michael and Anne. She supposed they'd have a big wedding or maybe it would be a small family affair like this wedding. She wondered if they'd set a date yet. The music swelled, and she realized the mass was over. She rose to her feet and watched the radiant couple stride up the aisle followed by their beaming parents.

Guests wandered into the rose garden as the picture taking drew to a close. Logan leaned down and whispered in her ear, "How long do we need to stay?"

Serena widened her eyes and bit her tongue to avoid the angry words that popped into her head. "I like Mary Lou and Steve, and I want to celebrate with them."

Logan nodded but said, "You know this isn't a good idea. It's appropriate that I congratulate them but not that we party with them."

"This is a wedding. Not an orgy. There are plenty of military men here. What are you so worried about?"

"The others are all chiefs or not from our ship. I told you before, fraternization is frowned on. We are leaving on deployment soon, and it is important that the men don't think I'm playing favorites."

Serena walked away and headed for the reception line. Logan watched her go. She hugged Steve and kissed Mary Lou and greeted their parents warmly, laughing and chatting with each. Logan wondered how much time she'd spent with the McGuiness family this week. It looked like they were old friends. *At least it's not a sit-down dinner wedding,* Logan thought. *We can have a glass of champagne and get out of here.*

Brian watched Logan watching Serena. It was obvious that they were having an argument. He turned and saw his sister watching, too. It wouldn't do for lovers spat to disrupt Mary Lou's special day. He grabbed two champagne flutes and slipped through the guests to Serena's side. "You look like you need this." He handed her the glass, and she took a deep swallow. "So," Brain raised his eyebrow. "Trouble in paradise?"

"No, of course not. It's just a Navy thing." Serena was rescued from his questioning eyes by Gilda's arrival.

"Please find me a drink, Sweetie. And not one of those glasses of bubbly. I'm ready for a real drink." Brian hurried to fulfill his mother's request. Gilda laid her had on Serena's arm and guided her to a table. "Sit with me, honey. I need to rest my feet."

"Everything is very beautiful," Serena said. "It's a lovely wedding, and Mary Lou looks so happy."

Gilda surveyed the rose garden. "Yes, it's beautiful, but I always thought Mary Lou would be married from our home in New Orleans with all of our friends and relatives there to help celebrate. I think I've been dreaming about it since the day she was born." Serena wasn't sure what to say so she remained silent as Gilda continued, "When you marry your young man will you rush about or are you planning to go home to your family?"

"We aren't engaged, Gilda. I'm not so sure I want to marry Logan."

"Well then, don't. It's a terrible mistake to marry when you aren't sure. If he loves you, he'll wait." Gilda hugged Serena again. Brian appeared with her drink. Gilda tipped it toward Serena in a silent toast, and the women smiled at one another. "I'd better get back to the cake cutting. Come on,

Brian, you need to make a toast to your sister and her new husband."

Logan reappeared at Serena's side, and they stood together for the toasts and the cake cutting. "Are you ready to leave now?" Logan asked.

Serena nodded. "I want to say goodbye first." Logan stayed with her as she told each member of Mary Lou's family how much she had enjoyed meeting them. Gilda made her promise that she'd come to New Orleans to visit and Mary Lou whispered, "I'll call you as soon as the ship leaves."

In the cab, Logan pulled Serena close and said, "I know this is a tough time. It's always hard on couples right before a deployment. We only have four days. Let's not fight." He kissed her hair and Serena turned her lips up to meet his.

# Chapter Twelve

Serena sat in Union Square; eyes closed, her face tilted to the sun, and considered her options. Logan was gone, and she hadn't ended their relationship. She knew she should have. She felt guilty that she hadn't, now she'd have to tell him in a letter and the sooner, the better. Something blocked the sun, and she opened her eyes. Brian stood in front of her grinning.

"Hey, pretty lady. I didn't expect to see you taking a nap on a park bench."

"Hi, Brian, I wasn't napping, just eating my lunch and enjoying the sun." She grinned back at him. "I thought you'd gone home."

"Nope, I've stayed a couple of days to console my sis, what with her new husband leaving for months and all." He sank down onto the bench next to Serena. "I'd offer to console you, too but I expect that isn't necessary."

"What do you mean by that?" Serena bristled.

"Don't worry; your secret is safe with me. I know you wanted to break up with Logan." Serena started to protest. Brian waved her to silence. "I've been ditched a couple of times, and you were showing all the signs. Did you do it?"

Serena shook her head. "I know I should have told him I'll never marry him. I'm just not cut out to be a Navy wife. There are too many rules."

Brian laughed. "I hear you. This is my last night in San Francisco. Come out with Mary Lou and me tonight, and we'll figure out how to write a Dear John letter."

Serena laughed. "I don't think the letter is a good idea but a night out sounds great." She gathered the remains of her lunch and stood up, brushing the crumbs from her skirt. "Where are you going? I'll meet you there."

The Peppermint Tree Lounge on Broadway was rocking when the doorman pushed open the heavy glass door for Serena. She shrugged off her coat and handed it the cloakroom girl. "There's a great group of good looking guys here tonight," the girl said, as she handed Serena a bright pink claim stub. "Have fun."

"I will," Serena replied. "Thanks." The girl's pink feathered headdress bobbed as she turned to the next in line and Serena couldn't help but smile. Somehow the striped pink walls seemed brighter tonight, and the music seemed louder. She felt young and free and having a good time was exactly why she was here. She scanned the room looking for

Brian and Mary Lou, and when she didn't find them, she accepted a dance invitation from a handsome stranger and moved onto the dance floor. As *Do The Bird* blasted through the room, Serena found herself moving freely and laughing out loud. The booming music made it impossible to talk, and that was precisely what she wanted tonight – fun with no strings attached.

The song ended, and the stranger offered her a drink. Serena was about to say yes when the band played the opening notes for *Little Town Flirt*. Brian appeared, "I think that's my cue," he said and pulled Serena back onto the dance floor.

Serena spun and twirled and flirted with everyone. As did Mary Lou, her new shiny wedding band didn't stop her from having fun. When the band left the stage for a break, Brian collected both the girls from the dance floor and escorted them to a tiny, bright pink table where tall glasses filled with a beautiful, rosy, drink waited for them. Serena grabbed a glass and took a couple of big gulps. "Whoa, Sweetie. That's not fruit punch," Mary Lou cautioned.

Brian laughed as Serena took another deep drink. "I think you two have danced with every man in this club," he said.

"That's the idea," Mary Lou admitted. "Steve doesn't care how much I dance as long as I go home alone."

Serena giggled, "I love this place, and everything is so pink!" She waved her glass. "I don't even like pink, but I like this pink!"

Mary Lou clicked her glass with Serena, "Here's to pink."

"And to freedom," Serena added. Mary Lou and Brian exchanged a look but didn't say anything. With one more swallow, Serena finished her drink. "Whatever this is, I want another one."

"Yes, Mam," Brian saluted.

"Don't call me that. And don't salute."

"Okay, Sweetie." He waved at the waitress and ordered two more Singapore Slings and a Jamison and Ginger for himself.

Serena allowed herself to relax into the fun of being out with friends. The music began again. Mary Lou accepted a dance with a tall, dark man and moved onto the dance floor. "Come on, beautiful, dance with me," Brian said pulling her to her feet. "You need to take a time-out from breaking hearts."

Serena smiled up at him as she moved into his arms. "You're so nice to Mary Lou; I wish you were my brother."

"I'm glad I'm not," Brian murmured into her hair. He pulled her close, and they swayed together to the sound of *I Can't Stop Loving You.* Suddenly Serena remembered Logan saying, on New Year's Eve that "he'd always think of her when he heard this song" and she pulled away. "What's wrong," Brian asked.

"I think we need a different band. Let's get Mary Lou and go somewhere else."

Brian followed her off the dance floor. He caught Mary Lou's attention, and she quickly joined them. "What's up?"

Serena giggled. "I'm tired of pink. Let's go to the Top of The Mark and dance to that jazz band." She swallowed the last of her drink and headed for the coat check.

"I think we can safely assume that Lieutenant Logan is no longer in the picture," Mary Lou said as she hooked her arm through Brian's. "I'm going to call it a night, but I think you need to keep an eye on Serena. Make sure she doesn't do anything she'll regret in the morning."

"My pleasure, Sis."

The sun woke Serena. She threw her arm over her eyes to shut it out. Her head was thumping. Her mouth felt like a dry ditch. She needed water. She groaned.

"Morning, Sunshine," a man's voice drawled.

Serena gasped and sat up fast, causing the room to spin. She turned and found Brian next to her in bed. "Shit." She lay back down and pulled a pillow over her head. "Shit, shit, shit."

Brian laughed and pulled the pillow away. "That's not exactly what a man likes to hear in the morning." He pushed the blanket aside and stood up. Serena peeked. He was wearing boxers and nothing else. She groaned again. "Just stay still. I'll be right back." She heard him open and close the bathroom door. She tried to remember what happened last night.

The door opened again, and the bed sank as Brian sat down on the edge. She looked at him. "Here," he held out a glass of water. "Drink this and take these aspirin. I imagine you have quite a headache."

Gratefully Serena accepted the water and pills and sank back on the pillows. She felt Brian stretch out next to her on the bed. He picked up her hand and held it gently. "Go back to sleep," he said. "We can talk when you wake up."

Hours later Serena woke again to find Brian gone from the bed. She stumbled to the bathroom and then to the kitchen. Her headache was gone, but a glance out the window showed her the setting sun. She'd slept all day. No wonder she was hungry. On the counter, next to the toaster, she found a white bakery bag with a note written on it.

I thought an east coast girl like you, might need a bagel. There is a smear in the fridge. I didn't want to wake you, and I had to catch my plane. I had a great time last night. Hope to see you again. Brian

Serena read the note twice. She wasn't sure what it meant. Her memories of last night were all about dancing and laughing, and yet Brian had been in her bed this morning. She wondered exactly what they'd done. But he was gone now, and it didn't really matter.

Writing the letter to Logan wasn't as hard as she'd expected. It had only taken a couple of tries before she'd figured out a way to say that she was sure that she could never be a Navy wife and that she was sorry to tell him by mail that they were not meant to be.

Her letter crossed a loving note from him that she read with a heavy heart, hurting Logan seemed wrong but so did marrying him. There'd been no more letters so she was sure that he must have received her Dear John letter. She put Logan out of her mind, ready to move on.

"I thought you were a coffee drinker?" one of the lawyers commented as Serena fixed herself a cup of tea in the break room.

She smiled. "I am, but this morning it doesn't taste right."

He laughed, "My wife always switches to tea when she's pregnant. It must be a girl thing."

"I think I just want a change. I'm certainly not pregnant." She carried her cup out of the break room and back to her desk. The fragrant steam rising from the warm mug made her think of her childhood. *Her dad, adopted father,* she reminded herself, *had always given her tea in a mug when she been ill or sad.* She pushed the thought aside; she never let herself dwell on thoughts about her family.

"Are you feeling okay?" her co-worker asked. "You look a little pale."

"I'm fine. My stomach just seems a little off. Must have been the tuna sandwich I ate last night."

Serena sipped the tea and kept her thoughts strictly focused on work. But walking home, she had to admit to herself that something was wrong. She was nauseated all day, every day, and, she admitted sadly, she might be pregnant. "Damn, damn, damn," she muttered, causing older women to glare at her. Serena wished she were brave enough to tell the women to "back off," but she tried to smile apologetically, and hurried home.

Serena had no idea where to turn. She needed a pregnancy test and then she needed to decide what to do. She hadn't allowed herself to make friends with anyone in San Francisco, except for Mary Lou, and asking her for help was impossible. Now that she'd broken her connection to Logan, she wanted to stay away from anyone that was connected to the ship, or the Navy. Finally not knowing what else to do, on Saturday morning, she phoned the Spencer home and asked to speak to Arabella.

"Who may I say is calling?" Mrs. Spencer's cold tone was actually scary.

"This is Sarah, I'm a friend of Bella's, from school. I just want to ask about an assignment." Serena concealed her east coast accent with a bit of Mary Lou's southern drawl. She was sure that the quiver in her voice would keep anyone from recognizing her.

"One moment, please." Serena could hear Mrs. Spencer even though she'd put the phone down. "Arabella, someone named Sarah wants to speak to you. I don't know anyone from your sorority named Sarah." Serena held her breath, what if Arabella wasn't curious enough to come to the phone.

"Mummy, she's just a girl from school. She's new and doesn't know anyone, so I gave her my number."

"Hmm," Mrs. Spencer seemed to pause a long time. "That's very nice of you. Invite her over. Your father and I want to meet all your friends."

"Hello," Arabella's cheerful greeting didn't betray any concern as to who might really be on the phone. But, of course, Serena thought there could be a real Sarah at her school.

"Hi, Bella, It's Serena. Don't say my name."

"Hi, Sarah," Arabella almost sang the words. "I'm so glad you called."

"I told your mother I wanted to ask you about an assignment."

"I'd be happy to help you with the English assignment. Do you want to come over?" Serena couldn't think of a response, but after a pause, Arabella continued. "I'll ask my mother. Just a moment." Serena heard the phone placed on the table again. "Mummy, Sarah needs a little help with our assignment. We have a big paper due for English Lit. I invited her over, but she's taking care of her brother. May I just meet her on the Marina Green for an hour or so? Her brother can play catch with his friend, and I can show her how Mr. Gibbons want our work to look."

Serena was impressed by the smoothness of Arabella's story. She could hear Mrs. Spencer agree and drew a deep breath. Even though Arabella was young, she was very worldly, more so than Serena.

"Sarah," Arabella was back on the phone. "Mother says that I may meet you on the Marina Green."

"I can be there in twenty minutes."

"Perfect, I'll see at Marina Green Park in about thirty minutes." Arabella hung up, and Serena took a deep breath and blew it out. This might be a mistake, but it was the only idea she had.

❧

Arabella was easy to spot in the park. She sat perched on the edge of a picnic table swinging her legs and chatting to a couple of young sailors. Serena grinned in spite of herself. There was something about Arabella that was irrepressible, and she realized that she'd missed the younger girl. Serena raised her hand to wave, and Arabella jumped off the table and ran to her.

"I'm so glad to see you. I want to hear all about what you've been doing. Are you still dating the beautiful Logan?" She hugged Serena and linked arms with her. "Let's walk, just in case Mummy comes driving by. I'm eighteen now, but she still checks up on me."

Serena laughed. "You haven't changed a bit. Your mother said sorority. Are you in college?"

"I am." Arabella wrinkled her nose. "I wanted to go away, but Daddy insisted that I stay close, so I'm at Holy Names. Daddy thinks the nuns will keep me safe." She giggled. "I had no idea who was calling when Mummy said Sarah. I never would have guessed you, not in a million years. Tell me about you, what are you doing?"

Serena told her about her job and apartment, trying to make it all sound fun and exciting. She admitted that she'd recently broken up with Logan, "I'm just not ready to be married."

"I'm not getting married until I'm at least twenty five," Serena declared. "And, no babies until I'm thirty."

"Sometimes babies come when you least expect them," Serena cautioned.

"Not for me. I know how to take care of myself. My roommate and I went to Planned Parenthood and got fitted with diaphragms." She caught sight of Serena's face. "Don't look so shocked. Everyone does it."

"I thought you had to be married to do that."

"You only have to wear a ring and give a married name." Arabella stopped and caught Serena's arm pulling her around, so they were face to face. "Are you telling me that you aren't using any kind of birth control? You know that's just plain stupid, right?"

"I," Serena stammered, "I'm careful, and Logan always used protection."

"Well, before you get a new boyfriend go get your own protection. You don't want to have a baby. I have a wedding ring you can wear if you want. It's kind of icky, they do this awful pelvic exam to be sure you aren't pregnant, but then you get your diaphragm, and they teach you how to use it."

"What if you are pregnant?" Serena asked carefully trying to appear only casually interested in the process.

"That's the pits. If you are, they tell you congratulations and offer prenatal care." Arabella laughed gaily. "I think for the girls with no one to marry they might offer some kind of home for unwed mothers."

Serena shuddered. She'd managed to find out where to get a pregnancy test but she was sure she didn't want Arabella to guess that had been the reason she wanted to see her. Serena forced a smile and a laugh. "You are still the craziest girl I've ever met. It's so good to see you. I think about you often, and I always wonder if you've changed. I'd love to hear more about your life but, I hate to say this, I think it's been over an hour. Do you need to get back?"

Arabella looked at her watch. "Yep, the watchdog will be searching for me soon. I'd better go. Call me anytime "Sarah." I'll always help you with your assignments." Arabella giggled. "At least until I get kicked out of college."

"What?"

"Just kidding…as long as Daddy gives a big donation, I can get away with anything." She sobered, "Anything but getting pregnant. Daddy would kill me for that."

They hugged and parted, promising to stay in touch. A promise Serena knew she wouldn't keep. As soon as Arabella was out of sight, Serena went to a phone booth and looked up the address for Planned Parenthood.

# Chapter Thirteen

The trip to Planned Parenthood was awful. Serena was sure that everyone knew she was using a fake name, that she was wearing a dime store ring, and that she wasn't married. After the pelvic exam, when they doctor told her she was at least eight weeks pregnant but that they would do a urine test to confirm, she'd started to cry.

It was not a surprise to Serena that she was pregnant. She'd tried to convince herself it wasn't possible but with the doctor's confirmation and a positive urine test she had to accept it. She and Logan had always used condoms and been very careful. The one night with Brian haunted her. She had no memory of sex, but she knew it was perfectly possible that they'd done it. After all, he was in her bed, and they were both mostly naked that morning. If only she'd stayed awake, and talked to him before he caught his plane. But…if the baby was Brian's she didn't want to force Brian to marry her. And if it were Logan's… her thoughts spun. The lies were completely out of control. No one knew who or what she really was; neither of the men, not her family, and she wasn't sure she knew either.

*Maybe,* she thought, *I can get an abortion.* If she knew how to get an abortion, she could do that, unless it was too late. There'd been a girl in her senior class who was rumored to have had an abortion in New York but here, in San Francisco, she knew only Arabella who might know how and where. *How could she have been so stupid?*

Back at work, she found herself listening more closely to the chatter of her co-workers. Their talk was all about boyfriends and wedding plans until one afternoon she heard them whispering about one of the secretaries who was rumored to have aborted a child using a knitting needle. "Oh," Serena heard herself gasp. "How awful, doesn't that hurt?"

"Well, of course, it does. But if you are dumb enough to get pregnant, you have to either marry the guy or fix the situation. I hear that the father is married, so what choice did she have. It's not exactly like you can go to the doctor and tell him you don't want the child."

"I'd never do that," another girl chimed in. "You can get a terrible infection, and it doesn't always work. I knew this girl in college that tried it. She almost died, and she still had to have the baby. That's why I'll never have sex until I'm married."

The girls laughed, and Serena tried to join in. She felt one of the older women watching her and forced herself to smile widely. Nausea rose in her throat and she struggled to push it down. Her last period was almost three months ago. It was probably already too late to do anything. She wondered how soon her pregnancy would begin to show.

Leaving the break room, the women who'd been watching her, touched her arm, "Serena, right?" she asked. Serena nodded. "I'm Carol, Mr. Gibbons, secretary." Serena waited, not sure why she was being approached. "I'd like to talk to you. I think I can help you."

"Help me? With what?" Serena was perplexed.

"Let's go get a cup of coffee after work and we can talk?" Carol looked around and made sure that no one was listening. "I'm quite sure that you have a problem and I'd like to help. I'll meet you in the lobby at 5:30."

"But..." Serena protested.

"Really," Carol said firmly, "I can help. I'll see you at 5:30."

Serena watched Carol enter the elevator. She felt numb and disoriented and afraid. How had this woman known she needed help?

By 5:30 Serena had convinced herself that whatever Carol wanted to help her with had to be work related. It was impossible that she would know about the pregnancy. That belief was shattered as Carol steered her into a booth at the Koffee Kup on the corner, ordered tea for them both and reached across the table to gently clasp Serena's hand. "First, let me assure you that your secret is safe with me." Serena tried to withdraw her hand and protest, but Carol held her firmly both with her hand and the look in her eye. "Don't say anything, Serena. Just listen." Serena nodded.

"I want to help you." Carol continued. "I've been exactly where you are now. I was twenty-one, unmarried, and pregnant. The man who was the father was not someone I could marry. I tried to get an abortion, but no one could tell me how. As soon as my mother discovered I was pregnant, she arranged for me to go to a home for unwed mothers. When my baby was born, I never saw her, I never held her, and she was adopted the same day." Tears filled her eyes. "I have missed my child every day for almost thirty years." Carol dropped Serena's hand and took several sips of her tea as she regained control. "I believe that you are alone and that you are unsure of what to do. If you will trust me, I can protect you at work until you have time to decide what you want to do and I will help you with whatever decision you make."

"How did you know?" Serena asked, not bothering to deny the pregnancy.

"It isn't obvious, not yet. But you look different, and you walk with a slightly different gait. Have you seen a doctor? Do you know when the baby is due?"

Serena nodded. "I think about the middle of June."

"How about the father, have you told him?" Serena shook her head. "Do you intend to?" Serena shook her head again. "Okay, then. You need to tell me what you want to do and it's okay if you don't know. We can talk about all the options and then you can decide. If you wear loose clothing no one will notice until January or maybe even February."

Serena looked around to be sure that no one was listening and then poured out her story; the story she'd decided on. She admitted to realizing too late that Logan was not someone she could marry, but didn't mention the Navy. She left out all thoughts that the baby might be from a one night mistake with Brian and said that she was so estranged from her family that they would never help her.

Carol patted her hand and said, "Don't be hard on yourself. It is too late to consider abortion, but you could give the child up for adoption. If you decide to keep the baby, we'll figure out a way to make it work. But you need to decide soon because if you surrender the baby for adoption, you'll want to be sure that no one knows you're pregnant. There are several homes in the Bay Area where you can live while you wait for the delivery."

Serena wiped away the tears that were threatening to overflow. "I was a war orphan in England and was adopted by Americans. I've never known who my real parents are and I don't think I can do that to my child." She nodded decisively. "I'm going to keep the baby and raise it alone."

"Excellent," Carol clapped her hands together. "You are young and pretty; I doubt that you'll stay single long." Serena smiled back; suddenly she felt much better. Carol continued, "Now we need a plan. I assume you need to work as long as possible."

"I do," Serena agreed.

"Let me think about your situation for a few days. I have contacts who want to help girls like you."

"Dumb and pregnant?"

"No, young and scared, without family and supports. I promise it will be alright. You just need to trust me." Carol reached for her coat. "What are you doing for Christmas?" she asked.

Serena tried to laugh and failed. "Nothing," she admitted.

"Do you realize that the office is closed from noon on Christmas Eve until January second?"

"Yes, but I heard a couple of the attorneys saying that they'd need to work on cases and I thought I'd volunteer to come in. I think I'll need all the money I can save."

"True, but I have a much better idea. I'm driving up to a friend's house in Healdsburg, and I think you should come along." Serena started to protest. "Don't say no; say that you'll think about it overnight. It'll just be a group of my female friends. Promise you'll think about it."

Not knowing what else to do, she promised.

# Chapter Fourteen

Serena sat on the deck in the sun, gazing at the Russian River. The crisp, bright morning air smelled sweetly of the pines, and the tumbling river gurgled as it swept over and around large boulders. She sipped her coffee, glad that for once, her morning sickness was allowing her to enjoy something other than weak tea. She found herself thinking about her family. They'd all be gathered together, most likely at Sam and Helen's lake house; all her cousins, their spouses, and children, even her brother and father. *Adopted brother and father,* she reminded herself. By now, the presents would be opened, and everyone would be talking and laughing. Serena wondered if they'd think of her, or if she'd been gone so long that no one ever talked about her. She shook away the thought. Certainly, Michael would mention her name, perhaps tell an old story. Of course, they didn't know she was pregnant and unmarried.

The door behind her creaked open, bringing her thoughts back to this ramshackle house perched precariously on spindly wooden legs, and to the present. "Are you warm enough out here?" Carol asked.

"It's lovely in the sun." Serena smiled warmly at the older woman. "Thanks so much for inviting me along. Your friends are all very kind."

"They are," Carol acknowledged. "Women need to stick together and help each other. Breakfast will be ready soon, come in and join us."

"I'll be there in a minute. Just want to finish this coffee." Serena needed the minute to compose herself. When they had arrived last night, Carol's friends were drinking wine and trimming a tree. They loudly greeted Carol with hugs and kisses and accepted Serena's presence without asking questions, but over breakfast, Serena was sure they'd be curious. She set her coffee cup on the deck rail and took a deep breath to steady her nerves.

The view really was beautiful, down below at the river's edge a slender, dark haired young woman caught her eye and waved. Serena lifted her hand and waved a greeting. She picked up her cup and looked back, but the woman had disappeared. There must be a hidden path down there, Serena thought. Maybe she could explore it later.

The sunny yellow kitchen was warm and welcoming. The smell of muffins caused Serena's stomach to growl, and one of the older women grinned at her. "Sit," she said, pushing a bright blue chair out from under the table with her foot. "Barb is the best baker we know and these bran muffins are just what a pregnant woman needs. Lots of vitamins and all that good stuff." Serena sat. "Smear on some of this goat cheese. Barb and I raised the goats and made the cheese."

Serena wasn't sure about eating goat cheese on a muffin, or goat cheese on anything, but it seemed impolite to refuse. So she broke the muffin in pieces and spread a small amount of the soft cheese on a bite size piece and placed it carefully in her mouth. "Wow," she laughed, delighted at the taste. "That's really good."

"Surprised, huh?"

Serena nodded. "I never tasted goat cheese before or," she admitted, "a bran muffin."

"Welcome to the good life. I'm Pat. That beauty over there," she indicated, a barefoot woman with very long hair, who was wearing men's pajamas, "is Barb. We have a tiny little vineyard and an organic farm. I don't know if you got it last night, but this house belongs to Barb, she's with Carol, and we've all been friends since college."

Serena tried to process that; it seemed like Pat was trying to tell her something important. She reached for another muffin, and Barb refilled her coffee mug. "Behave, Pat," Barb said tapping Pat on the back of her head. "Let the girl get some food in her."

Carol appeared in the kitchen, filled her coffee mug, pulled out the bright green chair, and sat down. "I love this kitchen," Serena declared looking around. "I think it's so cool that none of the chairs are the same color."

"That was Carol's idea." Barb joined them with her coffee. "She's the artist in the group."

Serena took a good look at Carol. The stern older woman from the office had been replaced by smiling, relaxed, almost young looking woman. Her hair was loose and curled softly around her face. She too was wearing men's pajamas and had a soft blue shawl thrown around her shoulders. Serena spoke without thinking, "You look so pretty. How old are you?"

Immediately she blushed and started to stammer an apology but the other three laughed, and Pat said, "Yeah, Carol, how old are you?"

"Exactly that same age as the rest of you," Carol said. "I'm forty-seven, Serena. I know that seems old, but it really isn't, you'll see."

Always before, when someone had told Serena "you'll see" she had become defensive, but these women were all so nice that instead, she took a large bite to finish her muffin and stayed quiet.

"What about you, Serena," Pat asked. "How old are you?"

"I was twenty-three in October."

"So young, to be on your own," Barb murmured. "And, now you're going to have a baby."

Serena couldn't deny it. She knew that Carol must have talked to her friends. She dropped her eyes to the table and waited for the accusations to start. Carol took her hand. "It's alright, Serena. We are here for you. All of us have been estranged from our families for a long time, and we just want to help in any way we can."

"This is Christmas Day," Barb said. "I think we should just have fun today. I'm going to start the turkey. What are the rest of you going to do?"

"I'll help with the cooking," Carol and Barb said together.

"I'll dig out a jigsaw puzzle for later, and be in charge of the bar." Pat caught Barb's frown. "And, I'll set the table."

Serena thought about the young woman she'd glimpsed down by the river. "I'd like to take a walk if that's okay. I'm not much good in the kitchen, but I can help with the table."

"Dinner is hours away, and this kitchen is too small for so many cooks," Barb smiled at Serena. "You deserve some peace and quiet. Go enjoy yourself."

Serena pulled on a pair of capris. The waistband seemed tighter. Was she beginning to show? Her stomach still seemed flat, but maybe not, perhaps she did have a bit of a bulge. She unbuttoned the waistband. It was definitely better. She twisted her long hair into a ponytail and left the cabin. She'd think about how to conceal her pregnancy later. Right now she needed some fresh air.

The path down to the river was steep and a little slippery but once she was at the water's edge the path leveled out. Hugh redwoods towered over her. The sun sparkled across the rippling water, and the smell of pine and dry grass caused her to take a deep breath. As she exhaled slowly, Serena could feel her tension drain away. She dropped onto a rock outcropping and took another deep breath. A large, black, bird landed on a branch just over her head and gave a raucous croak. She wondered if it was a crow or a raven. *Grandmother Minette would know*, she thought. A wave of loneliness engulfed her. It wasn't often that Serena allowed herself to think about family but it was Christmas Day, she was with strangers, and she was pregnant. For a moment she wanted to weep. She'd loved her grandmother, probably more than anyone but Michael, and she knew they'd both be disappointed in her now. She stood up and walked downstream, pushing away thoughts of family and love. It was just her, and this baby, against the world now.

She ducked under the branches of a low hanging redwood. As she straightened, she gasped. Not more than three feet in front of her was the young woman she'd spied earlier from the deck. "Yikes," Serena stammered. "You scared me. I didn't think anyone else was out here." The woman smiled. Serena smiled back. "I love your slacks. Vintage clothes are so neat." She lifted her hand in a half wave. "I'm Serena."

"Valerie. I'm so happy you can see me."

"Huh?"

Valerie grimaced. "I meant to say that I'm happy to meet you. I don't talk to many people."

"It is pretty quiet up here, but it's beautiful. Do you live in one of these cabins?"

Valerie shook her head. "I don't really live anywhere."

"Nowhere? Everyone lives somewhere."

"I used to live in a house by a river, but it was a long time ago."

"My mother's name was Valerie," Serena blurted out. "She died when I was born." Serena placed her hand over her mouth. Where had that come from? She never told anyone the truth about her family.

"I'm sorry." Valerie's eyes filled with tears. "That must have been very hard. But you had a great father, didn't you?"

"Not so much. I was adopted, and I never knew my real father." Serena took a deep breath. "My adoptive father tried hard but," she shrugged, "you know. It's not the same."

"But..." Valerie stammered, "I thought you and Michael grew up together."

"How do you know about Michael? Who are you?" The large black bird flew out of the tree and Serena looked up at the sound. When she looked back, Valerie was gone. "What the heck?" She looked around but could see no sign of the woman. Serena shivered and pulled her jacket closed; suddenly it didn't seem so warm and sunny down by this river. She turned and hurried back to the cabin.

Carol looked up from chopping an onion. "You look like you've seen a ghost."

"Not a ghost. But I did talk to a really weird woman."

Carol laughed. "There are a lot of characters living up here. It's pretty much live and let live kind of place. People mind their own business and don't interfere."

"This woman acted like she knew me."

"Maybe you ran into one of our local psychics," Barb said as she slid the turkey back into the oven. "Some of them are pretty good. I had my palm read a couple of days ago, and she told me we'd have a lovely young guest for Christmas dinner. And here you are."

"Maybe, but it was weird." Serena wanted to mention that the woman had known her brother's name and that she had disappeared, but that just sounded crazy, and none of these women even knew that she had a brother.

Over dinner, Carol and her friends talked about everything except Serena's pregnancy. With the dishes done, they gathered in the living room. A fire glowed in the stone fireplace, popping and cracking, as it warmed the room. Pat poured wine. Serena watched as Carol leaned against Barb and they entwined their hands. Her eyes widened, they're a couple, she realized. She turned to look at Pat and Susan. They, too, were sitting together, Pat's arm draped casually over Susan's shoulders. Pat caught her eye and grinned, "Yup," she said, "we're all lesbians."

Serena couldn't think of anything to say. Finally, she just nodded and took a large gulp of her wine. Carol took pity on her and admonished Pat, "Don't tease her." She turned to Serena. "Sorry, I wasn't sure how to tell you that my partner is a woman. But, it doesn't change anything; I still want to help you."

"We all do," Barb chimed in. "We know how hard it is to have a baby when you are unmarried. And, it will be even harder for you because your family is not here to offer support."

"I was just surprised. I don't think I know anyone who is...gay."

"I'm sure you do," Pat said. "You probably just haven't noticed yet."

Susan tapped Pat's leg. "Down, girl. Let Serena process one shock at a time."

Serena looked directly at Pat. "Believe me," she said, "finding myself pregnant is much more shocking than finding out about your love life. I wasn't even in love, and now I'm having a baby."

The women chuckled together. "Right," Carol said, "about that, are you still determined to keep the baby and raise it yourself?" Serena nodded. "Then we need to find you a new job. Do you want to stay in San Francisco or are you willing to move?"

# Chapter Fifteen

For the first time since leaving home, Serena felt like she had found a group of friends. True, it was a little strange that they were all lesbians, but she felt safe with these women. She was invited to have dinner or coffee with them. They didn't judge her; they offered her support but didn't insist that she live her life their way. They didn't ask about her past or about her plans for the future, and because they didn't ask, she didn't have to tell them lies.

She was able to conceal her pregnancy by wearing bulky sweaters, but as January drew to a close, she knew that someone was sure to notice soon. On Saturday, January twenty-fifth, she sat in the laundromat reading the help wanted ads and waiting for her machines to finish. Lost in her own worries, she didn't look up when the door opened. "Serena Miller! I thought you'd died or something. Why haven't I heard from you since Thanksgiving?" The newspaper was grabbed out of her hands. "All my brother could talk about at Christmas was you, and I couldn't tell him a thing. How are you, Sweetie? What's happening?"

Serena jumped up and hugged Mary Lou. "I thought about you a lot. But I knew you went home for holidays, and I didn't want to bother you."

"You couldn't bother me if you tried. What have you been doing? No new man in your life?" Serena shook her head, as Mary Lou continued, "Have you heard from Logan?"

"Not since I told him it was over. I haven't been dating just working."

"So boring. Let's go get lunch and catch up."

"I have to finish my laundry," Serena waved at the spinning washer.

"Okay, dinner then. That's better anyway. We'll have more time. I feel like Italian. Let's meet at Original Joe's, about seven?" Serena nodded and Mary Lou was out the door as quickly as she'd come in. I probably should have refused that invitation, Serena thought, but she wanted to know about Brian. She wondered what he'd told his sister at Christmas.

It was bright, noisy, and smelled divine when Serena pushed opened the door to the restaurant on Taylor Street. Tony greeted her as if she were a long lost friend and escorted her to the leather booth where Mary Lou was waiting, sipping on a Joe's Manhattan and laughing with a waiter. Serena slid into the booth and kissed her cheek. "It is so good to see you."

"Bring my friend one of these, and I'll have another." She gestured to her glass as she spoke to the waiter. "We've got a lot of talking to do."

"Coming right up. Tell Steve I say hi next time you send him a letter."

"Do you and Steve know everyone in San Francisco?" Serena asked.

"No, Jerry was my neighbor before I got married. Steve and I come in here a lot because the food is so good, the portions are huge, and the drinks are strong. All the things a sailor likes in his favorite restaurant."

Serena laughed. "How is Navy life?"

Mary Lou sobered. "Kind of lonely, but I keep busy. I was hoping I'd be pregnant but no such luck. I'm going to meet the ship in Hawaii when they get an RR, and maybe it'll happen then."

Serena accepted her drink and clicked it against Mary Lou's. "Here's to pregnancy." *Yours and mine,* she thought. "Tell me about your holidays. Did you see your whole family?"

"There is no other way to have a southern Christmas. Aunts, uncles, cousins, grandparent's, second cousins, brothers, spouses, nieces, nephews, there were twenty-nine people for Christmas Eve and even more for Christmas dinner. Mama loves to entertain. Everybody that wasn't here for the wedding wanted to come by and hear all about Steve. And," she wound down, "Brian wanted to hear all about you."

"What did you tell him?"

"The truth, silly. That you'd finally called it off with Logan. That you were so busy that I hardly saw you and that as soon as I got back here, I'd find out if he has a chance with you."

Serena gulped her drink. "I, um..." she stuttered, "don't know what to say."

"Say you like him. It would be amazing if you ended up as my sister-in-law. We could have our babies together."

"I hardly know him."

"Yeah, but he's lovable."

*And, I'm pregnant and it might be his baby but it might not,* Serena thought. "I don't think I'm ready to date anyone right now."

"You didn't even love Logan, and he's been gone for months. I think it's past time for you to date again. Didn't you have fun with Brian?"

"I did, but this isn't a good time for me to get involved. I'm thinking about getting a different job, and I might have to move."

Mary Lou tilted her head and narrowed her eyes as she observed Serena. "So, Brian doesn't care where you live. This city isn't that big. You can tell me if you don't like him. He's my big brother, some days I don't like him."

"I like him."

"But..?

"I have too much happening to think about falling in love. Let me handle that first. So, tell me more about your holiday."

Mary Lou took the hint and stopped her match making. They ordered and ate, laughing and talking. Serena excused herself and headed for the bathroom. Mary Lou studied her, confused by what she thought she saw. When Serena returned, she asked, "Are you sure you don't want to tell me anything else?" Serena shook her head. "You can trust me you know." Serena nodded. "I'll be here for you if you ever need my help." Serena nodded again looking decidedly uncomfortable. Mary Lou decided not to push it, she was sure Serena was pregnant, but if she wasn't, it would be horribly rude to ask.

Serena heard the unspoken question. She realized that Mary Lou might have discovered her secret and now she knew, more than ever, that she needed to hide at least until the baby was born. After that, she'd think of something to explain its existence.

Sunday evening, Carol and Barb knocked on her door with a solution to Serena's problems. Carol had found her a job across the bridge in Oakland. Far enough away that she'd never run into anyone, like Mary Lou or Logan, accidentally. But close enough to see Carol.

Carol explained that she had a friend who was a Civil Rights lawyer. She would be his "Girl Friday," doing a little bit of everything. He knows that you are pregnant and believes that you husband is dead. "He'll keep you on until you can't work anymore and by then the weather will be warm, and you can go back up to the Russian River. You can live in our house until the baby is born and you are ready to go back to work."

Tears spilled from Serena's eyes, and she swiped them away with the back of her hand. Carol hugged her. "It'll be alright. I know a woman who lives close to where you'll be working. You can live over her garage until you are ready to move to the river."

Carol's kindness was overwhelming. Serena stammered her thanks and her relief. Suddenly her world was back on track; maybe she could do this after all. "I think you should start with Alan on Monday. I don't think anyone at work is suspicious yet but I..."

"I know. It shows now, doesn't it?"

The move was accomplished with a minimum of fuss. Serena knew that she owed Carol for everything and vowed to herself that she'd find a way to repay her. Alan Warren turned out to be a charming, laid back guy. He accepted her story, saying only that he was sorry for her loss, and put her to work.

Serena found the new life busy and interesting. The work Alan and his staff of interns were doing mattered, and she was proud to be contributing. She knew about Martin Luther King and had listened to his stirring "I Have A Dream" speech. She was against segregation and felt that all races should be equal, but she'd never lived near or even really known a black person before moving to Oakland. This was California, not the Deep South, yet every day, she worked with persons who were being discriminated against in ways that seemed inconceivable. Most mornings the office was filled people who had been disallowed employment, admission to school, or housing based on nothing but the color of their skin. By March, Alan trusted her enough that he had Serena do initial interviews with the new clients. The days flew by.

Serena bought a few maternity outfits at a thrift store and tried to ignore her changing body. Everyone knew she was pregnant but, believing that her husband had died. The young interns, and Alan, avoided talking to her about anything personal. She worked six and, sometimes, seven days a week saving money toward the coming baby costs. Fortunately, her new job provided insurance, so the doctor and the hospital were covered. She'd have to be off work for at least six weeks after the baby, and even with Carol's offer of free housing, she had no idea of how they would survive.

Carol and Barb came by almost every weekend. They invited Serena to spend time at the cabin, but she preferred to work and avoid thinking about what would come next so, instead, they stocked her cupboards with healthy food and prepared the cabin for a baby.

By the second week in May, Serena felt like a blimp. She couldn't find a comfortable position for sleep, and the dark circles under eyes caused Alan to suggest that she should stop working until after the birth of her child. He promised she could return to her job and Serena reluctantly called Carol and admitted she was ready to move to the cabin.

Serena was quiet as she and Carol drove north. Suddenly the birth of this child was looming, and motherhood was about to become a reality.

# Chapter Sixteen

The cabin on the Russian River proved to be the perfect place to wait for the birth of her baby. Each weekend, Carol and Barb arrived on Friday night with a car full of fresh, farmer's market finds and tasty treats. During the week, Serena was alone. She took long walks, napped on the deck in the sun and nibbled at the healthy food Carol and Barb provided. She found a copy of Dr. Spock's *Baby and Child Care* and read it cover to cover. Following the list included in the book, she shopped at the Healdsburg thrift shops and the Goodwill for baby clothes, blankets, bottles, and a sterilizer. She'd never before thought about all the equipment a baby seemed to need. Some of her meager savings went to buying diapers, new bottle caps and nipples and a darling mobile for hanging over the crib Pat and Susan had given her.

Sometimes she would see the young woman, in her vintage clothing, but by the time Serena was close enough to speak, she was always out of sight. It almost felt like the woman was watching her. Serena dismissed that idea as silly. She felt as big as a house, her back ached and her feet were swollen. The doctor kept assuring her that it was a perfect pregnancy. *If this is perfect*, Serena thought, *what hell would a non-perfect pregnancy be?*

When she sensed the first low tightening in the early morning of June nineteenth, Serena held her belly and felt the full terror of her decision to have this child and raise it on her own. *What am I doing? I can't even get my own life together, and now I'm having a kid.* She brushed the tears away and refused to think about it. *First things first,* she thought. *I have to call Carol and tell her the baby is coming.*

Michael and his father, John, stood next to one another, their images reflected in the large mirror over the mantle. Michael straightened his bow tie, and John did the same. They grinned at each other. "We look nervous," Michael said.

"You look wonderful," Minette swept into the room, her pale gray gown highlighted her snowy hair, "Both of you. I can't believe I'm old enough to be watching my grandson marry."

Henry followed her into the room; he too was adjusting his bow tie. Minette slapped his hand away, "Leave that alone, I just tied it." All three men fiddled with their ties again, and Minette laughed at their nervous behavior. "Open the champagne, John. I'm here with my three favorite men, and I think we should drink a toast to our family, who today will be increased by one."

Henry popped the cork and filled the flutes. Minette raised her glass. "To the mighty Augustus Clan."

"To family," John said, and they drank. "To Michael, the best son a man could have, and," he paused a second before finishing, "to Elizabeth, where ever she is." They drank again.

Henry raised his glass next and in his strong British accent said, "As Shakespeare wrote, 'A flight of blessings light upon thy back.' I only wish that you and Anne will always be as happy as Minette and I."

Minette kissed his cheek and the mood lifted.

⁀ৄৎ⁀

Despite his happiness and the beauty of his bride, Michael found himself looking around the reception crowd searching for Elizabeth. Anne squeezed his hand, and he forced himself to pay attention. Anne looked beautiful in her pearl encrusted white gown. He lifted her hand and kissed the palm. The guests tapped their glasses and cheered. Michael kissed his new bride and forced himself to stop wishing Elizabeth was there to share in this day.

Later, standing on the balcony with his cousin Chris, the two men lit cigarettes and gazed out at the city. "Do you think we'll ever find her?" Michael asked.

Chris didn't have to ask what he was talking about and he took his time before answering, "Honestly, I don't think we will, not until she wants to be found."

Michael flicked his ash over the railing. "I guess you're right. But, I can't get her out of my mind today. It's like when we were kids, I always knew when she was scared, or needed me. I can feel her crying. I know she needs help."

Serena lay exhausted in the labor room. It had been hours since the pain started and the nurses were still telling her it would be a while, she was dilating very slowly. They assured her that everything was normal and that sometimes first babies just took their own sweet time about arriving. Tears trickled from the corners of her eyes, and she brushed them away. The loneliness that Serena usually managed to ignore overwhelmed her. *Having a baby should be a happy event*, she thought.

Just after 10 PM, floating on a cloud of Demerol, Serena finally heard a nurse announce that the baby was ready. Carol kissed her cheek and squeezed her hand. Serena was moved to the delivery room. The doctor asked if she wanted a mirror to see the birth, but Serena shook her head and closed her eyes against the glare from the bright overhead light.

Someone lifted her legs into the stirrups. A wave of pain caused her to cry out and bear down. "Don't push," the doctor demanded, and Serena tried not to. Someone put hands on her shoulder. She opened her eyes and looked into the stern face of a nurse. The woman's mask was framed by large red button ear rings and her eyes didn't smile. Another pain began, and finally, she heard the command to push.

A baby cried. Serena opened her eyes. The same nurse was watching her. "She's back with us, doctor."

The doctor's face swam into her wavering view. "Every thing's fine. We're just putting in a few stitches, and you'll be good as new."

"Is the baby okay?"

"Fine and dandy, it's a girl. 7 pounds 3 ounces." The doctor patted her foot. "When we're done here, you can see her."

"Is she keeping the baby? I didn't see a husband."

"No husband, but this one says she's keeping the baby." Serena heard the doctor walk away and opened her eyes again.

The nurse with the red earrings was no longer wearing a mask. Serena was aware that she was being inspected. The nurse wasn't smiling. Serena wondered if she'd done something wrong. "How old are you, honey?"

"Twenty-three," Serena answered honestly, the Demerol haze, causing her to forget momentarily that she'd added two years to her age on all the paperwork. "I mean twenty-five," she corrected.

"And I suppose your husband couldn't be here today," the flat, skeptical voice continued.

"He died."

"Right." The nurse turned away. Serena's eyes filled and she took a deep breath, determined not to cry in front of this women.

"May I see the baby?"

"She's been taken to the nursery. Someone will bring her to you after you're settled in a room. Do you have family here?"

"Just my friend Carol." The nurse merely nodded, but Serena could see the disapproval in her eyes. She'd been so protected by Carol and Barb that she'd been able to forget that as far as the majority of the world was concerned, she was an unwed mother with an illegitimate child. "My husband is dead," Serena spoke firmly. "This is his child."

"You better practice your story, girl. If you intend to keep this child, you'll need to protect her from the truth."

Serena drifted in and out of sleep in the noisy hospital room. She still hadn't been given her baby to hold, and when a young nurse took her blood pressure, she asked again. This time her request was met with kindness. "We don't wake the mother's in the night. Someone will bring your baby in for the 6 AM feeding. Are you planning to nurse?"

"No, my doctor recommended Similac. He said it was better for the baby."

The young nurse picked up her chart from the end of the bed and glanced at it. "They gave you a lactation suppression injection in the delivery room." She flipped a page and then looked back at Serena. "This says father unknown, is that correct?"

Serena felt her face flood with color, but she answered without hesitation, "Of course not. I know exactly who the father is. He died. He's not unknown."

"Well then, we'd better correct this before they fill out the birth certificate." She clicked her pen and asked, "Mother's maiden name?"

"Serena Miller"

"Middle name?"

"None."

"Birthplace"

"London, England."

The nurse looked at her curiously but continued, "Birth date?'

"October 15, 1938," Serena remembered to subtract the two years from her real birth date.

"Father's name?"

"Brian Lee Walker. New York City, New York," without hesitation she combined the names of the two possible fathers. "His birth date was June 10, 1936. He is deceased."

"You didn't change your name when you got married?" For a second Serena thought she was trapped by her lie. The nurse patted her arm. "How modern of you." Serena swallowed hard and laid her head back against the pillows. "Have you chosen a name for the baby?"

"Yes. I'm naming her Kala Michele Walker."

"What a pretty name. Okay, that's everything. Get some sleep."

Lying in the darkened room, Serena drifted. Someone touched her arm. She opened her eyes and saw the young woman from the river. She startled and started to call out but the woman disappeared, and she realized it was just a dream. She wondered again why the woman seemed so familiar.

Promptly, at 6 AM, the sound of crying babies echoed down the halls of the maternity ward. Serena sat up and pushed a pillow behind her back, aware of how sore she was but anxious to meet her daughter. A different nurse arrived with the pink bundle in her arms. "Here you go, Mommy, she said. This little girl is hungry."

Serena hesitated, unsure of how to hold the baby. The nurse smiled. "Don't worry, she won't break. Let's just put this pillow under your arm." She pulled a pillow into place and adjusted Serena's left arm into a curve. "Remember to support her neck." She handed a warm bottle of formula to Serena. "Wiggle the nipple in her mouth, and she'll start sucking. Babies know exactly what to do even when the mommies don't." She watched as Serena followed her instructions. "There you go. After about an ounce, you'll want to burp her. I'll stay if you'd like."

"I've never held a tiny baby before," Serena gazed down at her daughter. "She's so little."

"She is but you'll be surprised how fast she grows. Set the bottle on the tray and place your right hand under her head and lift her to your shoulder. Then just rub her back until she burps." The baby burped and spit a bit. "That's normal. See how easy it is. I'll let the two of you get acquainted. If you need anything just ring the bell."

Serena gazed down at the tiny bundle in arms. She studied the miniature face and could find no resemblance to anyone. The baby opened her eyes, and Serena found herself smiling. "Hello, Kala. I'm your mom kid. I sure hope that nurse was right and that you know what to do." Kala sucked on the nipple and formula dribbled from the corner of her mouth. Serena wiped it away with her thumb. "It's you and me, Kala. Us against the world."

# Chapter Seventeen

Monday, August third, Serena returned to work at the law firm. It was exhausting to get up every four hours to feed Kala. Carol and Barb had helped the first three weeks, each taking a few days off to stay at the cabin. But now, Serena felt that she was drowning. The tiny garage apartment that had been such a refuge, seemed smaller now. Kala and all the baby supplies filled every corner and surface. The very low rent was all that Serena could afford, and she realized that she was lucky. Serena knew she should be grateful, but mostly she felt lost and overwhelmed.

She'd been the youngest child and had never been a babysitter or spent time around babies. After reading Dr. Spock, Serena had felt like she was ready but everyday, a new question seemed to come up. So far, Kala was thriving despite the worry and fear plaguing Serena. She'd found an older woman to care for Kala while she worked. It was close to the apartment, and she charged a reasonable rate. Everything was so expensive. She needed someone to talk to; someone her own age, maybe someone in her situation. *Although* Serena admitted to herself, *it would be hard to find another unwed mother, pretending to be a widow, who wasn't sure who the father of her baby was. Probably impossible.*

At work, Serena placed a double frame on her new desk with a picture of Kala on one side and on the other the image of an unknown sailor. She'd found the photo of the sailor in a thrift store, and it fooled her co-workers. They cooed over Kala's picture and commented on how much she looked like Serena. Occasionally someone would mention how sad it was that her husband had been killed before seeing his daughter. However, both the war in Vietnam and the death of her young husband made people uncomfortable and, for the most part, Serena managed to keep to herself and avoid questions.

At work, Serena felt capable and confident. At home, she sank further and further into misery. It seemed that she was always tired, always short of money, and having no fun at all. She lost weight and, even when Kala slept through the night, she found herself awake and depressed.

As August drew to a close, the usually cool breezes from the bay seemed to stop altogether. All day, Serena dreamed of the big lake house where she'd spent such happy summers with her cousins and her brother. She imagined the whole family gathered together on the wide porch, ice tinkling in tall cool drinks, children chasing and laughing, fireflies glowing as the sky darkened. A hand dropped on her shoulder, and Serena gasped and jumped.

"Sorry," Alan said. "I didn't mean to scare you."

Serena felt herself blush. "I was just thinking about..." She couldn't think of anything to say.

"It's okay. I was just saying that I'm closing the office early. It's too hot in here to get any work done anyway."

Serena looked around and noticed that everyone else was gone or quickly getting ready to leave. "Oh, okay," she stammered.

"I know you need to get home to your daughter." Alan paused. "But I'm going to get an ice cream at MacFarlane's, and if you'd join me, we could be comfortable while we talk about the Spaulding case."

Serena looked at the large clock on the wall. The ornate hands pointed to three o'clock. She started to shake her head, but the thought of a cool ice cream treat was just too tempting. "I believe finishing the day's work over ice cream is an excellent idea."

"Great. I can be ready in fifteen. I'll lock up and meet you in the lobby."

Serena covered her typewriter and quickly straightened the papers on her desk. She stopped in the ladies room to run a comb through her hair and touch up her lipstick. She smoothed her pale yellow sun dress and surveyed herself in the mirror. Realizing what she was doing, she admonished herself, "Stop it. It's not a date, it's a work session with your boss." She grinned at her reflection. "It's actually ice cream on a hot day and an afternoon off."

On the short walk to MacFarlane's, Alan stayed silent until they passed under the bright red and white awnings. "I won't keep you long."

"It's not a problem. I just need to pick up Kala by 6 PM."

The doors stood wide open, and ceiling fans created a welcome breeze. Alan nodded and stepped aside so Serena could enter. The sweet smell of ice cream and candy filled the air. Serena took a deep breath, "It smells like summer in here."

Alan laughed. "Where did you grow up?"

"On the east coast. In our family, ice cream was always a summer treat."

"We had ice cream every Sunday. My dad loved it."

They approached the glass cases. "Hey, Alan, are you playing hooky this afternoon? Want your regular?"

Serena laughed. "Sounds like you still love ice cream."

"I do. And I will have my regular, Joey. What would you like, Serena?" She walked slowly along the case trying to decide. It all looked so delicious, and it had been a long time since she'd allowed herself a treat. Ice cream wasn't really in her budget. "I'm having a banana split, all vanilla ice cream," Alan announced, "and I don't care if it spoils my appetite for dinner." His grin was infectious, and Serena smiled back.

"It's too hot to eat dinner anyway," Serena said. "I'll have the hot fudge sundae with strawberry ice cream."

"Coming right up. You guys grab a seat outside in the shade, and I'll bring them out to you."

Alan held her chair as Serena seated herself. His manners reminded her of her dad, and she looked at him closely. He was certainly older but perhaps not as old as she had imagined. Maybe forty she thought. "Do you bring your children here for ice cream?" she asked.

"No children, I'm not married." Serena almost asked why not, but Alan continued. "My mom would like me to hurry up, but after serving in the Army and law school, I just haven't met the right person."

"Did you grow up here in Oakland?" Serena changed the subject to something a little less personal.

"Alameda, actually. It was a great place to be a kid. I always thought I'd move to Manhattan and join a big firm, but now I think Sacramento is as far as I want to go."

"Sacramento?"

He nodded. "It's the state capital, you know. I'd like to see some real changes made."

Serena studied him. "I can see that. You could be a politician."

Alan laughed. "No, I couldn't. But I'd like to influence politicians. I'd like to make sure they are aware of what people in this state need."

The ice cream treats arrived. Serena smiled at the size of her sundae. "Wow. This is the biggest dish of ice cream I've ever seen."

Alan grinned and dug into his even larger banana split. "Ice cream on a hot day contains no calories." Serena frowned. "It's true. My Grandma told me, and Grandmothers never lie."

"My grandmother certainly didn't," Serena agreed and took a large scoop of chocolate fudge.

They talked easily over the ice cream, and then Alan pulled out the Spaulding file from his briefcase. Serena felt a tinge of disappointment that it was time to get down to work.

Over the weekend, the heat wave broke, but Serena's spirits didn't rise. Flirting a bit with Alan had reminded her of how alone she was. Now, she reminded herself, *I'm just another young woman with a fatherless child. I need to pull myself together.*

# Chapter Eighteen

In October, Serena gave up. She needed more support than Carol and Barb were able to provide, more money than she was earning and she wanted to have some fun. She needed a night out. Not knowing who else to call, she found a posting at the grocery from a teenage girl offering babysitting, called the number, and hired her, sight unseen, to babysit.

Serena rushed home from work. Put Kala into her crib and propped up a bottle, filled with formula and rice cereal. Serena had learned the cereal in the formula trick from the doctor, and it was proving to be a blessing. She showered quickly, burped Kala and returned her to the crib to finish the bottle. Kala seemed to watch Serena apply her makeup and brush her hair into a beehive. It reminded Serena of how she'd watched her mother from the doorway never daring to risk her anger by actually entering the bedroom but always hoping that Sylvia would turn and dab her nose with powder or spray a bit of perfume on her arm. It seldom happened but when it did, Serena would be sure that her adoptive mother was beginning to like her, perhaps even love her.

She picked up Kala and hugged her close. "Don't worry, sweetheart," she cooed. "I'll always love you. I just want to go out for a glass of wine and talk to some grown-ups. Okay?"

Kala grabbed her mother's hair and pulled. "Ouch," Serena yelped. A knock sounded and Serena hurried to open the door.

"Hi." A tall leggy, blond stood on the mat. "I'm Andy and this little cutey must be Kala."

She plucked Kala from Serena's arms. "I love babies. You finish getting ready, Kala and I will get to know each other."

Serena relaxed. Obviously, Andy knew more about babies than she did. Her guilt over wanting to go out disappeared and she began to look forward to the evening. Serena grabbed the bottle from the crib and gave it to Andy. "This is Kala's awake time. I hope that's okay. She'll need another bottle around ten and after that, she'll sleep through the night, but I'll be home before midnight."

"Seriously, we'll be fine. I have four brothers all younger, and the youngest ones are twins. I've been taking care of babies since I was ten. Trust me I know all about babies."

"Wow! Ten? Your mother let you babysit when you were ten?"

"Let, isn't exactly what I would call it. She needed help with the twins, and I loved feeling grown up. Now, I still love taking care of kids, and I like earning my own money. I plan to attend UCLA, and I'll need some savings. Scholarships don't pay for everything."

Serena took one more look in the mirror, told Andy to help herself to a coke or anything else she wanted, kissed Kala good-bye and hurried out the door. As she descended the stairs her spirits continued to rise. She wished she was headed into San Francisco to one of her favorite clubs but that would be too risky. Someone might recognize her. A local, neighborhood place would have to do.

It had grown dark as she walked from the apartment. She didn't really have a plan. She just wanted to feel like herself for one evening. A building with wooden shingles and shuttered windows caught her attention. The Alley on Grand looked perfect, a bit like a saloon from a movie. Its exterior seemed far too rough and ramshackle to attract anyone from her former life, or anyone from her office. Serena pushed open the door and was greeted by the smells of delicious food and the sounds of people having a good time. She hesitated, allowing her eyes to adjust to the low light.

The booths were full and the lacquered wooden bar was busy and crowded. A few people looked at her as she walked toward the piano bar, some smiled. Serena's spirits soared; it seemed to be a friendly place. "Hey, pretty lady," the piano player acknowledged her presence. Tipped his head at Serena and slid into a smooth rendition of *As Time Goes By.* One of the twelve bar stools around the grand piano was vacant. Serena claimed it, pushed an empty cocktail glass aside and looked around. The blue haze of cigarette smoke rose toward the ceiling; business cards were stapled randomly all over the walls. A man and woman directly across the piano from her tilted their glasses in her direction. She felt welcome. Her shoulders relaxed. An attractive cocktail waitress arrived to take her order. Serena pulled a pack of cigarettes from her bag and extracted one. Smoking was a new habit. She liked the way it gave her something to do when she wasn't sure what to do. A cigarette lighter clicked, and a warm, rich voice murmured, "May I?" Serena bowed her head to the flame, drew deeply on the cigarette, and raised her eyes to the man in front of her.

She exhaled slowly. "Thank you."

"My pleasure, Princess."

The cocktail waitress returned with Serena's whiskey sour. She placed it on the bar and swept up the empty glass Serena had pushed aside. "Another of the same, Joey?" she asked.

"Yes, thanks, kiddo." Serena opened her bag to pay for her drink. "Don't bother, Princess, it's on me."

"Thank you again." She extended her hand. "Serena Miller. And you really don't have to do that. I think I took your seat."

"Joey Coppola. And the pleasure is all mine." His large, warm hand enveloped hers in a gentle squeeze. "I can't think of a nicer surprise than finding you on my stool. Tell me," he lifted one eyebrow and grinned. "What's a nice girl like you doing in a place like this?"

Serena laughed. The piano tinkled, silver and china clattered softly, glasses clinked. It was lovely. Serena took a deep drink of whiskey and allowed it's warmth to numb her worries and fears.

A waiter tapped Joey on the shoulder. "Your table is ready Mr. Coppola."

"Please join me, Serena?" She started to shake her head no. "I hate dining alone. A girl needs to eat, and I can't think of a better way to get to know someone than over a good steak, come on."

Serena's mouth watered at the thought of a juicy steak. It had been months since she'd been out to dinner. She found herself sliding off the bar stool and accepting Joey's arm.

As they crossed the bar to a small booth in the corner, other diners greeted Joey by name, and he smiled at each of them returning their greeting but not pausing to talk. Joey took her coat and handed it to the waiter as Serena slipped into the booth, her back to the room. "We'll start with champagne." He ordered without asking and turned to Serena. "This place may look like a dive, but the cocktails are strong, the wine list is impressive, and the piano player is a legend."

A bottle of champagne materialized at their table, in a silver bucket on a stand. The waiter deftly uncorked the champagne and filled their crystal flutes. Serena almost giggled. It seemed she'd stepped into a dream world. She'd come out for a break from being a single mother, and suddenly she felt like a movie star. Joey lifted his glass, and she followed his move. "Here's to the beginning of a beautiful evening."

Serena touched her glass to his and allowed the bubbles to fill her mouth with their delicate explosions. He was too smooth, too practiced, probably; she looked closely at him, too old, but this sure beat washing diapers in the bathtub.

Serena relaxed and found herself laughing and flirting. She hadn't been out on a date since she'd discovered she was pregnant and it felt great to feel attractive and desirable. The conversation roamed from one topic to another. When Joey asked where she worked, she mentioned the firm and the type of law Alan practiced. He didn't question her about her past, and she didn't volunteer anything. Joey told her he owned some property and was in imports and exports and that he traveled to the Far East often. It sounded exciting and foreign to Serena.

They moved from the dining table back to the piano bar. Joey introduced her to the pianist, Rod Dibble, and to most of the others gathered around. Serena basked in their acceptance and their obvious admiration for Joey. No one asked who she was, or where she came from. It was fun to be with the most popular man in the room. When Rod played *I Only Have Eyes for You*, Joey took Serena's hand and in a rich, warm tenor sang directly to her. "Wow." Serena was overwhelmed. "That was beautiful."

Joey lifted her hand and kissed it gently. "You're beautiful."

Serena gazed back at Joey. His dark eyes crinkled a bit at the corner, and there seemed to be a slight dusting of gray in his hair, but he knew how to treat a lady, and she was having fun. Serena withdrew her hand and caught sight of the Boluva on her wrist. The tiny hands stood at 12:30. "Yikes." She jumped up, and for a moment the room spun. "I have to go."

Joey protested but she insisted. Finally he held up his hands in defeat. "At least let me drive you home."

"No really. It's just around the corner. I can walk."

"You don't have a husband waiting for you, do you?" Joey's eyes narrowed in suspicion.

Serena laughed. "No, nothing like that. No husband. No boyfriend. I just promised som...myself I'd be home by midnight."

"Okay, Cinderella. If that's what you want." He took her hand and held it as they walked to the coat room. She felt safe.

Serena smiled up at him. "I've had a wonderful evening, Joey. Thank you again for dinner."

He held her coat, as she slipped it on, and opened the door. Fog had rolled in from the bay. The air smelled of the sea. They stepped out together. Joey turned Serena toward him. Using one finger, he tilted her face up and kissed her gently. "Let's do this again."

Serena nodded. "I'd like that." Serena kissed him this time her lips lingering for just a second as his arms tightened around her. It felt so good to be hugged, to be close to someone. She pulled away. "I really do have to go."

Joey didn't protest again. He dropped his arms and Serena hurried away. She turned and looked back. The neon sign lit him from above, a cigarette glowed, he raised his hand and she waved as she turned the corner.

Serena floated through the weekend. Paying for Andy to babysit would leave her a little short of cash all week but it had been worth it. The show tunes Rod had played on Friday night, echoed in her head, and she sang aloud to Kala. The baby seemed to love the music too and giggled and cooed from her infant seat.

Monday, she was still smiling. Kala's care giver noticed and commented, "Had a nice weekend, did you?"

Alan grinned at her from his office. Serena called out a good morning, put her sandwich into the refrigerator and caught a glimpse of her desk. A huge bouquet of roses sat, square in the middle. "Looks like you have an admirer," Alan said coming up behind her. Serena stood perfectly still. "Or is it your birthday?" Serena shook her head. She reached out and touched a petal. The sweet scent filled the air.

"Where did they come from?" she managed to ask.

"They were delivered a few minutes ago. Don't you know who sent them?" Alan cocked an eyebrow. Serena shook her head. Alan plucked a tiny envelope from the arrangement and handed it to her, watching closely as she opened it and read the message,

"Joey Coppola," she whispered softly, but Alan heard.

"Coppola? The import guy? How do you know him?"

Serena's usual instinct to protect herself and her secrets failed her, and she answered without thinking it through. "I met him Friday night. We had dinner together."

"And..." Alan encouraged.

"And, he wants to see me again." Serena caught the look on Alan's face. "Why are you looking at me like that?"

Alan blushed. "It's none of my business. I was just surprised. I didn't think you moved in those circles."

"What circles?"

Alan started to answer, but the rest of the staff was arriving, and instead, he said, "We'll talk about it later. I have to get to court right now."

All day, people commented on the roses. At quitting time, she plucked a few flowers and ferns from the arrangement, wrapped their stems in a wet paper towel and used a piece of newspaper as a floral cone. I'd love to take the whole arrangement home, she thought, but there's no table big enough in my apartment to hold them. She carefully put Joey's card in her purse and headed for the door.

"Hello, Cinderella." Joey lounged against the fender of a shiny black car parked in the no parking zone in front of the building. "Your chariot awaits." He swung the door open and smiled at her.

Serena stood stalk still. "Joey, what are you doing here?"

"I told you I wanted to see you again." He waved at the flowers in her hand. "You didn't give me your number on Friday, and I thought it would be rude to disturb you at work, so here I am, in person, waiting to take you to dinner."

"I can't go to dinner."

"How about just a drink then?" Serena shook her head. "Why not?"

"It's complicated." Other people were watching them now, amused by the sight of such a romantic scene taking place on a busy street.

A man shouted, "Give him a break, girl." Joey laughed at the support.

"Nothing is complicated unless you make it that way," Joey insisted.

*True,* Serena thought, *but I made it that way.*

"Coppola." Serena was surprised to hear Alan's voice.

Joey turned, "Warren." The two men didn't shake hands. Serena could hear the caution in their greeting.

"Serena," Alan looked at her carefully, "everything okay here."

"Yes, of course, Alan. I was just telling Joey thank you for the roses, but I can't go out tonight."

"And, is that a problem?" Alan seemed to be asking her, but he looked at Joey.

"Not at all. I have to catch my bus or I'm going to be late."

Joey tried one more time. "Hop in; I'll take you wherever you need to go."

Serena hesitated but there didn't seem to be a graceful way out, and she supposed she'd need to admit to having a child if she was going to see Joey again. It had been so nice on Friday that she wasn't willing to call it quit; at least not without having a few more dates. She stepped forward and sank into the soft leather seat. Joey closed the door and moved to the driver's side. He nodded to Alan. Serena caught the look on Alan's face as they pulled away from the curb. She couldn't decide what he was thinking. Was he angry? Or maybe concerned? She'd need to talk to him. *I can't afford to lose my job,* she thought.

"Where to, Serena?" Joey swung the car into the afternoon traffic. "Are you sure I can't take you to dinner?"

"I need to tell you something, Joey." Her tone alerted Joey, and he reached across and squeezed her hand.

"It can't be that bad. Unless," he glanced at her, "you really are married."

"Not married, but," Serena took a deep breath, "I have a daughter."

Joey laughed. "That's no big deal. Half the women I know have children. How old is the kid? You been divorced long?"

"I'm not divorced, Joey. My daughter is almost five months old. I'm a widow."

"That's a tough break, but I don't see why that means you can't go out to dinner with me."

"Because…" Serena stopped to consider her answer and decided to tell the truth. "Because I can't afford a babysitter."

Joey laughed. "Serena, you are a beautiful woman, and I had a lot of fun with you on Friday night. If you'd do me the honor of having dinner with me, I'll gladly pay for a babysitter. Now, where am I taking you? I assume we need to pick up your kid from day care."

# Chapter Nineteen

Michael cradled his new daughter in the crook of his arm. He rocked her gently and spoke softly, "Hi, Little One. Welcome to the world." Raising his eyes, he smiled at Anne. "She's beautiful." Anne patted the bed. Michael sat carefully juggling the baby to keep his hand beneath her small head. "Dad and Grandmother Minette are waiting. Do you want them to come in?"

"In a minute." She lifted her hand and gently stroked the baby's face with one finger. "She's perfect."

"Just like her mother," Michael kissed his wife's hand. "Thank you, Anne. I thought the happiest day of my life was the day we married, but now I think this day may be the happiest." His eyes filled with tears and Anne brushed them away. He smiled. "I love you both."

"I know." Anne held out her arms for the baby. "Give her to me and go tell the family they can come in and meet the newest member of the Augustus clan."

Minette cuddled the baby and pronounced her absolutely lovely before handing her off to her grandfather. John gazed into the baby's face and remembered the birth of his daughter. A wave of longing swept through him, and he drew the baby close. "Have you decided on a name?" His voice quivered. Michael placed a hand on his father's arm and gave it a gentle squeeze.

"If she had been a boy it would have been another Michael Augustus but..." Anne smiled up at her husband's family, the family that was now as important to her as her own, "since we've had a daughter we need to decide."

"Didn't you even consider any girl names?" Minette looked surprised.

"I was sure it was a boy," Anne confessed. "When Michael or my friends suggested she would be a girl I just didn't believe them."

Everyone laughed. "Well, she's certainly a girl. You're much too pretty to be a boy, aren't you, Sweetheart?" John kissed the baby's forehead. She opened her eyes and gazed at him. "Look at how smart she is," John exclaimed. "She already knows I'm her grandfather."

"Well, we aren't going to name her John," Michael stated firmly. "How about Michele?"

"Too close to Michael," Anne said decisively. Anne held out her arms and John returned her daughter. "I think," Anne smiled at the baby and then looked at Michael, "she would like to be named

Rachel, after my grandmother and Minette after yours. Rachel Minette Augustus."

"Absolutely. Rachel Minette it is," Michael agreed, "a lovely name for my lovely daughter."

Now it was Minette's turn to brush a tear from her eye. "I'm delighted to have such a beautiful namesake." Michael hugged his grandmother. A movement next to his father caught his attention. He took in a quick breath. "What is it?" Minette lifted her eyebrow.

"Em, I em..." he stammered.

"Is Valerie here?" John turned to the space beside him. "She is, isn't she? Did she say something?"

"It was probably just the light," Michael protested. "I thought I saw someone, sorry."

Anne smiled calmly. "Don't worry, darling. You've been talking to Valerie's ghost as long as we've all known you. We don't think you're crazy. Did she say something?"

Michael shook his head. There was no way he was going to put a damper on his family's happiness on such an important day. The door opened, and Helen and Sam arrived. Michael welcomed the interruption. He could feel Anne watching him closely. He refused to meet her eyes as he smiled broadly and accepted congratulation from his aunt and uncle.

Rachel was passed from arm to arm and admired by all. At last, a nurse entered the room and shooed them all out so that both the new mother and the baby could get some rest. Michael kissed his wife and told her again how much he loved her. Anne hugged him tight. She knew Valerie had spoken and she knew he wanted to keep it a secret. She'd let it go for now.

Life with a new baby in the house was demanding. Anne had followed her mother's advice and hired a nanny to cover the night time feedings and the heavy work, but even so, she found herself exhausted. She forgot to ask Michael about Valerie's visit to the hospital.

When Michael came in from work, she tried to greet him with pleasure, but all she wanted was to sleep. Michael assured it was normal and to give herself time to adjust, but Anne worried. "It's just hormones," she told herself. "Keep busy, and this will pass."

If Anne had forgotten Valerie's visit, Michael hadn't. At the office, he kept his focus strictly on business and left as quickly as possible each day to get home to his wife and child. He didn't want to think about her words, but they never left his thoughts.

He knew Valerie had looked at him and said, "There is something wrong. Help her." Help who, he wanted to shout? If it was Elizabeth, he didn't know where to find her. If it was Anne she seemed fine, tired but fine. If it was Rachel, the nanny assured him she was a "bonny child," and if it was Minette, he hadn't noticed anything wrong. He decided to talk to his grandmother. Ever since she'd rescued him and Elizabeth after the war, she'd been his rock, much more of a parent than either John or Sylvia. He called and asked if he could stop by.

Minette's greeting was as warm as ever. She was delighted to see her grandson, and it made no difference to her that he was not a grandchild by birth. She drew him into the cozy living room. Henry rose from his chair, carefully placing his book on the table next to him. He gave Michael a warm hug and offered to excuse himself so they could talk.

"No, Henry. Please stay. I do want to talk about something. It would be good to hear your take on the matter."

Henry nodded gravely and resumed his seat. Minette offered refreshment. Michael shook his head. "No thanks, I need to get home." He took a deep breath and sank into a chair. Minette and

Henry waited patiently. The silence stretched between them.

A log broke, and Michael jumped. "I know this sounds crazy," he began. "I saw Valerie at the hospital." Minette and Henry nodded. "I don't see her very often, not like when I was a kid, but there is no doubt it was Valerie. She said something that is really bothering me. I can't figure out what she meant, and I don't know what to do." He rose and began to pace. "She said, 'There is something wrong. Help her.' But I don't know what that means. Who needs my help?"

Minette studied his face, "Who do you think she meant?"

"Probably Elizabeth. But maybe Rachel or Anne or even you, Grandmother."

"I assure you I'm fine, Michael. I saw Rachel yesterday, and she is thriving." She considered her words and spoke carefully. "Has Valerie ever spoken to you about anyone other than Elizabeth?"

Michael nodded. "Yes. She used to talk to me a lot." He looked at Henry. "I'm not crazy. I really do see her, and sometimes I hear her."

"You are definitely not crazy, Michael. The supernatural isn't understood, but it doesn't mean it's not real. If you see and hear a ghost, there is a reason you do, and we need to figure it out. While it is most likely that Valerie is concerned about Elizabeth and wants you to find her, it is certainly possible that she is trying to tell you something about someone else." Henry watched Michael absorb his words. "Minette is well. Rachel is well. I think you should start with Anne. Go home and talk to your wife."

With Rachel tucked in bed, her care given over to the nanny for the night, Michael suggested to Anne that they have a glass of wine. Anne started to demur. All she wanted to do was go to sleep, but she caught the look in his eye and knew that he had something he needed to say. "Sounds good, Honey," she agreed. "I just want to change into my pajamas."

"Go ahead. I'll bring the wine upstairs, and we can relax. It's chilly enough tonight for a fire in the bedroom."

Anne curled up on the chaise lounge, and Michael sat at her feet. He lifted his glass and looked at the fire's glow. "This is nice." He smiled at Anne.

"It is." Anne took a deep drink of her wine and sighed. Michael stroked her foot. Anne sank further into the pillows, "Okay, tell me, Michael. What did Valerie say?" Michael continued to stroke his wife's foot. "Just talk to me. It can't be that bad."

"She said, 'There is something wrong. Help her.', and I don't know who she wants me to help or what she wants me to do." Michael let go of her foot and stared into the fire.

Anne slid down the lounge and laid her head against his back, encircling him with her arms. "You took care of Elizabeth every day of her life until she wouldn't let you. Even now you worry about her and search for her. I know how much you love Elizabeth and if Valerie's ghost doesn't know that …" Anne gulped. "I sound crazy, that darn ghost is like a member of the family." A giggle escaped. "I guess, she is a member of the family. No one sees or talks to her but you but we all we believe in her and act like she knows all and sees all."

Michael turned and hugged Anne close. "But what if it isn't Elizabeth? What if it is Rachel, or Minette or you? I can't help if I don't know who to help."

"Michael, you aren't responsible for everything. Rachel is growing like a weed. I'm tired and finding it a big adjustment to have a child, but I'm fine, and so is Minette. It has to be Elizabeth and unless she wants to be found… what can you do?"

# Chapter Twenty

Serena pushed her way through the crowd gathered in the staff room celebrating Alan's latest win in court. She smiled at her boss. "I hear you scored a direct hit on housing discrimination today. Another win for the good guys."

"I doubt that your boyfriend will think it's a win," one of the associates scoffed.

Serena turned to ask what he meant, but Alan caught her hand, "You got a minute? I think we need to talk." Serena nodded. "Come with me." She followed him from the room and into his office. He closed the door and waved her to a chair. "Are you still dating Coppola?" Serena nodded again. "Okay, then we definitely need to talk."

"You're kind of scaring me, Alan. What's the matter?"

"How much do you know about Coppola's business?"

"I know he owns some property and that he imports all kinds of merchandise from China and Japan. Why?"

"The property he owns is low-income housing, all over the Bay Area but mostly here in Oakland." Alan paused and watched her face as she realized where this conversation was going. "He's one of the landlords we sued, the biggest one." Serena clasped her hands tightly to keep them from trembling. "The judge levied a $100,000 fine and a cleanup order against him today."

Serena stared at Alan, unsure of what to say. $100,000 was a lot of money. Joey was not going to like that. Finally, she said, "I didn't know you were suing him."

"This wasn't a case that you worked on. We filed when you went out on your maternity leave and when you came back to work nothing much was happening. Then, when I discovered you had a relationship with Coppola, I kept you out of the loop on purpose. I'm surprised he never mentioned the lawsuit to you."

Serena remembered the day after her first evening with Joey when the two men had met outside the office. "I guess you were both trying to protect me," she said. *Or yourselves,* she thought. "Thank you, for telling me now."

"I hope this doesn't cause any trouble for you, Serena." Alan watched her closely, and she forced herself to relax. She'd seen Joey's temper a time or two, but it had never been directed at her.

"I'm sure Joey won't think I had anything to do with the judgment. After all, I'm just a secretary here."

"You're much more than that, Serena. I couldn't run this office without your support. You'd make a great paralegal. You have a good, quick mind and the clients all open up to you."

"Thanks for the compliment, Alan. But I better get out of here and pick up my daughter. Don't worry about Joey. He loves me." She rose from her chair and turned toward the door.

"If you ever need my help, I'm here."

At his words, she glanced back and smiled warmly. "Thanks, Alan. I'll remember that."

"I hope you will," Alan muttered as the door swung shut.

⁕

Joey was furious. His attorney had assured him that a 'wimpy little guy like Alan Warren' wouldn't have the ability to cause him any trouble. And, yet, here he was looking at a $100,000 fine, at least another $100,000 in required repairs on his buildings, and, worst of all, his picture was on every channel's six o'clock news. Now, the damn tenants would think they could get away with anything, and his import/export clients would lose respect for him.

He tossed back a glass of whiskey, slammed out of his luxury townhome and headed for the bar.

Serena bathed Kala and tucked her chubby legs and arms into a soft, pink sleeper. She brushed her hand across the fine pale fuzz that covered her daughter's head. "Are you going to be a redhead?" Eighteen-month-old Kala shook her head, an emphatic no. Serena laughed aloud.

Motherhood was so much easier now that Joey was paying for Andy to babysitter three or four nights a week. He kept pressing her to move in with him, but he never mentioned marriage and Serena wasn't sure she was free spirited enough to take her child and live with someone she wasn't married to. True, it would be easier. Sometimes they came back to her tiny apartment to make love at the end of a night out but Joey always left afterward, and she knew he didn't like the need to be quiet so they wouldn't wake Kala. More often they went to his place and he put her in a cab afterward.

"Andy will be here soon. Mama needs to finish getting ready." She popped her daughter into her highchair and scattered some dry Cheerios on the tray.

A knock sounded. Kala banged the tray and yelled, "An, An, An."

"That's right. Andy's here." Serena pulled open the door, and Andy popped in, long golden hair swishing across the shoulders of a letter jacket that was much too big for her.

"Hey," Serena surveyed the girl, "what's this? Whose jacket are you wearing?"

Andy giggled. "Steve Rains. The most, good looking, sweetest, Olympian at Skyline High."

Serena laughed. "I take it you are now dating Steve Rains."

"You are correct." Andy dropped a kiss on Kala's head and tickled her foot. "How's my little princess tonight?"

"Tell me about your Mr. Rains while I get dressed."

"He's a senior, like me." Andy giggled. "He's tall, he's cute, and his eyes are blue."

"Well, that's everything a girl could ask for." Serena wondered if she'd ever been that young. Andy was eighteen while she had just turned twenty-five. *How in the world could seven years make such a difference?* Serena pulled a black sheath dress over her head and turned so Andy could zip her up. She smoothed the dress over her hips and adjusted the white bow that was placed just under her breasts. She smoothed her hair to be sure it was still in an up-swept beehive. "So, what do you think?"

"I think Mr. Coppola will find you beautiful."

Serena heard the hesitation in Andy's compliment, "But?"

Andy studied her carefully. "It's a beautiful dress, but it seems a little…a little old, I guess. Kind of like a dress from an old movie."

Serena turned back to the mirror and studied her reflection. "It does, doesn't it? I look like I stepped out of a Doris Day movie. Joey gave it to me for my birthday."

Another knock sounded on the door, and Serena quickly rearranged her features into a smile. "You look great, doll." Joey pulled her close for a deep kiss. Serena tried to pull away, embarrassed in front of Andy, but Joey kept a tight hold on her waist. "You ready?"

"I just need my bag." He loosened his hold and Serena crossed the room to retrieve the bag. She dropped a kiss on Kala's head and, avoiding Andy's gaze, returned to the door.

"Serena," Andy's voice stopped her, "do you mind if Steve comes over after Kala is down for the night? We need to study for the calculus test."

Joey snickered and answered for Serena, "No problem kid. Just don't do anything we wouldn't do."

His laugh set Serena on edge, and she wanted to tell him to stop, but instead, she smiled at Andy and said, "It's fine."

❦

At the car Joey kissed her again, hard and unrelenting, it didn't feel like a kiss it felt like a challenge. Serena wasn't sure what to say so she stayed quiet and kissed him back. He opened her door and barely waited for her to be settled before he slammed it behind her. As he started the car, Serena asked, "Everything okay?"

Joey didn't answer, slammed the car into gear and pulled out with a jerk, tires squealed as he turned out of the driveway. Serena searched her mind, trying to think of something to say that would break the tension and calm him down. She reached across the gearshift and placed her hand on his leg. "Where are we going to dinner?" she asked.

He shot her a sideways look. "We need to talk in private. I'll take you to my place, and we'll have a cocktail before dinner."

Serena nodded, afraid to say she didn't think he needed another cocktail. "That sounds good."

This has to be about the lawsuit, she thought. She managed to smile at him.

Joey stayed quiet as he maneuvered the car through downtown Oakland and pulled up in front of the Art Deco building on the corner of Twenty-First Street and Lakeside Drive. The reflection of the downtown lights caused Lake Merritt to glow in the dark. Neither one of them commented on the beauty of the setting. Joey jerked the parking brake into position with way more force than necessary.

"Let's go, princess." Serena reached for her door handle and swung it open. Joey's manners had never failed him before, but it didn't sound like he wanted to be chivalrous tonight. He held her elbow instead of her hand as they walked quickly into the building and silently, rode the elevator up to his townhome.

Joey slammed the door and strode quickly across the room to the bar. She watched him pour a generous shot and gulp it down. Serena removed her coat and hung it in the entry. She crossed the room to gaze out at the sparkling lake. In the window, she could see Joey's reflection pour another shot and toss it back.

She turned and smiled, "Mix me a drink, too, Joey. And then tell me what's wrong."

Joey made a vodka tonic for Serena and poured more whiskey into his own glass. Serena was relieved to see him carry the glasses to the coffee table instead of tossing down a third drink. She sank down on the sofa and reached for her glass. Sipping carefully, she studied him, and with relief saw his shoulders begin to relax.

"Why didn't you tell me about the lawsuit?" she asked.

"Tell you? Isn't the question why didn't you tell me what that damn Warren was up to? How could you let me be blindsided like that?"

"I don't know anything about the lawsuit that Alan won today. I knew he was in court, but it wasn't a case I'd worked on. I only found out this afternoon that you were one of the landlords that he was suing."

"Am I supposed to believe that?" He picked up his glass and swirled the alcohol. "That law firm isn't that big."

"I think," Serena said carefully, "that after Alan realized we were dating, he was very careful to keep me away from anything that included your name and you never mentioned that you were being sued by any one, much less by our law firm. You know I'm not a paralegal or an attorney; I'm a secretary, one of the several secretaries. Mostly I take dictation, type letters and file things."

She heard herself belittling the job she'd grown to love. It felt like so much more than being a secretary, she did feel like part of the legal team, but this wasn't the time to tell that to Joey. She needed him to calm down.

Joey sipped at his drink. "You know, princess, I like you, and you look good. But you're damaged goods. Not many men would be willing to call a woman with a kid and no ex-husband his girlfriend."

"I'm a widow."

"Right, princess. If you say so." Joey watched her closely. "I don't really care about your past, Serena. We all have one but don't try to feed me that widow story." He watched her absorb his statement. When it looked like she might protest he held up his hand to stop her, "Get this straight, princess. Either you're with me or against me. There is no in between. That bastard you're working for is sticking his nose in where it doesn't belong. I need to go talk to some people, and get this mess your 'darling Alan' has created for me, straightened out. No damn judge is going to tell me how to run my business. Drink up and let's get out of here."

"But we just got here. Why don't we just stay in this evening? We could order something or ..."

"Aren't you listening? I need to fix this and to do that I need to talk to some people. Let's move it."

# Chapter Twenty One

It was warm for November and Serena felt antsy. She couldn't stand to stay in the apartment another minute. "Would you like to go to the park, Kala?" Kala smiled and nodded. She still wasn't talking very much, but she knew exactly what she wanted. She ran to her bed to get her favorite teddy bear, a silly, floppy thing that Barb and Carol had given her when she was born.

"Is teddy going with us?" Kala held up the bear and shook her head no, but Serena knew that meant yes. She laughed at her daughter. "You find your shoes, and we'll go." Kala ran off again leaving teddy by the door.

Motherhood was actually fun now that Kala could communicate. But Joey was right, they did need to move to a bigger place. The garage apartment was just too small for the two of them. Serena quickly packed some snacks, twisted her hair into a high ponytail and found a picnic blanket. Kala sat perfectly still while Serena put on her shoes and then picked up teddy and stood by the door. "Are you ready?" Again the head shake. Serena laughed. "Okay, let's go."

She opened the door and gasped. Carol stood just outside, hand raised to knock. "Sorry." Carol dropped her hand. "It looks like great minds think alike. Barb and I thought you guys might like to go to Fairyland today. We packed a picnic."

"We were just going to walk to the park on the corner, but Lake Merritt would be wonderful. Kala hasn't been to Fairyland, and neither have I."

"Excellent, you're both in for a treat. Don't bother with the blanket. We have a whole car full of stuff. You know Barb; she loves to plan an event. There's enough food to feed an army."

Kala peeked out from behind Serena's legs, smiling broadly when she saw that the visitor was one of her favorite people. "Hi pretty girl," Carol said and held out her arms to lift the small child in a hug. Kala patted her cheek.

"Go," Kala said firmly.

They trooped down the stairs and squeezed into Barb's VW bug. "When are you going to get a phone, Serena? We'd call ahead instead of just dropping by if we could."

"As soon as I can afford one, but you guys can drop by anytime, you know you're always welcome. I'm so glad you came today. I really needed to get outside, and I've been meaning to explore Fairyland, but it is two bus rides away."

The three women chatted easily on the drive. They found a picnic place close to the Cinderella's Slipper slide, and a wide eyed Kala took Barb's hand and walked cautiously toward the playground. Serena slipped off her shoes and leaned back, watching her daughter's delight.

"You guys are so good to us," Serena smiled at Carol. "I doubt that I can ever repay you." They had been such a help during the pregnancy, and with Kala's birth Serena had known she could always trust them.

"Don't be silly. You certainly don't owe us a thing. We love seeing you with your child." For a second Carol looked sad, and Serena remembered why they had stepped in to help. She reached out and squeezed Carol's hand. "Just help someone else someday. In fact, working with Alan Warren, you're on the right track. I saw the story in the Examiner about his big win last week."

"Alan is one of the good guys," Serena agreed. "But," she hesitated, and Carol turned to look at her, "I think I may have to change jobs."

"I thought you loved working with Alan? What's going on?"

"I do love working with Alan. He's been great, and I've learned so much. I think his commitment to fair housing is honorable. But, I've been dating someone who doesn't agree, and he wants me to spy on Alan for him."

"Serena Miller! I can't believe I just heard you say that." Carol sat up perfectly straight and glared at Serena. "How can you date a person who would ask such a thing?"

"I know how bad that sounds and I would never tell anyone, not even Joey, what goes on in the office. But if I keep working there he'll keep asking."

"Do you mean you intend to continue dating this Joey? Who is this guy anyway?"

"Joey Coppola. I met him about a year ago. We have a lot of fun, and he's been very good to me." Carol waited as Serena considered how much she wanted to tell. "He wants us to move in with him."

"Why would you even consider moving in with someone who'd ask you to spy on your boss?"

"I know it sounds awful, but..."

"Hello, there. I thought that was you."

"Alan." Serena sprang to her feet. "What are you doing here?"

"Just walking through the park and I thought I recognized you and Carol."

"Sit down, Alan. I haven't seen you in ages." Carol smiled up at him.

Alan sat. Serena sank back down. She fiddled with the blanket fringe and tried to think what to say as Carol and Alan began to talk shop. She certainly didn't want to discuss Joey, or his request, with Alan.

Kala ran up, closely followed by Barb. Serena held out her arms and caught her daughter close, saved from further discussion by the interruption. Kala learned against her mother and studied Alan. He smiled at her, "Hi, you must be Kala. You're just as pretty as your picture." Kala tucked her thumb in her mouth and shook her head no.

"I'm afraid we are entering the "no" stage. She doesn't talk much, but when she does, it's usually to say no, even if she means yes."

"She's lovely, Serena. Did she get that red hair from her dad?"

Serena stroked her daughter's soft hair and remembered Mary Lou's wedding and the red headed McGuiness family. Logan's hair had been dark blond, maybe he'd been a redhead when he was young. Maybe, she thought, her own parents had been red heads. "I'm quite sure it will get darker as she gets older. Believe it or not, my hair was almost blond when I was a baby."

Carol, aware of the conundrum of Kala's parenthood, jumped in with a laugh. "Whoever she looks like, she's a lucky girl to have such a pretty mommy."

"I can agree with that," Alan said smiling warmly at Serena.

Barb opened the picnic basket and suggested Alan join them. He protested but was overruled, and soon they were feasting on egg salad sandwiches, tomato and cucumber slices, fresh fruit, and chocolate cake. Serena was relieved to hear the conversation turn away from her daughter. Sometimes, she thought, *it was just so hard to keep all the secrets.*

After the picnic, Serena and Barb took Kala back to the playground leaving Alan and Carol to talk on the blanket. Alan lay back with his hands behind his head and looked up into the leaves of a large oak. Without looking directly at Carol, he said, "Serena's a great asset to the office. I'm really glad you recommended that I hire her. She's bright and very organized. I'm thinking of promoting her to be the office manager."

Carol waited for him to finish his thought but when he stayed silent she prompted, "And..."

Alan sat up and turned to watch Carol's face as he finished his thought. "And…nothing. But she's dating Joey Coppola."

"Yes, she told me."

"Don't you think that's a problem?" Carol raised a questioning eyebrow. "Coppola's the slum landlord I just sued."

"Yikes." Carol bit her lip and considered what to say next. No wonder Serena had been asked to spy. "Does she know?"

Alan nodded. "I told her, about a month ago, when we won the case. Until then she'd had no idea. I thought she'd break up with him. I hoped she'd break up with him. What do you think she sees in him anyway?"

"I think," Carol considered her words carefully. She and Alan had been friends for a long time. She didn't want to lie, but she needed to protect Serena and Kala. "I think, she's lonely and this Joey is nice to her. She's a single mother on a limited income, and he probably pays for everything. Serena can barely afford rent and food for herself and Kala."

"If I offer her the job and she takes it, there'd be a decent raise. How much does she need?"

Carol laughed and shook her head as she said, "Alan you are too good to be true. Do you even need an office manager?"

"That didn't come out right. I really do need more help. I'm thinking of moving the firm to Sacramento so we can be active with the legislature. The housing laws in this state need reform."

"I'd heard a rumor about that," Carol admitted. "How soon are you thinking about making this move?"

"What move?" Barb asked as she sank down on the blanket. "A two-year-old is exhausting." She flopped onto her back and closed her eyes.

"Where are Kala and Serena?"

"Over there by the Crooked Mile. Kala is walking it for the hundredth time."

Carol laughed and patted her partner's leg. Alan sat up and stretched. "I've been looking for offices for a while now, and I think I've found something. There's a great old house on K Street that was converted a few years ago. It's a good location, and I like the feel of the place."

"What about your Oakland practice?"

"I'd keep it going and gradually turn it over to Jim Butler as the lead. Maybe make it a partnership. I'm still working out the details. I think it would take about a year to be fully up and running in Sacramento anyway so I have some time to iron things out." He frowned as he studied the playground.

Carol turned to see what he was seeing. "Is that Joey with Serena?" she asked. Alan nodded.

Barb sat up to take a look. "He's way too old for her," she declared. They watched in silence for a minute. The couple appeared to be having an argument. Serena walked away from Joey, he grabbed her arm, and she shook him off. Alan rose to his feet ready to intervene, but Joey turned and stormed off. Serena went to the wall and picked up Kala and headed for the blanket.

"Do you guys mind leaving? I think it's time to get Kala home."

"Absolutely, the temperature is starting to drop anyway."

Alan helped gather up the picnic supplies and carry them to the car. He watched Serena, trying to decide if he should say anything about the scene they'd watched. Carol caught his eye and shook her head. "Thanks for your help, Alan," she said. "I'll handle it from here. Let's talk in a day or so, and you can tell me the rest of your plans."

Alan nodded his agreement and understanding, hugged Carol and Barb, patted

Kala's tired head and said, "See you on Monday," to Serena.

Serena watched him walk away. "He really is a good guy, isn't he?" She climbed into the VW and settled Kala on her lap. "Did you see me talking to Joey?"

The others nodded. Barb said, "It looked more like an argument than a talk."

Each of the women kept their thoughts to themselves on the drive back to Serena's apartment. Kala fell asleep, and Carol offered to carry stuff up so that Serena could manage Kala. When Kala was safely in her bed, Carol held out her arms to Serena and hugged her close. "You know you can tell me anything, right? I'll never judge you or tell your secrets." Serena nodded and brushed tears from her eyes.

"I need Joey. If we move into his house, Kala will have a room of her own. I won't have to worry about money all the time. He likes me, and who else would want us. I'm a single mom who's never been married."

"Serena, you're an intelligent, beautiful young women, raising a child. Any man would be lucky to have you."

"But, Joey's right. When they find out I've never been married no one will want to marry me. Joey says I'm 'spoiled goods.'

"First, you don't need to be married. Second, who the hell does this Joey creep think he is to tell you that you are anything but perfect? He's practically a criminal. Everyone in the city knows that his businesses operate barely within the law."

"I don't know that."

"Well then, maybe it's time you took a better look at Joey Coppola."

"But he has a point."

"No, he doesn't, Serena. Whatever has happened to you in the past is over. You don't have to explain to anyone or tell them anything you don't want to tell them. All that matters is the life you make for yourself from now on. One day at a time. Got that?"

*But if you knew all the lies I've told you wouldn't think I was worth anything either,* she thought. Serena managed a wobbly smile. "Thanks, Carol."

"I'll call you at work on Monday, okay?" Carol hugged her again and left.

Serena took off Kala's shoes and socks and loosened her clothing. Kala murmured something and popped her thumb into her mouth. Serena hoped she'd sleep through the night.

She quickly tidied the apartment; glanced at the clock, and discovered it was only 8:00 PM. Serena poured a glass of wine and changed into her most comfortable pajamas. She paced the apartment thinking about the afternoon. Joey had been so angry at the park; she'd tried to explain that the outing hadn't been planned. That Alan had simply been in the park, had stopped to say hi. That he had joined them at Carol's invitation. There was no reason for him to be jealous but it seemed like he thought she'd invited Alan.

She'd asked him to meet Carol and Barb, but he'd angrily declared that he had no interest in dykes, and that she needed to change her attitude and help him get the information he wanted from Alan's files. *I can't spy on Alan,* she thought. *He's been so good to me, and I really like my job.* She pulled a magazine from the pile on the end table and tried to stop thinking.

The sound of banging on the door startled her awake. She hurried to the door wanting the noise to stop before Kala awoke. A disheveled Joey stood on the landing. "Hey, Baby," he grinned at her, "aren't you glad to see me?"

"Go away. It's after midnight, and you're going to wake Kala."

Joey pushed the door open further and peered past her, "What's the matter. You got your boyfriend in there?"

"You're drunk, Joey." Serena tried to block the door.

Joey slammed the door the rest of the way open, and it bounced against the wall. Kala sat up in her bed. "Damn it, Joey. Get out of here."

He grabbed Serena's arm and used it to twist her body out of the doorway. Serena cried out in pain and tried to pry his fingers from around her arm. "Where is he? Hiding in the bathroom?" He frog marched Serena across the tiny apartment and threw open the bathroom door. "Come out, come out, little Alan,"

Kala began to wail. Serena tried to break free again, but Joey tightened his grip on her arm and twisted the skin. Serena screamed, and Kala cried louder. "For God's sake, Joey, Alan's not here. I told you this afternoon, he's not my boyfriend. I just work for him."

"What is going on in here?" Serena's landlady burst into the apartment. "You," she pointed at Joey, "need to let go of that girl and get out of here."

"Or what?" Joey eyed the older women, taking in the faded blue bathrobe and the rollers in her hair. He jerked Serena's arm up higher and grinned when she gasped.

His eyes widened in surprise as the landlady pulled a small gun from her pocket and pointed it in his direction. "Or I'll blow your brains out." Joey let go and stepped forward. "If you're smart you'll leave right now. I've already called the police, and I know how to use this gun." She lifted it slightly so that it was pointed directly at his chest.

Joey lifted his hands in mock surrender. "It was just a little misunderstanding between me and my girl. Right, Baby?" He tried to smile in Serena's direction.

"Get out of here, Joey and don't come back. I never want to see you or hear from you again, ever."

"I wouldn't waste my time on you, Baby. You're a worthless piece of shit that no man will ever want." The sound of an approaching siren caused Joey to turn toward the door. "I'm leaving, but you owe me the information I need. I'll be in touch."

He ran down the stairs. Serena hurried to Kala and scooped her up, hugging her close. They could hear Joey greet someone, and then a voice asked, "Everything okay here, Mr. Coppola? We got a call about a breaking and entry."

"Every thing's fine. Just leaving my girl's place."

"You have a good evening, sir."

A car door slammed, and the women heard the cars drive away. "So, I guess that's that," Serena's landlady said. She slipped her pistol back into her pocket. "I don't want to know how you got involved with that piece of slime but I'd better not see him around here again."

"You won't," Serena promised. "If he shows up again, I'll call the police myself."

"I don't think that'll do much good. It sounded to me like the cops are on his side." She studied Serena for a moment. "You'd better put some ice on your shoulders. You're going to be mighty sore in the morning. Get some sleep if you can."

"Thank you." Serena opened the door and watched the landlady walk down the stairs and back into her house before she began to sob.

# Chapter Twenty Two

Serena dressed carefully on Monday, choosing a long sleeved, high necked sweater that covered the bruises on her wrists and arms. Her shoulders ached from being pulled up and back but she admitted to herself, she'd been lucky. If her landlady hadn't heard the ruckus, she wasn't sure what Joey might have done. She watched carefully as she walked Kala to the daycare and then headed for her bus. Everything seemed fine and she didn't see Joey's car but her stomach twisted in fear when she remembered his angry words.

Only minutes after arriving in the office, Carol called. "Are you okay?"

"I'm fine. It was just a little scary."

"When Mandy called this morning, she made it sound like more than that. You need to be careful."

"Really, Carol, I'm fine. I don't think he'll bother me again."

"What's going on?" Alan asked, coming up behind her with a stack of files in his arms. "Who's bothering you?"

Serena reached for the files, "No one important. What's all this?"

Alan explained what he needed, and Serena breathed a sigh of relief, thinking she'd avoided his question, but as he returned to his office, he said, "If you need help, Serena, just tell me."

*No one can help*, Serena thought, *I got myself into this mess with a bunch of lies, and now I have to stick to my story.*

At 10:30, a tap on her shoulder interrupted her concentration. She turned and found the receptionist holding a huge bouquet of roses. "I don't want those," Serena declared.

"Well, someone wants you to have them."

Serena snatched the card out of flowers and ripped it open.

# Baby, please forgive me. I acted like an idiot. You know I love you. Joey

She picked up the vase and headed to the large trash can in the break room where she dumped the roses, vase and all into the trash can and slammed the lid. She turned and saw every eye in the office watching her as she stomped back to her desk, but instead of sitting down she whirled around and went to talk to Alan.

She knocked on his door frame to get his attention, and as soon as Alan looked up, she said, "I need to tell you something about Joey Coppola." He waved her to a chair, but Serena remained standing. "He asked me to provide him with information about your case against him."

"And did you?"

"No. But I considered it." Serena lifted her chin and looked Alan squarely in the eye.

"Thank you for telling me. You haven't done anything wrong, and I know that I can trust you. I also know that Coppola is not a good man, so I'm not surprised that he tried to use you."

"I've broken it off with him. We won't be dating anymore."

"Good." Alan smiled at her and picked up his pen. Serena managed to smile. Her knees felt weak, she placed her hands on the desk and leaned on them. Her sweater pulled up slightly exposing the bruises on her wrists. "What happened to your arms, Serena?"

Serena stiffened her spine and pulled down the sleeves, "Nothing, I'm fine."

"You are not fine, Serena. Coppola did that, didn't he?"

"He was drunk and jealous; he didn't mean to hurt me. And anyway, it's over now. I told him to stay away from me."

"Men like Coppola don't take no for an answer, easily. Did you report the assault to the police?"

"No. My landlady called them, but everything was over by the time they got to the house." She sank into the chair. "Joey knew them. They didn't even check on me."

"You need to be very careful. Not everyone on the police force is in Coppola's pocket. If he shows up again, don't let him in and call the police right away. Do you want me to file a restraining order against him?"

Serena shook her head. "I don't think he'll be back." She twisted her fingers together and remembered the flowers she'd thrown away just minutes ago, maybe she was wrong.

◦⁀◦⌣◦

By the next week, Serena felt like she could relax. Joey had made no attempt to contact her, no flowers, no calls, and no visits.

Late in the day, on Thursday, Alan stopped to tell her that the judge had finished his review of Coppola's petition for relief from the levied fines, and would be issuing his ruling in the morning. "What do you expect?" she asked.

"Coppola has a lot of political pull in this town, so the judge may reduce the fine, but I expect he'll let it stand. The reporters will have a field day if Coppola is allowed to continue to neglect his building. During the trial, we proved how dangerous conditions were in most of the units."

One look at Alan's face the next day told Serena that he was disappointed in the ruling. She followed him to his office and closed the door before asking, "How bad is it?"

"The damn judge gave him a slap on the wrist. He called the original award onerous and levied only a thousand dollar fine, and a requirement that he installs a fire pull-box on each floor of each building that he owns within five years." He pulled his tie open and slumped down in his desk chair. "I hate this town."

Serena couldn't think of anything to say that might help. "I'll get you a cup of coffee," she said and slipped away to give Alan time to compose himself.

Returning she placed the coffee on his desk and turned to leave. "Stay, please. There's something I wanted to talk to you about.

Remember last summer when I told you I'd like to lobby in Sacramento for changes in the state's housing policies?" She nodded. "I'm going to do it."

"I think that's wonderful, Alan. Everyone deserves a chance to live where they want to live. Some of the stories I hear every day, in this office, make me want to cry. If anyone I know can make a difference, I believe it will be you."

"Thanks for your confidence." He tapped his pen on the blotter and sipped his coffee before continuing. "I've found an office location near the capital buildings, and I plan to move there in January."

"Wow, that's fast."

"Not really, I've been thinking about it and planning it for well over a year. I'll be keeping this office open. Jim Butler and I have formed a partnership, and he'll run this location. We both want you to stay with the firm. I'd like you to come to Sacramento with me, but if you prefer to stay in Oakland, that's okay, too. In either case, I'm promoting you to Office Manager, effective immediately."

"I'm not sure what to say."

Alan laughed. "Say yes to the promotion and the pay raise, and that you'll think about whether you want to move to Sacramento or stay here."

"Okay," Serena grinned. "Yes."

"Don't you want to know how much your increase will be?"

"Sure, and what does becoming the office manager mean?"

"Actually, you're already doing everything we need an office manager to do. I just want to pay you a fair salary and give you the title. I believe you are at $1.60 an hour now and I'm going to raise that to $2.25, how's that sound?"

"Amazing! Are you sure?"

Alan laughed. "You're a terrible negotiator. I'm sure. I'll announce your title change to the rest of the staff, but you just keep doing what you've been doing and think about moving to Sacramento."

Serena floated out of the office. An extra twenty-five dollars a week would make such a difference in her life. She'd be able to buy a Christmas tree and a few decorations, Kala would love it. And maybe she could find a bigger apartment and get a telephone installed. She wanted to tell someone her good news.

Still smiling she picked up the ringing phone on her desk. "Good afternoon. You've reached the law office of Alan Warren. How may I help you?"

"Hey Baby. Remember me?" Serena almost dropped the phone at the sound of Joey's voice.

"What may I do for you, Mr. Coppola?" she managed to ask.

"I miss you. Let me take you to dinner tonight. We can celebrate your boss's loss in court today." He chuckled. "You're boyfriend doesn't seem like such a winner now does he?"

"I told you not to call me anymore."

"I'll pick you up at eight."

"No. I won't be home. Goodbye, Mr. Coppola." She resisted the urge to slam the receiver back on its cradle, and when it rang, almost at once, she didn't pick it up. The excitement over her promotion disappeared in the face of her fear. She lifted the receiver again and called Carol. "I need to get away for the weekend. Can Kala and I come with you to the Russian River?"

Even if Carol was surprised by the request, she managed not to show it. "Sure. We'd love to have you. Barb's already up there. I'll pick you up. I was planning on leaving soon. Can you be ready by five?"

"I'll be ready. Thanks."

When Serena walked back into Alan's office, he noticed her pallor and the quiver in her voice as she said, "I need to leave now, okay? I'll be in early on Monday."

"Of course," Alan wanted to ask what was wrong but he could see she was struggling for control. "Have a good weekend," he said instead.

❦

Kala seemed to realize that something was amiss. She held her teddy bear cradled in her arm and watched Serena throw clothes into a suitcase. "Go?" she asked from around her thumb.

"Yes, Sweetie." Serena stopped to hug her daughter. "Just be good five more minutes, and Aunt Carol will be here to pick us up, okay?"

"No," Kala smiled and nodded her head. Serena laughed. She felt herself relax. They just needed to get out of here, and everything would be fine, surely she didn't really need to be afraid of Joey.

Carol arrived a few minutes early and didn't ask any questions. She carried the suitcase downstairs, and tucked it into the car, as Serena locked the door. Carol drove swiftly, maneuvering her car through the Friday afternoon traffic with ease. When they were on the Eastshore Freeway headed for San Rafael, she asked, "Do you want to stop and get something for Kala to eat? Barb will have dinner ready for us when we get there, but it'll be over an hour from here."

"I have a peanut butter sandwich and some snacks for her. If you don't mind that she eats in your car, we don't need to stop."

"Of course, it's okay."

Serena turned and reached over the back seat to provide her daughter with the sandwich. Kala offered it first to teddy and then took a bite. Serena handed her a picture book and turned back to the front. "Ready to tell me what's going on?" Carol asked.

"It's probably nothing, but Joey called, and he scared me." She told Carol about the conversation and then added, "I'm probably just overreacting."

"I think you did the right thing getting out of town this weekend. You're not overreacting. People like Joey Coppola are not trustworthy."

They were silent for a few miles and then Serena spoke again. "I have some good news, too. I got a promotion today and a pay raise. I think I can afford to look for a bigger apartment."

"Now that's something to celebrate," Carol grinned at her. "Barb will break out the champagne while we decorate the Christmas tree."

"I was just thinking today that I should get a tree and some decorations. It's only one week away."

"Why not plan to spend it at the river with us? In fact, if your office is closing, come spend the whole week between Christmas and New Year's with us. It would be fun to have Kala," Carol tapped Serena's leg, "and you."

"I'm not sure if I can get away. But, thanks for the offer. You guys are the best family I've ever had."

It had been a perfect weekend. Kala had loved every minute of the tree trimming and had rearranged the bottom ornaments a million times on Saturday and Sunday. Serena managed to relax and let all thoughts of Joey drift away. The friends had discussed Alan's offer of a job in Sacramento and how much they enjoyed living so close together. Serena admitted that she'd miss working closely with Alan but in Oakland, Kala had a great day care and now, with a bigger paycheck they could move to a bigger place.

Sunday afternoon they said goodbye to Barb and drove back to the city. Carol helped Serena unload her things from the car followed her up the apartment stairs. Serena stopped abruptly, causing Carol to bump against her. "What the hell?" she asked staring up at the broken door.

Carol peered over her shoulder. "I think someone broke in. Come on. We need to call the police." Serena started up the stairs again, "Serena, get back here. Whoever it is could still be in there. And if, they're gone the police will need to collect fingerprints and stuff." She pulled on Serena's sweater. "Take Kala and go to Mandy's house to call. I'll stay by the car and watch."

"It was Joey, wasn't it?" Serena had turned very pale.

"We don't know that. Go call."

Serena stumbled across the lawn to her landlady's house and knocked on the door. No one answered. She turned away to try a neighbor. Mandy pulled into the driveway and waved. Carol hurried over to explain what was happening. Serena sank down on the steps. "Ouch. Mommy," Kala said trying to slip out of her tight grasp. Mandy brushed past to go in and call the police.

At his request, Serena left Kala with Carol and followed the policeman up the stairs. "No one's in here now, Mam, but it's a real mess. I'd say someone was really upset."

Serena stood in the doorway. Everything she owned seemed to be on the floor. Her bed had been torn apart. The refrigerator door stood open, its contents scattered and broken. Cracked and shattered dishes appeared to have been thrown at the wall. Through the open doorway, she could see that the bathroom was in the same state of dishevel. Kala's crib was turned on its side, her favorite blanket covered in something that looked like grape jelly. She stepped inside and thought she smelled something burning. Her clothing was piled in the middle of the room. She looked at the policeman. "Did he try to burn my clothes?"

"Looks like it. Do you know who did this?"

"I think so." She took a deep breath. "I think it was Joey Coppola."

"Why him? You owe him money or something?"

"No, I don't owe him money. I used to date him."

"Oh," the policeman nodded, "lover's spat."

"I want to press charges."

"That's your right, but I'd advise against it. Why don't you take the night to think about it, and if you still want to, you can call the station in the morning." Serena started to protest, but he held up a hand to stop her. "Seriously, Mam. It won't do you any good to press charges against Coppola, and it could do you harm. You look like a nice girl. Why don't you just clean up this mess and leave it alone."

Serena wanted to cry. She wanted to scream. She wanted this to all go away. The policeman watched her emotions flit across her face. "You got somewhere to go tonight?" Serena shrugged. "I'll call a locksmith for you, and he'll come fix this door, and then tomorrow you can come by and clean up. Things always look better in the morning."

# Chapter Twenty Three

Monday morning, Carol drove Serena and Kala back to Oakland. The apartment looked just as bad as it had the night before. She walked to a phone booth and called Alan. After explaining the mess the apartment was in, she said, "I think I need that restraining order."

"I'll take care of it. Be sure you take some pictures before you clean everything up. If there are any additional problems with Coppola, you might need proof."

"That's a good idea, but I don't have a camera."

"I do. I'll be right over." He hung up before she could protest.

Carol and Serena sat on the stairs waiting for Alan. They watched Kala as she examined each fallen leaf. "How did I get myself into this mess?" Serena asked.

"It's life, not a mess. Everyone makes mistakes; it's what you learn from them and how you move on that matters." Carol pulled Serena in for a hug. "You have a good job and a beautiful daughter."

*And, I'm a fraud,* Serena thought.

When Alan arrived, he took in the mess at a glance and shook his head in disgust, "The man is a pig," he muttered. He snapped a roll of film, helped the women replace the mattress on the bed and right the crib. "I'll head back to the office and take care of the restraining order unless you need my help with anything else."

"We'll be fine, Alan." Carol hugged him.

"Do you want the rest of the week off, Serena?" he asked.

"No, I'll be in first thing tomorrow," she said as she thought, I can't afford to take a week off.

"Okay, see you then. The office will be closed from Friday at noon until January 3. Will you be alright here alone?"

"Barb and I have invited Serena and Kala to spend the holiday at the river with us."

"Excellent," he glanced around the small apartment. "After the New Year, you need to get a phone."

Serena agreed, but the one hundred dollar deposit for a new hook up was far out of her reach now that she'd need to replace everything Joey had ruined. She was hoping to move to a larger place soon. It would have to wait. In fact, she wasn't sure how she was going to replace the clothing or the food that Joey's rampage had destroyed, especially with an unpaid week between Christmas and New Year's. She pushed those thoughts aside and thanked Alan again for all his help.

By late afternoon the apartment was back in order. Kala's things were fine, but Joey's attempt to burn her clothing had resulted in damage to almost everything she owned. She'd managed to salvage one pair of shoes, and a few pieces of underwear. From the clothes on her back and the things she'd taken with her for the weekend, she'd have to figure out something to wear to work in the morning.

Carol looked around the apartment with satisfaction. "There," she said dusting her hands, "that's done. Now let's run over to Rhodes and get you a few necessary items."

Serena protested. "You don't have to do that. I'll wash out the blouse and underwear I wore Friday. Kala and I can just walk down to the corner store and buy what we need for dinner and breakfast." The Cheerios in the cupboard had not been dumped, and Kala wouldn't mind eating them for every meal. *I'll just need milk and bananas*, Serena calculated.

"No way. Come on. I'm buying you an early Christmas present. I insist."

Over Serena's protests, Carol choose two blouses, a gray wool pencil skirt, a garter belt, hose, and underwear. She gaily piled everything on the checkout counter and surveyed her choices as the clerk rang up the sale. "Do you need a suit instead of just a skirt and blouse? You are the Office Manager now."

"Carol. Stop.   You're being incredibly generous.  I don't know how I'll ever repay you as it is."

"I think of you as family. You don't owe me anything, ever."

Tears filled Serena's eyes and threatened to spill over. She rubbed them away and hugged Carol. "You're the best, much better than family."

"Right," Carol blinked away her own tears. "I'm just going to add this cardigan." She placed a soft white sweater on the pile and paid.

"One more stop, the supermarket. You can get what you need there. It will be cheaper, and you won't have to carry it home.  I don't know about you, but I'm ready to sit down and have a glass of wine. So, let's get this finished."

The short work week and the festive mood in the office combined to make the days speed by. Serena had decided not to put up a tree since the river house was completely decorated and Kala was too young to ask why they didn't have a tree, but she was determined to buy something for Carol and Barb. She owed them so much.

Shortly before noon, Alan strolled through the office wishing everyone a happy holiday. When he reached Serena, he asked if he could talk to her for a minute. She followed him to his office. He perched on the edge of his desk. Serena waited impatiently. She needed to find a gift, wrap it, collect Kala from day care and be ready for Carol to pick them by four.

"Is everything okay?" Serena nodded. "Have you heard anything from Coppola?" She shook her head. "I just wanted to warn you that he will be served with the restraining order today. I took the liberty of asking the police to keep an eye on your place while you are out of town. I don't think he'll try anything but, just in case."

Serena's voice was steady. Her stomach quaked as she said, "Thank you. I really appreciate all your help."

"Not a problem. And I wanted to give you this." He handed her an envelope. "You've been doing the job of Office Manager for months now, so I felt it was fair to go back six weeks and pay you for the job." Serena started to protest. "You earned it, Serena. Enjoy the holiday. Tell Carol and Barb hello for me." Serena smiled her thanks, afraid to speak for fear she would cry. "Oh, one more thing." He pulled a gaily wrapped package from behind the desk. "This is for Kala. Tell her it's from Santa."

Back at her desk, Serena covered her typewriter and grabbed her coat. She was alone in the elevator, so she ripped open envelope. Instead of the expected payroll check, Alan had given her a Christmas card. Serena pulled it out a gasped. Five crisp twenty dollar bills were enclosed, and Alan had added a note.

*Back pay and Christmas bonus. Thank you for all your hard work. Please consider moving to Sacramento, the office there will need you. Alan*

*Oh, my God,* Serena thought. When she'd been growing up, she'd never had to think about money, and now it seemed to be all she thought about. One hundred dollars would make things so much easier, and now every month she'd be earning more. The elevator door slid open. Serena grinned at the security guard by the door. "Happy Holiday," she said.

"Happy Holiday to you too, miss." Touching his hat brim, the guard returned her smile.

Serena floated down the street and turned into Walker Scott. She quickly chose leather gloves, brown for Barb and black for Carol, and waited for them to be gift wrapped. She asked for a bag big enough to carry the gloves and Alan's gift for Kala and hurried upstairs to the toy department. She selected the Fisher Price Music Box Lacing Shoe with its set of Little People. She knew Kala would love it. It's going to be a good Christmas, she thought, despite Joey Coppola.

Carol had spread the word, and her friends cleaned out their closets. All week long they came by the house on the river bringing clothing for Serena. It was an overwhelming display of caring. "Look at this," Serena pointed to the clothing piled on her bed. "This is so much more than Joey burned. I can't believe how generous your friends have been."

"People want to help others, Serena. You just need to tell them what you need and allow them to help."

"Maybe, but these clothes are lovely. I'm going to be the best-dressed Office Manager in Oakland. I haven't had a closet full of clothes since," Serena realized that she had almost said since I ran away from college and quickly amended her words to, "since I don't remember when."

Carol laughed. "You can dress like a professional woman in the office but it's New Year's Eve. These stirrup pants will look great on you, why don't you wear them tonight with that sparkly sweater Barb found in the back of her closet."

The river house was overflowing with women, all shapes, sizes, and ages. The stack of LPs, on the stereo, kept music flowing through the rooms. Kala had been hugged and admired and finally tucked into bed, too tired to keep her eyes open another minute. With midnight approaching, Barb popped the corks on bottles of champagne and Carol turned the television to the countdown in Times Square. Serena helped pass the full flutes making sure that everyone held a glass. The ball drop began, and the woman counted down together. The shouts of Happy New Year echoed in the room. Serena sipped her champagne and realized that she was the only one in the room with no one to kiss. Last year she'd attended a fabulous party with Joey and this year she was alone again. She opened the door and stepped out on the deck.

A bright moon hung just above the trees. The sky sparkled with a million stars. She walked to the railing and looked down. A movement caught her eye. The dark haired woman, she remembered seeing when she was pregnant, stood on the river bank. For a long moment, they regarded each other. Slowly the woman raised her hand in greeting. Serena thought she heard her ask if everything was okay, but that was crazy, they were too far apart to hear each other. Serena raised her hand and whispered, "I'm fine." *I am fine,* she thought, *everything is going to be fine. I can do this.* She turned and went back into the house.

"Is it cold out there?" a woman asked. "We're going to do the burning bowl ceremony now. Will you join us?"

"I don't know what that is?" Serena admitted.

"It's simple and very effective. Take these slips of paper and on each one write something you are ready to get rid of; old hurts, grudges, habits, regrets, anything that you feel is holding you back anything you want to relinquish. We place our slips of paper in the burning bowl and light them on fire. The ashes float away, and with the ashes, you release those things that have been holding you back. You'll find that it clears your mind so that you can make and keep new promises to yourself."

Serena accepted the slips of paper. I hope this works, she thought. Serena quickly wrote Joey on the first slip but then she stopped. If she was honest with herself she knew there were some habits she should change but nothing that she was willing to change. She folded her paper and tossed it into the copper bowl and walked to the deck with the others. The papers flared up at the touch of a match. The ashes floated on the breeze. Serena looked down at the river, hoping to see the woman again but she was gone.

The party moved back inside. The conversation turned to resolutions; everyone seemed to have at least one. Serena had never made a real resolution, but this year it seemed like a good idea. When her turn came, she said very slowly, choosing her words carefully. "I'm resolving to change my life. I am going to tell Alan that I will move to Sacramento and run the new office for him. But, I'm also going to tell him that I want to study law and become an attorney." The women burst into spontaneous applause.

Carol hugged her tight. "That's the best resolution I've ever heard. We will miss you when you and Kala move away but we will see you often, and I resolve to support you any way I can."

"Hear, Hear." Everyone applauded and cheered. "1966 is going to be the best year ever."

❦

In the city, Michael awoke with a start. He looked at the clock, 4 AM, New Year's Day. Rachel wasn't crying. He wondered what had caused him to wake so fully and so quickly. Beside him, Anne slept peacefully. He eased himself out of bed. Pulling on a robe and slippers, he first looked in on Rachel and then went to the kitchen to make a cup of coffee. He knew he wouldn't go back to sleep.

Ever since the day Rachel was born, when he'd heard Valerie say 'Help her,' he'd been afraid for the females in his life. He remembered how Valerie had known that Beth would die and now someone he loved was in trouble. Whatever Valerie had tried to tell him, he knew it was important. The coffee started to perk. He turned down the flame. There must be some way to find Elizabeth, some way to find out if she was okay. He reached into the cupboard for his favorite mug and turned back to the cook top. Valerie stood next to the refrigerator. She smiled and held out a hand. "Elizabeth is going to be okay. She has made a wise decision."

"Where is she?" Michael demanded.

Valerie shook her head sadly. "She's in a safe place now." Her image faded and Michael expected her to disappear, but then the image grew clearer and stronger. "She loves you, Michael."

"And I love her." A wave of intense sadness gripped him. "I want her to come home."

"I know you do, Michael. I promise she'll come home when she is ready. For now, take care of your family and try not to worry."

"Are you talking to someone, sweetheart?" Anne yawned.

"Not anymore."

# Chapter Twenty Four

When Serena told Alan that she would move to Sacramento, he grinned, shook her hand, and told her he was delighted. "But," Serena continued, "I don't want to be your office manager for long. As soon as I can I want to become a paralegal or," she took a deep breath and finished, "maybe an attorney. I know it sounds crazy, but I want to make a difference, especially a difference for women."

"That's a great idea. What can I do to help?"

"I haven't figured anything out yet. As soon as we have the office up and running and I get a few things straightened out in my life, maybe you would help me decide how to proceed."

"Absolutely. For now, let's start with, how soon can you move? I signed the lease for the property over the holiday, and I've found a house for myself."

"Wow, you really are in a hurry. I've never even been to Sacramento." Serena was suddenly overwhelmed with what this move might entail. "I haven't given notice on my apartment, or thought about how to accomplish the move."

"The law firm will pay your moving expenses, after all, you are doing this at our request, so don't worry about that. I think we should meet with Jim together and find out who he wants you to train for your job here. I'll be coming back and forth, but I'll need you full time in Sacramento as soon as possible."

Serena's head was spinning. When she'd made her resolution, she hadn't taken into consideration what it really meant. Alan kept talking, "If you can get someone to care for Kala on Thursday, we'll drive over early, and you can use my car to look around and see where you'd like to live, maybe even find a place. If we leave at 7AM, we'll be there by 9. I'll show you the new office, and then you can do your thing and meet me back at the office at 5 PM, and I can drive you home by 7 PM. Will that work?"

His enthusiasm was contagious. Serena laughed aloud. "That might work if I can find a babysitter and if I knew how to drive."

"You don't drive?"

Serena shook her head. "I've always lived in cities. I never needed to learn." And, my father always had a driver, she thought.

"Well," Alan nodded, "that will need to be one of the first things you do. If you are going to take care of your child, work and study you'll need a car. Sacramento isn't like Oakland. Okay, so you find a babysitter, and I'll find an intern who drives to go with us. How does that sound?"

Back at her desk Serena called Andy, and asked, "Is there any chance you can babysit for Kala on Thursday? After school, you could pick her up at her day care, and I'll be home about 7 or 8 PM."

"I can't, Serena. I'm really sorry but my mom heard about what happened at your apartment, and she won't let me babysit for you anymore."

Damn Joey, Serena thought. But aloud she said pleasantly, "I'm not dating Mr. Coppola anymore. I need to go to Sacramento with my boss, just for the day."

"Hang on, I'll ask." Serena heard the receiver being laid down and Andy calling to her mother. She crossed her fingers.

"Mrs. Miller, this is Andy's Mom, Arlene Kline. I know how hard it is to get a babysitter on short notice. I really don't want Andy to babysit at your apartment anymore. I'm afraid it isn't safe." Serena tried to formulate an answer, but she knew in her heart that it might not be safe, wasn't that why she was moving to Sacramento? Arlene didn't wait for her to speak. "Andy doesn't have school this week, so if you can bring Kala to our house in the morning and pick her up from here when you get home, I think it will be alright."

"I could certainly do that, but I'll need to drop her off early, about 7 AM and I won't be back until 7 or 8 PM."

"That's not a problem; the twins are up and tearing the house apart by then. Andy adores Kala, and it will be fun to have a little girl around. I'll give you back to Andy, and you can arrange everything with her."

"Thank you, Mrs. Kline. I'm sure Kala will love being with Andy instead of at day care."

"You're welcome." She hesitated and then said softly. "Stay safe."

Serena completed her arrangements and went in to tell Alan that she'd been able to arrange a babysitter. "Great," he said. "I was thinking it would be best if I pick you up at your house at a few minutes to seven, we can drop Kala, pick up Larry, and get on our way without coming to the office. How's that sound?"

"Like you just solved all my transportation problems. Thank you. I'll be ready."

With Larry as her driver, they looked at a variety of apartments in the downtown area, and Serena began to relax. It seemed so far from Joey and the Spencers and from everyone else she'd lied to. Maybe she could make a new start here. They stopped for lunch in a neighborhood café with a notice board.

While they waited for their food, Serena read the For Rent notices and jotted down a few number she could call. The waitress noticed her interest in the board and asked, "Are you two looking for a place to rent?"

"I am." Serena acknowledged. "I'm moving here for my job, and I need to find a place fast, like today, if possible. Somewhere downtown because I don't have a car yet."

"Is it just you?"

"Myself and my two-year-old daughter."

"What kind of job?"

Serena was a little taken aback by the questions, but she figured the woman meant no harm. "I'm the office manager for a small law firm on K Street."

The waitress nodded. "Okay, you look alright, like a responsible person so I think I might have a place for you. Two of my morning regulars are a really nice couple that lives just a couple of blocks from here. They just told me this morning that their tenant had moved out over the holiday, and they were looking for someone to rent the back house."

"I can't afford a lot," Serena said.

"I don't know what they are asking, but it won't be a lot. I'll write down their names and number, and you can call them when you finish lunch. Just tell them Nora sent you."

Nora's name had indeed, been a great introduction. Serena was invited to come over right away and take a look. The owners, Gary and Lois Anderson, reminded Serena of Minette and Henry. They were charming and seemed delighted at the thought of having a small child playing in the wide garden that separated the large front house from the small cottage on the alley.

The cottage itself had once been a carriage house, but now it contained everything Serena wanted; a bedroom for herself and a tiny extra room that could be Kala's room. It came with kitchen appliances, a washing machine and nothing else, but she had Kala's crib, and she was sure she could find everything she needed at garage sales or thrift stores. It was within walking distance of the new office. "It's absolutely perfect. But I'm not sure I can afford it. How much is the rent?"

"We planned to charge fifty-five dollars a month," Lois said, carefully watching Serena's reaction. "Utilities are included, except for the telephone. Would that be alright?"

"That would be amazing." Serena wanted to spin in circles and jump up and down. "I can give you a deposit today and a list of references to check."

"Oh no, dear. We don't need that. Gary used to be a minister, and he always knows who we can trust. When would you like to move in?"

"I'm not exactly sure. This has all happened so fast that I haven't arranged for anyone to move my things and I don't have a car yet."

"I'll give you the key right now, and you can consider the place yours. You can pay the first month's rent when you move in. We'll love having you and your daughter here. It'll liven up this place."

Lois laughed and patted her husband's arm. "Our daughter and grand-babies moved to San Diego, and we miss the kids. You just give us a call when you know your plans. If there is anything we can do to help you, let us know."

"I do need to find a good nursery school for Kala."

"Let me think a minute." Lois cocked her head. "You said your office will be at Eighth and K, and our cross streets are Second and O. Gary, what was the name of that place on L Street, where

Lynda's daughter is the teacher? I think they have a preschool program. Wait right here, I'll call Lynda."

Gary smiled fondly as his wife hurried toward the kitchen. "She never takes a breath," he said. "Better get comfortable, this could take a minute. Lois loves to solve problems."

Gary chatted easily as Serena filled out her information on the rental agreement. She hesitated for a moment and then used Carol for her family reference. Gary kept the conversation away from personal questions and concentrated on all the things to do and see in Sacramento. Lois returned with a slip of paper. "Here's the address. It's a Montessori School, and they have a toddler program that has an opening for Kala. I told them you'd stop by today, I hope that was okay."

"Of course, it was. I can't begin to tell you how grateful I am for all your help and for renting the cottage to me."

Lois waved her thanks away, "It's nothing. We hope you and Kala will be happy here. Run along now and check out the school. We'll be waiting to hear from you. Move in any time."

Back in the car, Larry grinned at her. "You must live a charmed life."

"Hardly," Serena grinned back, "but today it feels like I do."

On the drive back to Oakland, Alan and Larry talked about a case Larry was researching for the firm. Serena wrote a list of things she needed to accomplish both at home and at the office. It was going to be a very busy couple of weeks.

# Chapter Twenty Five

For Serena, the first months in Sacramento flew past. She loved her job. Kala loved her nursery school. Gary and Lois had met Carol and Barb when they helped her move and were always delighted to see them when they drove over for a visit. Serena felt like she had created a real family for herself and Kala.

Lois took control of the need for furniture, and the cottage was soon furnished with items she found here and there. It seemed that Lois knew everyone in the neighborhood and soon everyone knew Serena and Kala.

Serena didn't talk much about her past, and the Anderson's didn't pry. She was determined to get her license to practice law and knew that she needed to get a few things straightened out first, beginning with a name change.

The change proved to very easy. She simply went to the courthouse, filled out the necessary forms, paid the sixteen dollar fee and waited the four weeks required before appearing in the court where the judge asked only if she was changing her name for any illegal purpose and in a matter of minutes she was no longer named Elizabeth Augustus. Serena wanted to tell someone but, of course, that was impossible. Instead, when Gary found her hanging laundry on the line, he asked her what she was grinning about, and she told him her desire to pass the bar.

"What a grand idea! You'll make a splendid attorney. Do you want to practice with Alan, doing Equal Rights work?"

"I haven't planned that far in advance. But I know I want to help women. It will take years more of college, and it'll be very expensive."

"Where there's a will there's a way. Lois and I will help in anyway we can. We consider Kala our grandchild, and we'll be happy to babysit whenever you need us."

"We certainly will," Lois arrived in the garden with coffee and a plate of cookies. "You two looked so serious. Come on. Sit down and tell me what's going on." The adults sat down. Kala climbed into Lois's lap and reached for a cookie. Serena repeated her desire. Lois looked thoughtful for a moment. "I think," she said, "that in California you don't have to go to law school to get a license. I know I read that somewhere. You should talk to Alan."

"I will but right now, my next big thing is that I want to learn to drive. Will you teach me, Gary?"

Lois laughed. "You don't want him to teach you. I'm a much better driver. Gary can take care of Kala while we practice. Do you have your permit?"

"I got it yesterday." *It's the first thing with my new name on it that is completely legal;* she thought and couldn't help smiling.

"Excellent. First thing Saturday morning I'm giving you your first lesson. Read the rule book before then."

Kala clapped and said, "Me, too." The adults all chuckled.

"You will have to wait about thirteen years for your lesson," Serena said sternly.

Lois was right. In California; it was possible to become a lawyer by "reading the law" which, simply put, meant studying and apprenticing in the office of a practicing attorney or judge. After her driving lesson, Serena went to the library and read everything she could find about the process. She wrote a formal proposal of her request to Alan, asking that he act as her supervising attorney, during the four years of apprenticeship. She included everything she knew about the process, the monthly exams he would need to give, the bi-annual progress reports that he would have to file with the California Bar. The fact that she would need to pass the law students exam at the end of her first year, and that during the entire four years she would need to work directly with him for at least eighteen hours a week. She included a copy of the completed registration form, that if he agreed and signed, she would file along with a fifty dollar fee.

At the last minute, she added a summary of how she felt she could handle her current job during the apprentice period. Back home she collected Kala and requested that Gary read over the proposal to be sure it was clear and covered everything.

Having spent the entire weekend worrying about Alan's reaction to her request, his actual response was anti-climactic. "Serena, this is brilliant. Of course, I'll be your supervisor." He signed the registration form with a flourish. "Send this in right away, and we'll get started. Grab your jacket. Let's celebrate. I'll take you to lunch at Frank Fat's. You might as well begin to meet the other lawyers in this city."

Serena had heard about the legendary Chinese restaurant where it was rumored that all the real business of the state legislature took place and she was not disappointed. Everywhere she looked there was someone she recognized from the news. "I hope you like Chinese." Alan said flipping open his menu.

"I love it." Serena studied the room from behind her open menu. She didn't see another woman, anywhere. "Aren't there any female lawyers in this town?" she asked.

"A few, but not many work with the Assembly or the Senate."

"I may have to change that."

Alan saluted her with his tea cup, "If anyone can, I believe you can, Serena." He stabbed a dumpling with his chop stick. "I cannot get the hang of these things." He watched Serena deftly bring a dumpling to her mouth. "Where did you learn to do that?"

"My grandmother taught us when we were very young. She was a stickler for good manners."

"We? How many siblings do you have?"

"Just one brother. We aren't a close family." Serena changed the subject. "Lois is teaching me to drive. I like walking to work, but now that I'll be studying I think I'll need to find a law library that I can use, and a car will make it easier and faster to get around."

"That's a good idea, and you will have full access to my law library, too. Have you found a car yet?"

"Gary has. He knows someone who has a 1957 Nash Rambler station wagon that Gary says is in great condition. I'm going to look at it next weekend."

Alan watched the emotions flit across Serena's face. She really was a beautiful woman, even more so now that she was taking charge of her life. "I'm lucky Carol sent you to my firm instead of to any of the lawyers she knows in San Francisco. Now, let's talk about your job." Serena sat up straighter. "I think you need to hire another full-time person, someone you can train to take over as Office Manager. If I'm going to supervise your law education, I want to be sure you have time to learn everything you need."

"But, it only requires that you supervise me eighteen hours a week."

"True, but the first year is the hardest. If you can work alongside me in a student/intern/assistant kind of way, I bet we can knock this thing out in 3 years, or less. What do you say? Shall we give it a try?"

# Chapter Twenty Six

Serena sat at a picnic table in William Land Park, her books and notes spread out in front of her. Kala, and her friend Jamie were playing something that involved a great deal of giggling. Serena kept an eye on them while she studied, ready to jump up if they needed her.

It was a good life. Kala, work, study and daily chores kept Serena so busy that she seldom had time to dwell on the past or think about dating. When she did feel lonely, she pushed it aside. There would be plenty of time later. For now, she was proud of her daughter and enjoyed every minute they spent together. A five-year-old was so much more interesting than a baby, she thought.

Then she turned her eyes back to her notes. Alan was sure she was ready to take the bar exam this year, but she was worried. Everyone kept telling her how hard it was, but they'd said that about every test and so far she passed them all, even the dreaded first-year test.

"Elizabeth?" Serena looked up. A tall, slim, Air Force Officer looked back at her. "Elizabeth Augustus?" Serena couldn't speak. "It is you, isn't it? Oh my god, Elizabeth. It's so good to see you."

Serena wanted to protest to say, no, you've mistaken me for someone else, but the words didn't come. She knew that she'd given it away by her silence and by the look she was giving this almost stranger. "Chris?"

"I can't believe it. Your dad and Michael have been looking for you everywhere and here you are right in plain sight."

"Chris, sit down." He sat and glanced at the books and papers. "How is Michael?"

"Married, he married Anne about five years ago. He still works for the family business. He misses you. We all miss you."

"Chris, I'm not going back. Not now, maybe never. I don't belong to the Augustus family. I'm just the adopted kid, the war orphan with no past, stuck in a family where the only thing that matters to them is family."

"I don't see it that way, and I know Michael doesn't either. He loves you."

"No, he wants to protect me, to take care of me, he thinks he owns me. Just because a ghost gave me to him doesn't mean I belong to him."

Chris studied her face. "You kind of look like an Augustus and maybe a little bit like a young Minette."

"No, I don't. I never have and I never will. I probably look like my birth father and John always said I looked like Valerie." She shook her head. "None of that matters. They aren't my family, and I'm not going back. I need you to forget that you saw me today. Just walk away and go about your life. You have to promise not to tell Michael or anyone else that you saw me."

"Do you live here in Sacramento?"

"It's none of your business, Chris. Promise me you won't tell."

"I can't promise that, Elizabeth. I won't call them and tell them but if someone asks me I won't lie."

"Thank you. Now go and leave me alone." Serena glanced at Kala, but she and Jamie were still busy, paying no attention to the adults. "And, don't try to find me, Chris. Today was an accident, something that should never happen again."

"The day he married Anne, June 19, 1964, he told me that he knew you were in pain, somewhere, that he could feel it just like he did when you were kids."

*Kala's birth,* she thought, *I was in labor by myself.*

"Michael still talks to Valerie sometimes. When his daughter was born he saw her at the hospital, she told him you needed help," Chris continued.

Serena thought of the dark haired woman by the river. *I sometimes see Valerie, too,* she thought. "I'm glad he has a daughter. I'm sure he's a great dad. When was she born?"

"Not sure exactly, but it was late 1965." Chris watched the shadow cross Serena's eyes.

Joey Coppola, she thought. Valerie had known bad things were happening.

"A bond like yours and Michael's doesn't break, Elizabeth. It might bend, but you will always be bound together."

Serena shook her head. "Just go, Chris. None of that matters."

"I'll go and leave you alone, but if I keep your secret, you need to promise me that you'll think about going home. Minette and Henry are getting old, John isn't very healthy, and you are the only person Michael has left."

"He has a wife."

"It's not the same thing." Chris reached for her and Serena allowed herself to be hugged. "Please, promise to think about it."

Serena nodded, determined not to cry, "I promise." Chris hugged her again, turned and walked away. He didn't look back. If he had, Serena might have run to him. But this was better, she couldn't go home, she couldn't admit that running away had been a mistake.

Kala ran up. "Who was that soldier, Mommy?"

"Just someone I knew a long time ago." She knelt and pulled Kala into a hug. "I love you very much. You know that, right?"

"Silly mommy, I love you too. Come on Jamie. Let's swing."

# Chapter Twenty Seven

In February 1970, Serena took the arduous, eighteen hour, three-day bar exam. When it was over, she wasn't sure she could remember a single question that had been on the exam. She had no idea if she had done well or failed miserably. All she wanted to do was sleep for a week.

She waited, on pins and needles, for the results to arrive. When the letter finally appeared in the office mail, she tucked it into her purse and walked up to Capital Park, where she could open it in private. She sat on a bench facing the portico. Her hands were trembling. Serena knew that it was common to fail on your first try and that if she'd failed she could take it again. Taking a deep breath, Serena ripped open the envelope and drew out the single sheet of elegant, heavy, paper. She scanned the message quickly, dashed a tear from her eye and hurried back to the office where she burst into Alan's office without knocking.

He turned from the bookcase where he was standing and smiled at her. Serena rushed over and hugged him close, "We did it, Alan, we truly did it. I passed the bar!"

"I think you did it, Serena. Congratulations. You're a full-fledged lawyer now."

Serena laughed, "I still have to be sworn in." She realized she was still hugging Alan. "Sorry, I'm just so happy," she said and stepped back.

"I'm so proud of you, Serena. Jim and I have been waiting for this day; we want to make you a full partner. We hope you'll accept."

"Are you sure? I haven't even handled a case on my own yet."

"We're sure. Jim and I have been watching you learn and grow for four years, five if you count the time before you started studying, and we think you'll be a great asset, both here and in the Oakland office."

"I'm so proud to work with you. I know how much work you do building and strengthening the community. That new legislature for Fair Housing would never have happened without you."

"Jim and I couldn't have done it without you, Serena. I know you want to concentrate on gender discrimination, particularly women's rights, and we want you to bring that interest and all of your strengths to the law offices of Warren, Butler, and Miller. What do you say?"

Serena grinned, "I say, oh my God, yes!"

"Come on then, let's go tell the rest of the staff." Alan led the way to the lounge, announcing a meeting as he went.

Gary and Lois were as excited as Serena. They insisted on taking Serena and Kala to dinner to celebrate. Kala chose the Black Angus because she loved the dessert and the others acquiesced. The hostess led them to a large private booth and commented, "You all look very happy tonight. Are you celebrating something special?"

Kala bounced up and down. "My Mommy just turned into a real lawyer," she announced, "and GG and Grandy and I very proud of her. Right, GG?"

"Right," Gary agreed. He loved the nicknames Kala had bestowed on them when she had decided they were grandparents. "We are all very proud, but we aren't surprised. Serena is going to be the best lawyer ever."

"I'm proud of you, too." The hostess smiled at Serena. "I'm doing pre-med at Sac State. Powerful women will change the world."

"Hear, hear," Lois said.

"Hear what," Kala asked.

"Enough," Gary said. "Let's celebrate. Wine or cocktails, ladies?"

Late that night, Serena sat on the cottage deck, wrapped in a soft blanket. The orange trees were in full bloom, and their delicate scent filled the air. High in the sky, the lights of an airplane winked off and on. Somewhere an owl called. She pulled her blanket closer and thought about her other family.

Chris must have kept his promise not to tell anyone since no one had come looking for her. She wondered if Michael would be surprised that she'd chosen the law. He'd always said he wanted to teach, but like all the Augustus family, he'd done what the family wanted and joined the family business. Sometimes she found herself reading the Wall Street Journal, scanning for news of AmCo just to see if there was any reference to the family. However, like Great Grandfather Walter had decreed, the only mention of the Augustus family was on the society pages when someone was born, married or died.

*I'm probably the first Augustus woman with a real career*, she thought. *Of course, I'm not a real Augustus. And, I'm certainly the only one with a child born out of wedlock.* The owl hooted again. Something moved in the garden. The woman from the river stood just inside the gate. Serena held her breath as she watched her move closer. Her long dark hair was combed to one side and cascaded in waves to her shoulders. Her wide legged trousers and shoulder pads were straight out of the 1940's. She stopped and smiled. "Valerie," Serena whispered. The woman watched her. "Mother?"

Serena stood up and moved down the deck stairs. She felt no fear. As long as she could remember she'd heard the story of how Valerie had died when giving birth and then come back as a ghost to tell Michael to take care of her. If this was her mother's ghost, Serena knew that she meant no harm. Serena wanted to hear her speak; she wanted to hear the voice of her mother. But Valerie only smiled and disappeared. "Damn," Serena muttered. "What the hell was that?" *My mother,* she thought, *that was my mother.*

Michael woke with a start and looked around the room, expecting to see Valerie. Maybe it had only been a dream. He tried to go back to sleep, but he knew he was awake for the day. He might as well get up. He plugged in the new olive green, electric percolator, took his favorite cup from the cupboard and moved to the window to watch the sky brighten over the river. He thought he heard an owl hoot. That didn't seem possible. He could feel Elizabeth. *How was that possible?* It had been more than ten years since she'd disappeared. He'd call Ron Schwartz today just to see if the detective had any new leads.

Hearing footsteps he turned from the window and found his five-year-old daughter watching him. "Good Morning, Rachel. Did I wake you up?"

"Nope, I heard the owl. Did you see it?"

"I don't think we have any owls in the city, honey. Maybe you dreamed about an owl."

"There are owls, Daddy. When I'm a scientist, I'll find them and show you."

"Okay, but right now, how about a cup of cocoa?"

"No thanks, I was just checking on you. I'm going to sleep now." Rachel spun about and left the kitchen. Michael shook his head in wonder. Every day, he was amazed by his child. How could she be so smart and so sure of herself when she was so young?

Anne laughed at him for thinking she was smarter than others her age. Minette called her an old soul, and her teachers said that she was precocious.

John said she reminded him of Michael as a child, but Michael didn't remember being sure of anything when he was a child, except that he needed to take care of Elizabeth, and he'd failed at that. He poured his coffee and carried it into his den.

Serena found it exciting to be a full partner. She often worked long hours and worried that she might be neglecting Kala, but Kala never seemed to mind. She was a happy, outgoing child who knew everyone in their neighborhood. She accompanied GG on his evening walk, and they stopped to talk to every dog, cat, and human they met. Serena loved to watch them together. When Kala asked about her father, Serena stuck to the lie she'd told everyone except Carol; her father had been named Brian Lee Walker, he'd died before she was born, he'd never seen her, but he would have loved her because he was very happy Serena was having a baby.

When Kala turned six, she asked why her last name didn't match her Mommy and Serena explained that not all women change their name when they get married. At seven Serena had needed to add to her story that the fictional Brian had been killed in the Vietnam War and that she didn't have any "extra" grandparents because they lived far away. Whenever possible, Serena changed the subject as quickly as she could.

Serena still loved the cottage, but Kala needed a bedroom of her own not just an alcove. She knew she should look for a larger place, perhaps even try to buy a house, but she hated to disrupt the living arrangements that worked so well for all of them.

Gary and Lois had been thinking much the same thing, and in the summer of 1973, they found the perfect solution. Lois called a family meeting. Gary started by saying, "Lois and I are concerned about a couple of things. We are getting older, and this house is much too big. The neighborhood isn't the same as it was when we raised our children here. Many of the houses have been torn down, and the lots have been filled with commercial building and parking facilities. We'd like to move to a single level home with a smaller garden."

Serena's heart sank. She knew she was being selfish but if they moved she would miss them terribly and so would Kala.

He continued, "Kala needs a room of her own," Kala nodded, "and you need a home office space, Serena." Lois reached for his hand as he finished, "Lois and I have been looking at houses, and we think we've found the perfect house. We'd like to show you what we've chosen."

Serena's eyes filled with tears, she brushed them away. "Of course, Gary. We'd love to see the house you've chosen, right Kala?" Kala nodded, she could tell that her mother was upset, but she wasn't sure why.

"Okay then, everybody in the car." Gary was beaming, and Lois kept smiling and patting his arm.

They were all quiet as Gary navigated through the side streets toward William Land Park. He turned onto Bartley Drive and pulled into the drive of a charming, half brick rambler. "It looks lovely," Serena managed to say.

"Just wait until you see it. Everybody out."

A real estate agent opened the door and greeted Gary and Lois warmly. "I see you've brought your daughter and granddaughter to see the house." Gary introduced everyone, and the agent led the way inside. "Serena, your Mom, and Dad were very specific about what they wanted to find. I think you see that the house they've chosen has everything they asked for. I'll wait on the porch. You folks look around, take your time there's no rush."

It was lovely, the rooms were spacious and light flooded. The hardwood flooring gleamed. "Now," Gary said after they'd looked at all three bedrooms and Kala had opened every closet and cupboard, "Let me show you the garden." He opened the wide sliding door in the dining room and gestured for Serena and Kala to go first.

Kala jumped up and down. "You have a pool at your house. Lucky you. Jamie is going to be so jealous." She hugged GG.

"Lucky us," Gary said hugging her back. "Notice anything else?"

Kala spun in a circle and considered. "This house is bigger out here than it is in there."

"You're right." He turned to Serena. "It doesn't have a separate address, but the former owner added a completely separate Mother-In-Law apartment."

He led the way around the pool and Serena realized that what she has assumed was the bedroom wing was actually a wing added to the front house. Gary opened the door and waved them in. "Lois and I are hoping you'd want to buy this property with us. Lois and I will buy this part, and you and Kala can buy the other half. We'll get to move to a smaller place, and you and Kala will get a bigger place."

Kala clapped, "And we'll all live happily ever after."

Lois hugged her close, "Yes, we will."

"But," Serena protested, "what about your real daughter?"

"Mom, don't be silly. You're a real daughter, too."

Gary laughed. "You certainly are. Don't worry Serena, we talked to her, and she's fine with this arrangement."

"Then I'm fine with it, too. Where do we sign?"

"Maybe you would like to take the time to look around the city and see if you find something you like better? Or, at least take the time to decide if you want to continue living so close to us."

"I don't need to look at anything else. Kala and I love living close to you guys. This is a great neighborhood in a good school district. But, I guess I should ask the price. I've never purchased a home before, and I don't know if I qualify for a loan."

"Gary thought of that, too," Lois said. "If you don't, we'll buy the whole property and sell half to you in a sale by owner."

"Then I guess it's a deal. Let's take another look around. Now that I'm not afraid that we are losing you, I need to see it all again."

The financing and mortgage were smoother and quicker than Serena had imagined. Each time she passed through a situation without her deceptions and lies being exposed it was easier to believe that she had never been anyone but Serena Miller.

❧❦❧

Kala's circle of friends expanded, but Serena's own circle stayed limited to Carol, Barb, Jim and Alan. She loved Gary and Lois and considered them her family, and they concurred, always introducing her as their daughter and Kala as their granddaughter. Serena never accepted a date, and when an escort was necessary, she simply chose to attend the event with Alan. Lois tried to tell her that she should get out more, reminding her that they were always happy to have Kala spend the night with them. Serena pleaded that her work load was too great and she just didn't have the time or energy to date.

As Serena became known for her support of the Women's Movement, increasing streams of clients choose their firm to help them fight job discrimination and salary inequality. It was exciting exhilarating work.

Serena knew they were making a difference. She seldom found a need to go into either Oakland or San Francisco, but late in 1974, she was asked to speak at a regional meeting of the National Organization of Woman being held at the Fairmont Hotel. She booked two rooms for overnight and Lois, and Kala accompanied her, excited to have a chance to shop for Christmas on Union Square.

Her speech was well received, and as the meeting broke up, women gathered to shake her hand and ask questions. Serena thoroughly enjoyed herself. When someone said her name, she turned with an out thrust hand to greet the woman. "Serena Miller, as I live and breathe. I never thought I'd see you again." She was pulled into a tight hug and then pushed back so that the woman could get a better look. "I wondered if it was you when I saw your name announced."

"Mary Lou McGuiness, where did you come from?"

"Mary Lou Martinelli, remember?"

"Of course, I remember. I was at the wedding. How are you? Do you live here now?"

"Steve is headed out for another West Pac cruise. So, I'm just in San Francisco to wave goodbye. He's stationed in Long Beach."

"How is military life?"

"It's good. Great actually. Since I saw you last, we've moved twice, Norfolk and then Washington State. Still no kids, but it's not for lack of trying. Tell me about yourself. I never would have expected you to be a big shot, lady lawyer. Did you marry Logan or someone else?"

"I haven't seen Logan since I broke up with him and I'm not married."

Mary Lou considered this for a moment, "Why not? You're certainly pretty enough. I'd offer to introduce you to some eligible guys but the only single men I know are Navy men and I remember how you felt about that."

Serena laughed. "I've been busy."

"Mom," Serena turned at the shout and watched her daughter rush across the room. "Wait until you see what Grandy bought for me to wear on Thanksgiving. It's the most beautiful dress you've ever seen, and we found shoes that match." Kala skidded to a stop and threw her arms around Serena. Her bright red hair was tumbled about her flushed face, her wide eyes sparkled with excitement. "And Grandy took me to a luscious place for lunch, and I had a Shirley Temple." She stopped talking and noticed Mary Lou. "Hello," she said, "I'm Kala."

Quickly Serena recovered, "Mary Lou, this is my daughter Kala Walker and our very good friend Lois Anderson. Kala, Mrs. Martinelli is a friend of mine from a long time ago."

Kala put out her hand, "Hello, Mrs. Martinelli. It is a pleasure to meet you." She studied Mary Lou carefully. "You have hair exactly like me."

"It's a pleasure to meet you Kala, and I was just thinking the same thing. Our hair is the same color."

"And, yours does the same poofy thing on the side that mine does. I have to wear a barrette in the exact same place. Did you know my Dad?"

"Kala Walker, I think perhaps I do...did." Mary Lou searched Serena's face for some sign that she would explain, but Serena gathered up her purse and speech notes and wouldn't allow Mary Lou to catch her eye.

"Come on, Kala. It's time to leave. It was lovely running into you Mary Lou. Will you be in the city long?"

"Long enough for us to have a long conversation just like we used to, how about having dinner together?"

Serena started to protest, but Lois stopped her. "That's an excellent idea. You deserve a night off, Serena. Go out to dinner with your friend and forget about everything. Have some fun. Kala and I will order room service and watch a movie in our pj's. Go," she shooed them away. "Come on, Kala."

Mary Lou raised her eyebrow. "I guess you have been busy, Missy. You've got some explaining to do." Serena opened her lips to speak, but Mary Lou held up her hand. "Not yet. I'm pretty sure this is going to be what the McGuiness family calls a conversation that needs lubrication. Remember the Hurricane Bar? It's still the same, and the drinks are still great. Come on."

Serena wanted to just walk away but part of her was glad to see Mary Lou, and suddenly she needed to know about Brian. She followed Mary Lou to the Terrace level and into the opulent Tonga Room. The maître d' greeted Mary Lou by name and when she requested a quiet booth, he held them to a secluded spot away from the band.

"I see you haven't lost your touch." Serena smiled. "Are you staying here?"

"I am. And you? Are you and your family staying here, too?" Serena nodded. "Good because even if I have to get you drunk I'm going to get you to tell me what is going on."

With their cocktails in front of them, Mary Lou started, "How old is Kala?"

"She was born in June 1964, she's nine going on ten."

"And, her last name is Walker?" Serena nodded. "That," Mary Lou said emphatically, "is not Logan Walker's daughter." She studied Serena. "Why didn't you tell me you were pregnant the last time I saw you?"

"I knew I wasn't going to marry Logan and I didn't want anyone to know I was pregnant. I was still considering having an abortion." Mary Lou drew in a sharp breath. "I know you don't approve, but I was a single twenty-four year old with a dead end job. I really didn't see how I could raise a child on my own. I couldn't tell Logan, he would have insisted that we marry and that just wasn't a possibility."

"Because you weren't sure if he was the father?"

"Partially, but I'd already broken it off before I found out I was pregnant and I really didn't want to marry him."

"And yet, your daughter is named after him."

*And after Brian*, Serena thought, as she nodded and then took a long drink from her gin and tonic. Mary Lou studied her. "Okay, I guess I get it. You didn't want to marry Logan but ... you know Kala isn't his child now. So, why not tell the father? You didn't sleep around, Serena. I know that. But I'm guessing that you slept with Brian that night we all went to the Peppermint Lounge."

"Kala believes that her father died before she was born, everyone believes that. People say terrible things about unwed mothers, and they do not accept children that are born out of wedlock. I won't subject my child to that."

"But think of how you would you feel if you didn't know your father?"

"I don't know my father, Mary Lou. I know exactly how it feels to search and never find your father. Kala believes that she knows who her father was; she'll never have to search. She knows his name and that he loved her. She accepts that he is dead. End of story."

"But what about Brian? Doesn't he deserve to know that he has a child?"

"Kala is not anyone's child but mine. Just because she has red hair doesn't make her Brian's child. If, and you note I said if, we slept together it was one time. I was young, and I'd had too much to drink. I choose to believe that Logan was Kala's father."

"Okay, I'll drop it. Let's order dinner, and you can tell me how you became an attorney and I'll tell you what you missed by not marrying a sailor and becoming a Navy Wife."

# Chapter Twenty Eight

Kala and Serena sat across from each other at the large, leather topped, partners desk that Serena had found for the home office. They often spent an hour or two in the evening this way; Kala doing her homework or drawing and Serena working on a case.

Tonight Serena had trouble keeping her mind focused. She and Mary Lou had stayed in touch with occasional short letters. Serena knew it was a risk, but she really liked Mary Lou, and it felt good to have a friend. Certainly, she thought, if Mary Lou hadn't told yet, she would keep her word and not tell Brian her suspicions about Kala's parentage. Sometimes, Serena looked at her daughter and saw herself but, she admitted, more often she saw Mary Lou.

How, she wondered, was it possible that a child who has never spent time with a relative could sound, laugh, and move like just like that relative. "Damn genetics," she muttered allowed.

"What did you say?" Kala looked at her mother.

"Nothing important, I'm just frustrated."

"Sounded a lot like a swear word to me." Kala grinned. "Do you need help with your homework?"

"Mind your manners, smarty pants. Show me what you're drawing?"

Kala held up her sketch pad. Serena could see that it was a portrait of the two of them. In the background there appeared to be dark shadows. "It's for my portrait class. We have to create a family portrait showing multiple generations. I'm trying to figure out a way to show that we have no one except us but, of course, we do or we wouldn't be here." She turned the pad back to herself. "Ghosts don't seem right because I don't feel haunted by the past."

*I do,* Serena thought.

"I know you don't like to talk about your family, but maybe you could tell me something about my Dad that would help me draw this."

*Fourteen was such a tough age,* Serena thought. *It was probably right about then that I began to fight for knowledge about my birth father.* She remembered how angry she'd been when, every time she asked questions, she'd been told that there was no way to trace him. John had sworn that he only knew Valerie and had never met her husband. Michael had been certain that he didn't remember anyone but Valerie, John, and a nanny, named Annie. It had never made sense, and it still didn't.

Serena put down her pen and studied Kala. "Your father was smart and funny. I think you look a lot like him. I wish I knew more about him or his family, but I only knew him a very short time and then he was gone."

Kala doodled with her charcoal stick. "Where did he come from? Didn't his family come for your wedding or his funeral? Didn't you tell them when I was born?"

"You know this, Kala. Brian was from Pennsylvania. There was no funeral, no service of any kind because there was no body. I'm sure the military told his family but they never contacted me, and I never contacted them."

"It's not fair, you know. Everyone else has a family."

"You may not believe it, Kala, but not everyone does. You are actually luckier than many kids. We have a family we created, and sometimes, that's better than a birth family. GG and Grandy love you, Carol and Lois love you, Alan and Jim love you, Jamie and her parents consider you Jamie's sister, and I love you."

"I know, but I want to know who I am." She scratched out her doodle. "I guess I'll just draw some vague people shapes and a tall, red haired guy, walking into an explosion." She turned back to the sketch pad and retreated into her own thoughts.

Minette looked up from her book and smiled at Henry. "Do you remember the day we met, and how you helped me find Michael and Elizabeth in Wales?"

"Of course I do, love. I remember every day I've spent with you. The twenty-eight years we've been married have been the best years of my life."

"Mine, too, Henry. But what I was thinking about was the stories and lies this family has told themselves and others. I'm almost ninety years old. I want to see my granddaughter again before I die. I want her to know I have missed her, and hoped for her return, every day since she disappeared. I want her to know that John is her father. And, I want Michael to know that he was a good brother, that he did everything he could. I want him to stop seeing that damn ghost."

Henry smiled at her use of the word damn. Minette never swore, absolutely never. "Well, love, if you feel that strongly about all of this perhaps you and I need to take control of the search instead of letting others handle it."

"Do you think we are too late? That we waited too long?"

"It's never too late." Henry kissed her cheek. "I guess you have a plan."

"I think I do. Hand me my notebook, please. We need to give a dinner party."

Minette sat at the head of the table, a chair usually reserved for Henry, but tonight they had exchanged places. Every adult member of her family, the people she loved, with the exception of Elizabeth, were gathered around the large table. As always, when the family was together the conversation was lively, and everyone enjoyed the feast Minette had arranged.

When dessert was served, and each person had a glass of brandy or a cup of coffee, Minette raised her glass and said, "I'd like to offer a toast." The family turned toward her. Henry caught her eye and smiled his encouragement. Minette hesitated, and the family waited. She lowered her glass and took in a deep breath. "I want to make a toast to our family. It is a wonderful loving family but we are still missing Elizabeth, and we will not be complete until she is found and until she knows the truth about her birth. So, until we find Elizabeth and bring her home, I cannot make a toast to the family. Instead, I would like to make a pact with you all that we will find her now." She raised her glass again. "To Elizabeth's safe return."

Glasses clinked, and her pact was repeated. Minette sipped her brandy. She turned to her son, "John, I know you and Michael have searched more than fifteen years to find Elizabeth. I think it apparent that she is hiding from us, but I do not believe that she doesn't want to come home. I think she is afraid."

John started to protest, but Minette waved him to silence and continued, "I think she is afraid that we will judge her and find her unacceptable. We need to reach out and be sure that she knows we love her no matter what or how she has been living. Can you do that?" Minette's eyes moved slowly from person to person.

"Henry and I are going to devote our time and resources to the search. We have hired another detective, Charles Williams. We are hoping that fresh eyes will make it easier to discover where she is. Each of you will need to be completely honest when you talk to Mr. Williams. This is not a time to keep family secrets. Agreed?"

"Agreed," voices spoke in unison and glasses clinked again.

"Mother," John said, "there is nothing I want more than to find Elizabeth and bring her home, but we have found no trace of her since the day she disappeared."

"I have a belief that sometimes the impossible is possible, John. Remember when you found my mother for me, and she forgave me for my mistakes? I should have told the whole world my story, but Walter didn't want the world to know, and I felt like I owed him my silence in payment for the protection he had provided to you and me.

"The keeping of secrets is just too large a price to pay. Each secret begins because we think we need to protect something or someone, but every time we don't tell the truth, it gets harder and harder to dig out from beneath the secret. How many of you have ever told anyone that Elizabeth is missing?"

The looks on their faces confirmed that no one talked about it outside the family.

John looked at Michael and then at Sam, considering what to say and how to say it, "Mother is right. It's hard to keep secrets. It's difficult to keep straight exactly who you've told what. Walter taught us all to keep everything within the family and, even within the family to share only when absolutely necessary. Elizabeth ran away because I was afraid to tell her the truth. She knew that her mother had died the night she was born but, like us all, she wanted to know more, she wanted to find her father." He swallowed.

"I lied to her, and to everyone, I told her over and over again that I had never met her father, that he was gone away fighting the war. I went so far as to adopt her to cover the fact that I was her father."

He brushed a tear away, "Valerie and I were living together in London. We loved each other very much, and yet I abandoned my own daughter, and ran away."

Every person in the room was silent watching John as he continued. "And, then after the war, when I learned that Mother and Henry had found the children and brought them home, I compounded the lie by continuing to deny that Elizabeth was my child. I'm disgusted with my behavior, and I know that Valerie would be, too. When Elizabeth comes home, I will tell her and beg her forgiveness."

For a long moment, no one spoke. Michael rose from his chair and approached John. He placed his hands on John's slumped shoulders and squeezed gently. "Dad wasn't just protecting Elizabeth or himself. He was also protecting me. Sylvia was making everyone's life a living hell, and he did what he thought was best at the time. Secrets are like that. One just leads to another." Michal returned to his chair and smiled sadly at Anne. "I'm actually not an Augustus at all. John isn't my birth father. Sylvia took her secret to her grave, and I will never know who my father was."

Anne gaped at him, caught completely by surprise at his admission. Sam took control of the conversation, "John is named on your birth certificate. Legally you are an Augustus, and what's more? We have always loved you and been proud of you. Never concern yourself with your heritage again."

Anne pulled him close in a hug. "I love you," she whispered into his ear.

"I have a secret, too," Chris cleared his throat and looked around the table. "I saw Elizabeth five years ago in Sacramento." Everyone held their breaths and stared at him.

"Son, how could you keep that a secret?" Sam demanded. "You knew how much Michael and John wanted to find her."

"I know but I promised her I wouldn't tell. After I had time to think it over, I tried to find her again, but there was no phone listing. I must have gone back to that park a hundred times, but she was never there. Then, I came home on leave, and I thought about telling you but," he looked apologetically at Michael, "you said Valerie had told you Elizabeth was doing well and would come home when she was ready, and I let it go."

"It's not your fault. I stopped pushing then, too. But now we have a new clue, a big one. When can we meet with your detective, Grandmother?" Michael asked.

Valerie appeared behind John. She smiled warmly at Michael. He heard her say, "She's ready."

Michael grinned. "Valerie says she's ready to be found."

"That damn ghost," Minette muttered.

Everyone laughed, and the tension was broken. The mood lifted. Excitement at the thought that Elizabeth might soon be home filled the air.

# Chapter Twenty Nine

John and Michael joined Minette and Henry for their appointment with Charles Williams. John was relieved to see that, despite the fact that Williams' hair was long enough to brush his collar, it was well groomed, and was wearing a "normal" business suit and not one of those tacky leisure suits. Williams had a confident air and a firm handshake. He greeted Minette with a few words in French and made sure that she was seated comfortably before offering chairs to the men.

When everyone had been offered and declined coffee, Williams settled behind his desk and took a moment to assess the family. "I understand you have decided to use my services to locate Elizabeth Augustus."

John and Michael nodded. Minette murmured, "Please."

"Mrs. Smythe mentioned that you have some new information, but before we get started, I would like to explain some things. Miss Augustus disappeared almost twenty years ago. That is a long time, and she will have changed a great deal. During the 1960's when young girls ran away they often joined communes, and many of them were caught up in the drug culture or sex trade. I will find her, but I cannot guarantee if she is alive or under what circumstances she will be living."

The color drained from Michael's face, "Elizabeth is not like that. I know she's okay. Valerie told me."

Williams' drew his notebook toward him and jotted Valerie on the empty page. He ignored Michael's outburst and continued, "The fact that she, herself, has had no contact with the family is a strong indicator that she doesn't want to be found or that she is no longer alive. Assuming she is alive, and since there has been no official word otherwise, it is likely that she is hiding something." He looked toward Minette and smiled. "Mrs. Smythe has indicated that it is her desire that I find her granddaughter and let her know that the family loves her and wants her to come home."

"We want you to bring her home," John said.

"I can't do that. You all must understand that there has been no crime committed. Miss Augustus is an adult. I can find her, and I can give her your messages, and I will tell you when I do. But without her permission, I will not tell you where she is or how she is living. In fact, I will do everything possible to protect her privacy."

John flushed, and his jaw clenched, "But we're paying you to find her."

Williams nodded, "You are, but that changes nothing. Do you understand?"

Minette watched John struggle to come to grips with what he was hearing. "We understand, Mr. Williams. I'm ninety years old. Try not to waste any time." She smiled, and Williams chuckled.

"I'll do my best, Mam." He picked up his pen and tapped the notebook. "Mrs. Smythe provided me with copies of the reports from your prior search, and I've made notes from those files." He looked at John. "You and I will need to go over that information, but for now, why don't you tell me about the new information."

John quickly filled him in on Chris' sighting and conversation in Sacramento. "I know it is still a long time ago but…"

"But, five years is better than twenty. I'll need to gather a complete list of family names and phone numbers beginning with Chris' information." He swiveled his chair to look directly at Michael, "But let's start with Valerie. Who is she and when did she tell you Miss Augustus was alive and well?"

Michael blushed. He knew how ridiculous people outside the family thought it was that he believed that he saw and talked to a ghost. "Valerie was Elizabeth's mother."

"Was?" Williams raised an eyebrow.

"She died the night Elizabeth was born."

"So, let me be sure I understand," Williams said carefully tapping his pen on the open page, "your knowledge that Miss Augustus is alive and well comes from a ghost." He leaned back in his chair. "Tell me how that works."

"Mr. Williams," Minette decided to intervene and support Michael, "While it may be unusual, the entire family is aware that Michael sees and hears Valerie. He has done so since the night Elizabeth was born. We do not doubt that this is true nor that Valerie seems to always be right."

"Nothing surprises me, Mrs. Smythe," Williams smiled at Minette. "If you think this ghost is credible, I'm willing to hear the story. Go on, Mr. Augustus, tell me about your ghost, when and where did you see her last and what did she say?"

"Two nights ago, at Grandmother's, she had just told us about engaging you to find Elizabeth. Valerie appeared behind Dad and said 'she's ready.' I told everyone, and she disappeared."

"And you think that means Miss Augustus is safe and okay?"

"Not just that. I've always seen Valerie when Elizabeth is in trouble or needs help. When we were young, she'd tell me what Elizabeth needed and where to find her. After Elizabeth disappeared, she never again told me where to find her or how to help, just that she needed me. During the last five years when I see her, she only," he glanced at John, "hovers behind or around Dad. If she says anything at all it's something like, 'Elizabeth is fine or happy. Stuff like that."

"All right, I'm not saying I believe, but I am willing to accept that you do, and I expect you to inform me if and/or when you see this ghost and what if anything that she says, agreed?" Michael nodded. "Good.  Now, what's this new information?"

༖

Serena, GG, and Grandy watched with pride as Kala held her long red hair out of the way and blew out the fifteen candles on her cake with one exhale. Her friends cheered, and Kala grinned. "What did you wish for," Jamie demanded.

"None of your business," Kala giggled.

"I bet you wished for your first kiss," Jamie taunted.

"As if...I don't need a wish to get a kiss."

"You better not be kissing anyone until I meet them," GG said, trying to look stern.

"Don't worry, GG," Jamie kissed his cheek. "There's no boy at our school who would be willing to kiss Kala."

"You're just jealous because I'm getting my permit tomorrow and Grandy has promised to teach me to drive."

Serena watched the tomfoolery delighted, that for this evening, Kala was happy and not asking questions. She was quite certain that Kala's wish had been to know about her birth father and Serena wasn't sure if she would be able to sustain the lie she'd been telling. *She's so bright and beautiful,* Serena thought. *She'll hate me when she finds out I've been lying. I can't tell her and risk losing her. I just can't.*

GG smiled at Serena and raised his glass of tea in a toast. Serena pushed her worries aside and joined the fun.

⚬❀⚬

Serena took the first week of July off and they headed for the Russian River to spend time with Carol and Barb. Kala's driving skills impressed her mother. "Did you know I didn't learn to drive until I was almost twenty-four years old?" Serena asked.

"Really? Why not?"

"I grew up in a city with taxis and a subway system. My father had a driver, so I just didn't need to drive."

Kala concentrated on the road. Her mother seldom mentioned her childhood, and this was new information. She stayed quiet hoping Serena would continue. When she didn't, Kala prompted, "Who taught you?"

"Grandy. When we moved the office here, I needed to drive so that I could go to law school and get around."

"I'm glad I don't have to wait until I'm old to learn."

"Twenty four isn't old," Serena smiled.

"Duh, to get a license it is. When did you have your first date?"

"I was sixteen. And you can wait until then, too."

"Tell me about your first boyfriend. Was he cute? Did your parents like him?"

"My first date was a friend of my brother's."

"Whoa," Kala couldn't help herself from exclaiming, "I didn't know you have a brother."

Damn, Serena thought, I didn't mean to say that. "It's not important. Let's listen to some music." She leaned forward and flipped on the radio. Tuning it to a rock station, she turned it up loud. Then tipped her seat back and pretended to drift off to sleep. Serena pictured Michael as she'd last seen him, waving goodbye at the airport when she left for college. *I wonder what he looked like now. He'll be turning forty-three on the 4ᵗʰ of July. Maybe he's bald.* She almost giggled at the thought.

⁓⁂⁓

After breakfast, Carol sent Barb and Kala into Guerneville to pick up a few things she claimed to have forgotten. As soon as they were gone, she poured fresh coffee and asked Serena to join her on the deck. "You know Barb and I love you, right?" Serena nodded. "You and Kala are family to us, and we would do anything to help you."

"Carol, I know that. We love you, too. If it weren't for your help and love, I wouldn't have Kala, or a law degree, or be in partnership with Alan and Jim. Our whole life, and my career, is thanks to you and Barb."

"No, it isn't, Serena. You are an amazing woman. You built this life, and it's a good life but..." she paused.

Serena waited, unsure of where this was going. Finally, Carol continued, "I don't want to interfere, but Kala is getting older. She wants to know who she is. She deserves to know."

Serena shook her head.

"I need to tell you something," Carol started again. "Last Friday a detective came to the office. He had a picture of you...of you at about age eighteen." Serena set her cup down carefully and sat perfectly still, she waited. "I said I didn't recognize the girl. But, of course, I did. If he knows where you worked fifteen years ago, sooner or later he will find you."

Serena didn't bother to dispute that a detective might be looking for her; instead, she gazed straight ahead, watching the water rush over the rocks, as it headed for the ocean. "It's a long story, Carol," she finally said.

"I'm sure it is, Serena. I want you to know that Barb and I will always love you. We've watched you grow and change, and we are as proud of you as it is possible to be. I think of you as my daughter. That will not change, no matter why you are hiding from your past. You can tell me anything, and I will help you if I can."

"I haven't done anything wrong, Carol. I ran away and I did some dumb things, but I got my act together pretty fast when I realized that I wasn't cut out for street life." She stared down at the river and found herself hoping to see the woman in the vintage clothes, but, today no one was there. "Did the detective seem to know much about me?"

"He only had that old picture, and he asked about Elizabeth Augustus but," Carol frowned, remembering the conversation, "he must know something because he came to my office, and you haven't worked there in fifteen years. I'd guess he's talked to someone who said that a girl that looked like you used to work there. He never mentioned Serena Miller, so I don't think he's learned that name."

"But," Serena took up the thought, "once he's sure I was in San Francisco, I'll be easy to find. I changed my name legally and when I did I had to file in the newspaper. The filing shows the change from Elizabeth Augustus to Serena Miller. He'll be able to find that. I wonder who he talked to and how he found my trail."

"I'd guess, he's good at his job. I don't think it will long until he finds you…and Kala."

# Chapter Thirty

Serena knew that patience was not one of her virtues. Every time her secretary, Joan, announced a call she felt sure that it would be the detective. Alan commented on her distraction and asked if anything was wrong. Serena called it the "summer itch" and laughed it off. When a second week went by without Williams appearing she began to relax and think that perhaps he hadn't found her trail after all.

The following Monday, Joan appeared with a business card in her hand. She handed the card to Serena and announced, "There is a Private Detective, named Charles Williams, in the reception area. He doesn't have an appointment, and he declined to say what case he is working on, but he'd like a few minutes of your time. What should I tell him?"

Serena studied the card. Both his address and his phone number were from her home city. She squared her shoulders. This is it, she thought. "I'll see him, Joan. And, please hold my calls until we finish."

Serena walked around her desk, hand extended, to greet Williams. For a long moment, they appraised each other. "Ms. Miller, it's a pleasure to meet you."

"How may I help you, Mr. Williams?"

"May I sit down?" Serena weighed her options and decided she would need to hear whatever he had to tell her. She nodded and slipped behind her desk,.

He seated himself and began, "I was contacted by Mrs. Minette Smythe a few months ago. She requested that I renew her family's search for her granddaughter, Elizabeth Augustus." Serena could feel him watching her closely and kept her face expressionless. "Mrs. Smythe is approaching her ninety-first birthday and would very much like to see her granddaughter again."

Still, Serena didn't speak, so Williams continued, "I met with Mr. John Augustus and his son Michael and they, too, are very anxious to reconnect with Elizabeth. I informed the family that Elizabeth is now an adult and that if I found her, and she was not in danger, I would only tell the family that she is safe and well. I would not reveal her whereabouts, not even her general location unless she agreed."

Serena nodded her understanding. "I appreciate your discretion, Mr. Williams."

"You should also know that your cousin Christopher Augustus has admitted that he saw you five years ago, here, in Sacramento." Serena noticed he was now speaking directly about her instead of about an unknown person. "I understand that you have a teenage daughter and that you have built a full life and career. It is not my intention to disrupt your life."

"Thank you." Serena stood and walked to the window. "No one knows." Williams waited without moving. "I would like to see Grandmother and Michael, but I'm someone else now."

"Take your time. Talk it over with someone you trust." He moved to her side. "I'll explain to your family that you need time." Serena tried to smile at him. "I have learned a lot about you, while I searched. You are a strong, capable person and if I can be of any help, please call."

This time Serena did smile. "Thank you. I need a time to decide what to do. What to tell my daughter."

She spent a sleepless night and then asked Alan if he had time to talk after the office closed for the day. She called Kala and told her she'd be home late. Then she called Grandy to let her know that Kala would be home alone. As always, Grandy and GG were delighted to have Kala to themselves and urged her to enjoy her dinner with Alan. *As if,* Serena thought.

She tapped on Alan's door just after five. At his invitation, she stepped in and closed the door. Alan looked up, "Closed door meeting after hours, this must be important."

"I need to tell you something, Alan. Something I don't want others to hear."

"Did you take out a contract on Judge Clampett?" Serena shook her head. "Okay, then whatever it is can't be all that bad. I was going to suggest we go out to dinner and talk but maybe we should have a drink here first. Make yourself comfortable."

Serena kicked off her high heels and sat on the sofa staring out the window at the summer sky. *It should be gray and cloudy or maybe even flashing lightening,* she thought. Drinks in hand, they sipped a moment. Serena could almost hear Alan waiting. "I don't know where to start?"

"Try the beginning."

"First, I need to say, I think when Carol introduced me to you and Jim and you hired me to work for you was the luckiest day of my life."

She took a gulp for courage and began, "I'm not who you think I am. Well. I am, but my name used to be Elizabeth Augustus. I ran away from my family in 1960. I thought I wanted to live free, be a hippy, so I changed my name and joined a commune. I wasn't very good at it. I missed everything, hot showers, clean beds, meat." Alan chuckled but didn't interrupt.

Serena avoided making eye contact, as she continued. "I left the commune, lied about my age and education, and took a job working for a wealthy family in San Francisco. One thing led to another, until I found myself unwed and pregnant. After that, you are involved in the story." She finished her drink.

Alan got up to refill their glasses. He handed her the glass. "Look at me, Serena." He waited until she did. "I've known you more than fifteen years. There is nothing you can tell me that would make me think less of you. You are bright, hardworking, a very fine lawyer, and my good friend."

"But I lied about so much."

"Have you legally changed your name?" Serena nodded. "Then your name is Serena Miller. It doesn't matter to me if Kala's father is alive or dead, although I'm sure it will matter to Kala."

"I am Serena Miller," she agreed. "I've lived all my adult life as Serena. There is no way I can go back to being Elizabeth Augustus, I don't even want to but...the Augustus family is rich and powerful. I don't think they could accept me as I am now."

"Do you want to get in touch with them?" Alan asked, wondering where this was going.

"They hired a detective to find me." Serena locked her eyes on Alan's. "He found me today."

"Wow, no wonder, you're so upset. Do you know what you want to do?"

"I have no idea. He promised that he wouldn't tell the family where I live but I doubt that I can hide forever."

"Do you want to?" Alan looked into his glass.

"Part of me does, I like my life. Kala is curious about her father but she has always accepted that he is dead." She hesitated and started again, "A part of me wants to tell Kala the truth about her father and in order to do that I'd need to tell her the truth about me. And if I tell her the truth then GG and Grandy need to know the truth, too."

She stood and began to pace, a habit she'd picked up when prepping for a case. "I am Serena Miller. I will never be Elizabeth Augustus again. Somehow – I think I need to figure out a way to combine the two. Although," she admitted, "I don't see any way to do that."

Serena deliberated about how to tell Kala. Both Carol and Alan suggested that just being honest and telling the truth was probably best. But the truth was hard, after fifteen years of telling her daughter that her Daddy had died in the war she'd now have to admit she'd lied.

Yet, Serena knew that she, herself, had run from the Augustus family because she was angry when they wouldn't help her find her birth father. She was sure that Kala would be at least as angry. If she was going to tell Kala the truth, she needed to tell Brian first.

# Chapter Thirty One

Serena wasn't sure where Brian was living or what he was doing so she called Mary Lou, just to chat, and casually asked if her whole family still lived in New Orleans. "Absolutely, Mama wouldn't have it any other way. Steve and I are the only ones who aren't home every Sunday for dinner. And, if he ever retires, Mama's already informed him that we'd best be moving home."

Serena laughed. "What does Steve think of that?"

"Oh, he loves the whole family. My brothers have oodles of kids now, and they all love Uncle Steve."

"I'm going to be in New Orleans, and I wondered..." she hesitated long enough that Mary Lou interrupted.

"You better find time to go see my mama. If she finds out you were in town and didn't visit, she'd be hurt, and I'd never hear the end of it. When are you going? Hey, you should stay over Sunday and then you could see everybody."

Serena was going to ask about Brian but seeing him with the entire family seemed easier. "That sounds like fun, maybe I will. I think I'm going next week. Give me your mother's phone number, and I'll call her."

Mary Lou rattled off the number. "I'm going to call her right now and give her a head's up, so you have to go. Is that pretty daughter of yours going along?"

*Not likely*, Serena thought. Aloud she said, "Not this time," and got off the phone.

Serena booked her flight, leaving Saturday afternoon and flying home Monday morning. She told Kala and GG that it was a business trip and spend most of the week, and the entire flight, rehearsing ways to tell Brian that he was the father of her daughter. She wished she had dared ask Mary Lou if Brian was married and if he had other children.

Between worry and the time change, Serena was up early. She dressed carefully in a conservative white sun dress that she knew complimented both her dark hair and her slender form. She strolled from her hotel to Café Du Monde where she was seated at an outdoor table. She ordered beignets and a coffee and chicory au lait and settled to people watch.

Serena walked around Jackson Square, looking at the art work on display and stopping to pet one of the carriage horses who wore a particularly spectacular headdress. Serena, remembering the stories Mary Lou had told of her childhood, caught the St. Charles Avenue streetcar and rode through the Garden District mansions to the McGuiness house.

The moment she stepped down from the streetcar, Mama McGuiness grabbed her in a hug, and a swarm of red headed children swept her up onto the wide, welcoming, porch. Serena found herself laughing along with the family as she tried to make sense out of which child belonged to which brother. Mama shooed everyone away and pulled her in for another hug, "Bless your heart, girl. You're just as pretty as a picture, isn't she, Brian?"

Serena turned as Brian came through the screen door, letting it slam behind him. For a moment neither spoke. Brian grinned his infectious grin and Serena grinned back. "If anything you are prettier than ever, Miss Serena. Welcome to New Orleans. Long time no see."

He stepped forward and opened his arms. Serena moved into his embrace and felt his tall body press against hers. She sighed, and Brian whispered, "I never thought I'd see you again."

Serena pulled back. Brian let his arms drop, "Mary Lou tells me you never married that Navy guy of yours or anyone else."

Serena shook her head, "That's true.   How about you?"

"Never found the right girl, I guess."

"Although he's tried," his brother teased. "Every unmarried girl, from twenty to forty, wants to capture and tame the wealthy, dashing Brian McGuiness." Mama swatted at him, and Serena joined the laughter.

"What do you do that makes you so eligible?"

"Well, the dashing part just comes naturally." His brothers groaned. "And, I'm an unmarried doctor so, I guess, that makes me eligible."

"More important," Mama declared, "you're a lovely man.  Come on in and fill your plates."

❧

The McGuiness family was as charming and friendly as Serena had remembered from Mary Lou's wedding. Everyone seemed to know that she lived in Sacramento and practiced law, but Mary Lou had kept her promise and never mentioned Kala. Lunch over, Mama provided the perfect opportunity to give her time to talk to Brian alone by suggesting that they take a walk. "Show her some of the historic homes in the neighborhood," she insisted.

Serena protested that she would help clean up until Brian grabbed her hand and pulled her down the steps. They walked together lightly swinging their clasped hands. Serena hated that she needed to disrupt the pleasure she was feeling in his company, but it was now or never. They were out of sight of the porch and passing a tiny park. "Let's sit for a moment."

Brian sat with his arm stretched along the back of the bench. Serena wanted to lean into his embrace. *He smells so good,* she thought. When his hand cupped her shoulder, Serena pulled away, sat up straight, and turned to face him. "I need to tell you something."

Brian waited. She tried to remember everything she'd rehearsed. His clear blue eyes crinkled as he smiled his encouragement. "I have a child," she blurted, dropping her gaze from his.

He tilted her chin with one finger forcing her to meet his eyes. "Boy or girl?"

"Girl, Kala Michele. She's fifteen." Serena watched him process the age.

"So, you didn't marry the sailor, but you kept the child."

"Not exactly. Logan isn't her father. You are."

Brian winced and drew back, his eyes wide. "But we only made love once." Serena smiled and nodded. "Are you sure?" he demanded.

"If you mean have I had a blood test done, no, of course not. But Kala looks exactly like Mary Lou."

"Why did you wait so long to tell me?" Brian took his arm from the back of the bench. "She's fifteen years old, for God's sake. Who does she think is her father?"

"I made up a father's name for the birth certificate. At first, she didn't look like anyone, and when her hair came in red, I tried to believe that it was just a coincidence. I told Kala her father was dead."

"Dead, what the hell were you thinking?"

"I was thinking that it would be harder to be an illegitimate child than a child whose father had died in the war."

"Didn't you think I'd want to know, didn't you even consider telling me when you found out you were pregnant?"

"Brian, we weren't a couple. I wasn't even sure we'd had sex." Brian shook his head in disgust. Serena bristled, the color rising in her cheeks. "It wasn't like you ever called me again. You left a cavalier note and then you were gone."

"You told me you needed time to get over Logan. I waited six months, and when I still hadn't heard from you, I went back to San Francisco. I didn't find any trace of you. Mary Lou said she'd seen you, but she was sure you wanted to be left alone."

Serena thought of that last night in San Francisco, when she'd been afraid that Mary Lou had guessed her secret. Perhaps she had and assumed, like Brian, that the baby was Logan's. After that, it had been years before they met again and when they had, Serena had been adamant that the baby wasn't a McGuiness.

"I want to meet Kala. If she's my daughter, I want to know her and allow her to know me and my family. She deserves both sides of her heritage."

Serena nodded. "I came here to tell you. Now I need to tell Kala who you are and that you are alive."

"Do it fast because I'm coming out, to Sacramento, as soon as I rearrange my schedule." His fists clenched and unclenched as he tried to control his anger. "I don't understand why you did this Serena. Even if we weren't couple, we made a child together. Are you so ashamed that you had to hide me from your family, from everyone?"

"I'm not ashamed of you Brian or of Kala. She doesn't know anyone from my family either."

"I don't know what game you have been playing Serena, but I want to meet my daughter, ASAP."

*It's a game called survival,* Serena thought. She stood and brushed off the back of her dress. "Tell your mother, thank you for the lovely meal. It was great seeing your family again." She dug in her purse and took out a business card. "Here's my number. Give me a call when you know your schedule. I'm going to leave now, and I'll tell Kala tomorrow night." She began to walk toward the streetcar stop.

"Serena." His voice stopped her footsteps. She turned to look at him.. "I'm very angry, and I need to think about this. But, I'm sorry you had to go through this alone. You should have told me. I'll be in touch." She nodded. Brian turned and walked back to his family home.

Serena watched him go. He didn't turn around.

# Chapter Thirty Two

Serena had planned to go straight to work from the airport since the time change would allow her to arrive at noon. Instead, she left a message for Joan, on the new office answering machine, telling her to cancel all of her appointments and to let Alan know she wouldn't be back until Tuesday.

On the flight home she wrote out her arguments for Kala, ticking off all the points she needed to cover, but somewhere over the Rockies she realized this wasn't a law case; this conversation would determine her relationship with Kala forever. She put down her pen and allowed herself to think about the Augustus family, her family.

*I was so stupid,* she thought. *There was never any reason to hide. I knew Michael always loved me and I know I love him. All my best memories include him and his stories about conversations with my ghost mother. I miss Michael and all the cousins. Sylvia doesn't matter anymore. She didn't like me, but she didn't love her own child either. As for John, he might have been distant, but he tried to be a father to both Michael and I. Grandmother Minette, never showed any of us anything but love. All I wanted to do was feel like I belonged to a family and all the time I did. I need to tell Kala all of this in a way that she will understand.*

The stewardess stopped by Serena's seat and asked if she needed anything. Serena realized she was crying and brushed the tears away as she shook her head. She picked up her pen and a legal pad. This time she listed the names of the Augustus family, names she'd been trying to forget for twenty years.

Kala and Jamie were on the patio in the middle of a complicated beauty session, curling their hair, painting their nails and giggling. They waved to Serena as she stepped from the car. "Hi, Mom," Kala called.

"Hi yourself, don't I get a welcome home hug?"

"Mom, my nails are wet."

"I'm going to take my suitcase inside, and then we need to talk, Kala. Finish up quickly and come in."

Kala stopped painting her toes and looked at her Mom. "What's wrong? Am I in trouble?"

"No, of course not, I just want to tell you something."

Grandy waved to Serena from the house. "Welcome home. I have some chicken salad I made for the girl's lunch. Do you want some?"

"No thanks, I'll be over later. Kala hurry up. Tell Jamie goodbye and come in."

"Can't Jamie stay?"

"Not this time." Damn, Serena thought, this is already hard.

Serena popped open cans of Diet Rite soda and filled two glasses with ice. Kala slumped down in a chair at the kitchen table and regarded her mother, "Have you been crying?"

"A little." She sat opposite Kala and began, "I went to New Orleans this weekend to see someone I haven't seen in a long time."

Kala waited.

Serena reached across the table and touched Kala's hand. "I need to tell you some things and I want you to listen, okay?" Kala nodded.

"I was born in London, England during the second world war," Serena began. "My mother died when I was born."

Kala watched her closely and didn't speak. This was the story she'd always wanted to know.

As Serena's story unfolded she could see Kala becoming more and more excited, finally she could wait no longer. "A ghost, that is so cool. Are these people still alive? Will we go see them? Can we go now?"

"We'll talk about all of that later, right now I need you to listen a little longer."

"I lied to you about your father." Kala's mouth opened to make a protest, but Serena kept talking. "There isn't an easy way to say this. When I met your father, I was dating someone else. After they were both gone, I found out I was pregnant. Carol and Barb helped me, and I was able to keep you. And that's the best decision I've ever made. I love you with all my heart, and I'm sorry I lied about your father."

"Is he alive, who is he?"

"His name is Brian McGuiness. Yes, he's alive. I went down to New Orleans to meet him and tell him about you. He wants to meet you."

Kala's leaped up, her chair crashed backward, she stared open mouthed at her mother. "You knew all this time, and you never told me. I hate you!"

Kala slammed out the door and rushed across the patio and into Grandy's arms. Serena followed.

Grandy hugged Kala close and patted her back. Her eyes questioned Serena over Kala's head. Serena tried to pry Kala from Grandy's arms.

"Don't touch me. Leave me alone. You're nothing but a big fat liar."

GG came into the kitchen to see what all the commotion was about. "What's going on in here?"

Kala swiped at her tears, "My Mom's a liar, and I hate her."

Ever the peacemaker GG said calmly, "Let's all sit down and talk about this."

"No. I'm never going to talk to her again."

"Never is a very long time, sweetie. Why don't you stay with Grandy for a bit and your Mom and I will leave you two alone." Kala gulped and nodded. "Let's go over to your house, Serena."

He led the way, and Serena followed. Back in her kitchen he righted Kala's chair and made himself a cup of coffee. Serena sat at the table, hands over her eyes, weeping. GG placed a box of tissues in front of her and sat down. "Now then, do you want to talk about it?"

Serena shook her head. "Kala's right. I am a liar. A big fat liar. I don't think she'll ever forgive me."

"Of course she will. You're a great mother."

"A great mother doesn't tell lies, especially lies about everything important." GG waited, sipping his coffee. After a long minute, Serena spoke, "You are going to hate me, too."

"I doubt that very much. Lois and I think of you as our daughter. We will love you and help you no matter what you think you have done."

"It isn't something I think I've done. It's everything I've done. I'm not who you think I am."

"Then why don't you tell me who you are."

Serena blew her nose. She was so tired of keeping secrets. At last, she began again, "I was born in London, England..."

⟶ ⟵

Sam and John Augustus met for breakfast, as they often did, now that they were both retired. "Do you remember the first time we had coffee here?" John asked. Sam shook his head. "It was the day Michael was born. I'd just realized that Sylvia had lied to me and that whoever that baby's father was, it wasn't me."

Sam nodded.

"Now I can't even imagine why I cared. Michael is the best son a father could want; I never should have rejected him."

Sam nodded again.

"When Valerie died, I ran away from my responsibilities and rejected Elizabeth, too. If it hadn't have been for Minette, I might never have seen my children again. I was always afraid to stand up to grandfather; I should have acknowledged Elizabeth as mine. But, instead, I did as I was told and pretended she was a war orphan and adopted her. I've been a terrible father, Sam."

"It's not too late. You and Michael have cleared the air and I know he considers you his father in all ways. Elizabeth will come home. I'm sure of it."

"What makes you so sure? That detective, Charles Williams, told us she didn't want him to reveal where she is living."

"I know that, but I think it has to be somewhere in the California Bay Area. Chris saw her in Sacramento, right?" John nodded. "It's almost Minette's birthday. I think we should plan a big party."

"Sure, we should have a party but how will that help find Elizabeth?"

"Remember that gossip columnist, Sharon Chatsworth?"

John chuckled. "Of course, I do. Grandfather hated it whenever she mentioned our family in her column."

"There aren't any national gossip columns anymore, but let's see if we can stir up enough gossip to get it heard all the way to the west coast."

John waited to hear Sam's idea.

"Everyone is tired of the gas crisis. Let's announce a party, the biggest and grandest party we can imagine. We can invite everyone who ever knew Minette and a few celebrities. Then we can advertise in the Bay Area papers, and perhaps we can convince Elizabeth Augustus to come home for the party. We'll buy a page and make a 'congratulations to Minette on her ninety-four birthday' announcement. Her marriage to an Augustus and then her work in the French Resistance, plus her finding Michael and Elizabeth in Wales; it all makes a great human interest story. The media will love it."

"That might just work. If we are interviewed, or when Minette is, we can all say we want the entire family to come home for the party."

Grandy and GG agreed that Kala could stay in their guest room for a few days, but they insisted that Serena eat with them and that Kala should be civil to her mother. Mostly Kala chose not to speak, but she listened closely as GG encouraged Serena to talk about her childhood.

It only took two days for Brian to arrange for time off to come west and meet his daughter. He called Serena at her office, keeping the conversation brief, only requesting the home phone number and informing her that he intended to call Kala and invite her to meet him.

"Kala is very angry," Serena admitted. "Would you like me to be there when you meet?"

"Of course, she's angry. What did you expect?" Brian didn't wait for an answer. ""Unless Kala suggests it, I'd rather meet with her alone. I don't really think you and I have anything to say to each other."

Jamie watched as Kala dressed carefully for her date with this man who was suddenly her father. "What if he doesn't like me?"

"Silly, he's going to love you. Everyone does."

"Not my mother, if she loved me she wouldn't have lied to me."

Jamie reached for the hair brush, loyalty to her best friend kept her from protesting; that parents usually tried to do what they thought was best. "Let me fix your hair."

The doorbell rang, and Kala rushed to open it. A red-haired stranger stood on the porch. They stared at each other, and then each stroked their hair.

"We're related alright." Brian held out his hand. "Hello, Kala, I'm Brian McGuiness, and I'm very happy to meet you."

"Wow," Jamie said from the stairs, "you're really handsome. No wonder Kala's so pretty."

Brian laughed. "Thank you, and who are you?"

"This is Jamie. She's my best friend. I knew I didn't look like my Mom but I sure look like you."

"You do, and when you meet the rest of the family, you'll see that you look like my sister and all of your cousins. If you are ready to go, let's go to lunch and get acquainted."

"Grandy," Kala called, "I'm leaving."

"Just a second, GG and I want to meet your Dad."

The formalities over, Jamie hugged Kala and whispered in her ear, "This is so cool. Tell me everything when you get home." Brian and Kala walked to his rental car. Serena watched from the gate.

Brian and Kala spent the next three days together. Kala still refused to talk to her mother but her excitement was evident, and she bubbled over, to Grandy and GG, with praise for her dad. Brian called Serena and told her he wanted to take Kala to

New Orleans to meet the rest of the family. Reluctantly, Serena agreed, she didn't think she had a choice.

Brian encouraged Kala to call her mother from New Orleans, but Kala adamantly refused. She did call Grandy and GG, who passed her reports about the McGuiness family and the wonders of New Orleans on to Serena.

Serena tried not to let it bother her, but it felt as if she'd lost her daughter. Suddenly she realized how much she had hurt her family by disappearing and refusing to contact them.

Kala finally called her mother at the office and demanded that she be allowed to stay in New Orleans, live with her father, and complete school with her cousins. Serena was furious. She managed to control her temper with Kala and simply said she missed her too much to allow that to happen. Kala slammed the phone down, and Serena immediately dialed Brian. "What do you think you are doing?" she demanded without saying hello.

"Serena?"

"Yes, Serena, the mother of your child. I agreed to let her visit you and your family but I didn't give you custody."

"Whoa," Brian said. "Back up and tell me what you are talking about?"

Serena told him of Kala's request.

"I admit I'd love to have Kala live closer to me. My whole family adores her, and she seems to love having a big family around her, but I didn't ask her to move here. I know she has a life with you. She's a great kid, so I know you've been a good mother. I expect to share custody and we'll need to make that a formal agreement, but moving, nope, not my suggestion."

"Sorry, I jumped down your throat. I was just upset. I really miss Kala, and I want to clear the air between us, but I don't seem to be able to get through to her when she is so far away."

"I'll talk to her tonight and explain that we both feel she needs to live with you until she finishes high school. But I'd like to be able to tell her that she can spend her Christmas break with me in New Orleans."

"Brian, we always go to the Russian River with friends for Christmas and New Year's."

"But this year she has a father, and I'd like to show her the McGuiness way of celebrating." The phone hummed as he waited for her answer. "You could come, too. My family loves you."

"I doubt that." Serena tapped her pen against the phone. "I can't imagine that your mama approves of a woman having a child out of wedlock."

Brian laughed. "My mama is the most practical woman you'll ever meet. If she blames anyone, it's me. Mostly she's just delighted to have another grand-baby."

His words made Serena chuckle, she remembered how much she'd enjoyed his company those few hours they'd spent together in San Francisco and New Orleans. "Okay, you can tell Kala I said she can spend her holiday with you."

"Great. And you think about coming, too. I swear Mama will be delighted." She imagined his smile. Her own lips smiled in response to his happiness.

# Chapter Thirty Three

It had been a tough fall for Kala and Serena, but gradually, with Jamie's prodding and GG's support, Kala began to ask questions; questions that Serena was careful to answer truthfully.

Serena made herself tell Carol and Barb, and Alan and Jim the whole truth, and was amazed by their acceptance and understanding. By Thanksgiving, the extended family that Serena and Kala had created for themselves had drawn closer than ever.

Kala asked if she could invite Brian to Thanksgiving. Grandy and GG, who were hosting, immediately said yes. Brian only hesitated a moment before agreeing but asked to speak to Serena. Kala reluctantly handed the phone to Serena but hung around to eavesdrop on her parents.

They exchanged polite greetings, and then Brian said, "Mary Lou and Steve are in Monterey while he attends language school before going overseas. They haven't met Kala yet, and they'd really like to do so. Perhaps they could drive over there on Friday or Saturday if that would be all right with you."

*Mary Lou*, Serena thought, *she'd been such a great friend before everything went wrong in San*

*Francisco*. She had kept Serena's secret. Without thinking further, she said, "Why don't you invite them to spend Thanksgiving with us? There's plenty of room for two more."

Stunned silence greeted her invitation, and she almost took it back, but she heard Grandmother Minette saying "C'est finis, " and she decided to let the invitation stand.

"If you're sure, I know they'd love to come. I'll let you know. If they decide to come, I'll fly into San Francisco on Wednesday, and we'll drive over on Thursday. Will that fit with your dinner plans."

"I think that would be great. Grandy likes to serve dinner at six. It's about a three-hour drive so you might want to get a hotel here for Thursday night." They completed the arrangements and hung up.

Kala was dancing around impatiently, demanding to know who else was coming for dinner. "Another aunt and uncle, your Aunt Mary Lou was my friend before I met your father."

"Hurrah. I heard all about them in New Orleans. I didn't know you knew them, too. Why, if you knew all the McGuiness family, didn't you tell them about me?"

"It seems silly now, but at the time I was embarrassed and afraid. I had too many secrets."

Kala squinted her eyes at her mother, "Got it. Kind of dumb though. I'm going to go tell Grandy and Jamie that they are all coming."

She slammed out the door and ran across the yard.

Thanksgiving was a great deal of fun. Now that everyone knew her secrets, Serena could relax. She giggled, with Mary Lou, about their time in San Francisco. Serena swelled with pride as Mary Lou marveled at the wonder of this beautiful, smart, teenage niece, who was as she kept saying, her spitting image.

Everyone liked Brian, and it was delightful to see how happy Kala was as she introduced her new relatives to Carol, Barb, Alan, and Jim. With the main meal over, Grandy and Carol shooed everyone else out of the kitchen so they could clean up a bit before dessert.

Mary Lou suggested to Serena that they take a walk around the block to help digest the delicious food. They strolled off together in the growing dark. "So," Mary Lou started, "I guess I know why Brian never married."

"He didn't know about Kala."

"No, but that boy has been carrying a torch for someone, and it's pretty obvious that someone is you."

"Don't be silly, Mary Lou."

"Say what you want, I can see the way he looks at you and what's more, Missy, I can see the way you look at him. I'm a Southern woman. I know stuff. I'll bet you thought about him plenty these last sixteen years."

"Well, of course, I did. I gave birth to a red-headed child, and I only knew one red-headed man."

Mary Lou smiled wisely and tucked her arm through Serena's. "Let's hurry up before that red-headed man of yours, and my darling husband, eat all the pecan pie."

⁂

Serena tried not to cry as she hugged Kala one more time at the boarding gate. "I'm going to miss you so much."

"I'll miss you, too. But remember, I'm expecting Santa to leave a pile of presents under our tree."

Serena laughed. "More likely a lump of coal." She hugged Kala again. "Have a wonderful time.

Say hi to everyone, and I'll see you in the New Year."

Kala handed her ticket to the gate attendant, waved to Serena, walked down the jetway, and disappeared from sight. Serena wanted to run after her and bring her back. *Or perhaps I want to go to New Orleans and have a McGuiness Christmas too*, she thought.

Exiting the terminal, she stopped at a newsstand and picked up a Sunday edition of the *New York Times*. The idea of finding out what was happening in the city appealed to her. Maybe the Augustus family has made the society pages. She wondered if the family rule was still to avoid publicity all costs.

Back at home, Serena settled herself on the patio with a glass of wine and the paper. Already the house seemed too quiet. GG came out with a book and a cocktail of his own, Grandy waved from the kitchen. Serena opened the paper and scanned the headlines, but international or even New York State or City news wasn't where her interest lay. She scanned the business section and read one article that outlined a merger that Michael Augustus, CEO for AmCo was considering. So, Michael went into the family business, after all, she thought. I wonder if he's happy.

She glanced over the engagements and a few weddings, took a look at obituaries and was relieved not to find a name she recognized. She picked up the Style Section and there on the front page was a picture of Michael and Anne. She studied it carefully. She'd recognized them instantly. It was surprising how much the forty-year-old couple resembled the twenty-year-old couple of her memories. She was glad to see they were holding hands and looked happy. She flipped open the section and gasped. GG looked up, "Everything okay?" he asked.

Serena didn't answer. Instead, she stared at a large picture of Grandmother Minette. It was a picture she recognized. Minette, looking beautiful and glamorous, stood on the gangway of a large ship. A small boy clung to her hand, and an even smaller girl held tight to the boy. She touched the boy's face and murmured "Michael."

GG looked up and considered her expression. He wondered what she was looking at.

Bit by bit, Serena let herself remember those early days in the states when Michael was her hero, and Minette seemed to be an angel. *We were so young,* she thought, *only seven and four. But, we were so happy until Sylvia came home.* She forced herself away from those thoughts and concentrated on the rest of the page. "Wow!" she said aloud.

This time GG felt he could ask, "What are you reading?"

Serena handed him the paper. "That's my grandmother."

"And are you the little girl?" Serena nodded. GG studied the picture. "Your grandmother was a lovely woman. When was this taken?"

"The day we arrived in the United States. Minette found Michael and me in Wales and brought us home with her. Michael's dad, John Augustus, and his wife Sylvia adopted me."

GG was reading the rest of the full page story. "This is very interesting. Minette married and came to the US after her husband was killed when she was only seventeen. She actually worked with the French Resistance. Did you know all this?"

"I probably heard it, but you know how kids are. She was my grandmother. I loved her, and I knew she loved me. She took us places and we always had fun. I remember when she married Henry, my mother was furious and wouldn't allow Michael to go to the wedding, but I helped him hide in the car and he went with us."

GG raised his eyebrows at such strange behavior but didn't interrupt the flow of her memories.

When I came out to California she was the one I missed most." Serena sighed. "Actually, I missed Michael most, but I was too mad at them all to admit it."

"It says here that, on January fifth, the family is throwing a big party to celebrate your grandmother's birthday. They are hoping all members of the family, no matter whom they are or where they are, will attend the party." GG looked over his glasses. "I think that may be an invitation meant just for you unless other members of the family are missing."

"Do you think so? They could have just asked that detective to deliver the message."

"I think they want you to know that they want you to come."

"But why would they place this item in the *New York Times*?"

GG chuckled. "How many times have you heard someone say, once a New Yorker always a New Yorker?" He gestured toward the paper. "And they were right. But just to be sure, they placed this ad in the *Sacramento Bee*, too. I saw it this morning."

"Chris must have told them where he saw me. Why else would they choose our local paper?" She hugged herself as she pondered the thought. "I wonder where else this ad is running today?"

"Does it matter? They wanted you to see it, and you have. Now you need to decide if you are going to accept the invitation."

GG stood up and offered his hand to pull her from her chair. "Come on, Grandy has dinner ready by now. We can talk about it while we eat."

Minette held up a copy of the ad and shook her head at Sam and John. "Your grandfather must be rolling in his grave. I can just imagine how angry he'd be at this much public exposure. Whose idea was this?" The two men looked guilty, John because his mother was questioning them, Sam because it had been his idea.

Minette laughed. "You look just like you did when you got into mischief as boys. I don't care whose idea it was, I think it was brilliant. Do you think Elizabeth will see it? Do you think she will attend?"

# Chapter Thirty Four

Carol had convinced Serena to follow their tradition and spend Christmas week at the Russian River despite Kala's absence. She drove up Saturday morning, acutely aware that Kala was not chattering beside her. She'd left Kala's presents at home under the tree. With only her small bag and the presents for her friends, the car was too big and too empty. She knew Kala would be having fun and, most likely, wasn't even thinking about her. Serena could think of nothing else. *I wonder if any Augustus missed me as much as I miss Kala,* she mused.

Christmas Eve day started early with the ringing of the phone in the cottage kitchen. Serena, who was already up, drinking coffee and watching the sun rise over the river, grabbed it quickly.

Her tentative hello was greeted with Kala exuberant greeting. "Guess what, Mom?" Kala didn't pause for an answer. "We went to this store called Maison Blanche yesterday, and they have this crazy snowman named Mr. Bingle, but the cool thing is that we had our picture taken with Santa Claus, I mean we all had our picture taken, like a hundred of us. I love having a family. Mama says she'll send me a copy so I can remember this first Christmas forever."

Serena wanted to ask, what about all of our Christmases together. Instead, she said, "I'm so glad you're having a good time."

"I wish you were here. Everybody says such nice things about you." Serena heard someone call. "Okay, I gotta go. I have to help Mama in the kitchen. Nobody here is eating today but then we're going to Midnight Mass and afterward there'll be a big dinner called Reveillon. Love you, Mom. Happy Christmas Eve."

Serena put the phone back slowly. She remembered the fun and excitement of Christmas Eve at her childhood home. The whole family used to gather at Sam and Helen's big house. She and Michael had spent so much time with their cousins that they really were one family.

She'd tried to give Kala a family, a warm loving family of friends, but perhaps it was time to admit that they had another family. But, what if we go to the city for that party and no one is glad to see us, she worried.

Serena slid open the kitchen door and stepped out onto the deck. Steam was curling up from the river and the scent of pine filled the air. It was cool and crisp, with the promise of a beautiful day in the air. A movement down by the water caught her attention. The woman in the vintage clothes stood on the opposite bank watching her. Serena raised her hand in greeting and to her surprise the woman blew her a kiss. She felt a soft touch on her cheek. Shut her eyes for a moment and when she opened them the woman was gone.

Carol came out on the deck. "Who is that woman?" Serena demanded.

"What woman?" Carol looked around confused.

Serena looked carefully at the water but saw nothing. "Maybe I'm seeing Michael's ghost. Do you think that's possible?'

"Serena, when it comes to you and the story of your life, I think anything is possible. Come on in. Barb is making her famous Good Morning muffins." She hooked her arm around Serena and gave her a hug. "Let's plan your upcoming trip."

"Trip, what trip?"

"Don't try to kid yourself; you know you're going home for that party. It's time for Kala to meet the other half of her family."

Christmas Day, after exchanging greetings with half the McGuiness family and listening to Kala's excited recounting of mass, dinner, the bonfire for Papa Noel, and the presents she received, Serena asked to speak to Brian.

The warmth of his Merry Christmas made Serena blush. Carol, who'd been eavesdropping on the conversation, grinned and theatrically fanned herself. Serena shook her head and mouthed, shut up. "Hi, Brian, Kala's having a wonderful time."

"She's a great kid. You've obviously been a good Mother. She has nothing but praise for you and GG and Grandy. We are all enjoying getting to know her."

"I know I promised you that Kala could stay until January seventh but I want to take her to New York with me."

Brian was silent, and Serena realized that, after sixteen years, she needed to learn to share parenting decisions.

She apologized and explained about the party notice in the paper. "It's Friday the fifth. I talked it over with GG and Grandy, and they agree that I need to face this and that Kala deserves to know my side of the family, too."

"I agree, but I do have one idea." Brian paused. "I think it might be easier for Kala if I tell her about the change in plans. I'll call you back in a couple of hours, and we can coordinate things."

Kala was the one that called back. Despite her initial misgivings, Brian had convinced her that there was no such thing as too much family and she was actually quite excited to finally be meeting Serena's family.

"Dad bought me a beautiful blue velvet dress for midnight mass, with shoes to match. Mama says that should be appropriate for the party. What do you think?"

"I think we can trust Mama's advice when it comes to social matters. I'll get you a flight home, and then we can fly to New York together."

"Actually, Dad has a better idea. He's going to get tickets for us to fly up together. We're going to get hotel rooms and go to Times Square to see the ball drop. We might even get to see a play on Broadway. I invited him to the party, I think we need one friendly face, we can count on, just in case."

"Wow!" Serena was stunned.

Brian took the phone from Kala. "You should come early and join us. You'd have time to get reacquainted with your city, maybe show Kala some the sights."

Serena started to protest when Kala's excited voice interrupted, "Yeah, Mom. That would be great. We could go shopping for a dress for you; I know what's in your closet and you need to step it up. You want to make a good impression, right?"

Brian took the phone back. His voice was filled with laughter. "That's a girl with an opinion. I guess I'd better make sure my dinner jacket is up to her standards. Seriously, you can share Kala's room. It will be fun, unless, you have other plans for New Year's Eve?"

In the background Serena could hear Kala, "I told you she doesn't have plans, she never goes anywhere but work." And there goes any chance of Brian thinking of me as a desirable woman, Serena thought, surprised that she cared.

Carol and Barb were excited by the joint trip and urged her to go. "We'll miss you at our New Year's Eve party, but maybe we will see you and Kala on TV during the ball drop."

Serena flew into New York on the thirty-first, and Kala insisted that she and Brian should meet the flight. On the way to the gate, Brian picked up a bouquet of flowers. Serena exited the jetway and Kala flew into her arms. Others smiled at the picture they made. Brian hugged Serena quickly as Kala started to talk, "Dad got us rooms at the Heloise hotel. Isn't that cool? I told him those were my favorite books, ever."

Serena smile at the memory of reading to her sleepy daughter, "I remember."

"Dad, give her the flowers. I told him to buy white carnations because I know you love the way they smell. Right, Dad?"

Kala's exuberance reminded Serena of a much younger child. She realized that her daughter was nervous. "Thanks, Honey, and thank you, too, Brian. I'm sorry you had to cut your vacation short."

"We really aren't cutting it short; we're just changing the location and the itinerary. I made reservations for dinner tonight at a restaurant in Time's Square. Then we can enjoy the crowds and watch the ball drop."

"And," Kala picked up the schedule, "Tomorrow is a holiday, so we'll walk in Central Park and have tea at the Palm Court. Tuesday we shop for your dress and shoes. Wednesday you can show me some of your favorite things. Thursday we can do museums and Friday we have to have manicures and hair and all that stuff."

Kala paused to take a breath. Serena and Brian looked at each other and laughed. "That's quite a plan."

Kala nodded proudly, "Jamie helped me. She thought it would be good to keep busy so we wouldn't get nervous."

❧

By 7PM, Friday, Serena was nervous despite the schedule. They had found the perfect dress and Brian had whistled appreciatively when she twirled to display her choice. So she knew she looked right. Kala looked beautiful in her sedate blue velvet. They met Brian in the lobby. He also looked wonderful, his jacket and slacks fit to perfection.

"I'm escorting the two most beautiful women in Manhattan tonight." He offered his arm to Serena and felt her tremble as she tucked her arm through his. For a second he pulled her closer and whispered. "Stick close. I'll protect both of you." Serena smiled up at him. He offered Kala his other arm, and they headed out for the party.

Brian had the doorman hail a taxi for the very short ride from The Plaza Hotel to the Waldorf Astoria. "This is my grandmother's favorite hotel," Serena told Kala. "We always celebrated special events here."

Kala took in the opulent uniform of the door man and the gold leafing on the entrance. She whispered to her mother, "Remind me to ask you exactly how rich this family of yours is."

*Rich isn't everything*, Serena thought and swept into the lobby on Brian's arm. They had deliberately arrived after the cocktail hour had started in hopes of avoiding having to awkwardly stand around waiting for someone they recognized to arrive.

She hadn't needed to worry; Chris was standing just inside the room obviously watching for her. He spotted her at once, "Elizabeth," he said pulling her away from Brian and into a hug. "I was sure you would come."

Serena wasn't sure what to say, she settled for, "No one calls me Elizabeth anymore." Chris looked quizzical. "I changed my name to Serena years ago."

She grasped Kala's hand. "My daughter, Kala and her father, Brian McGuiness. This is my cousin Christopher." The men shook hands, and Kala smiled shyly.

Brian took her hand, "Okay, Serena Elizabeth, let's do this." Kala took her other hand, and together they entered the room.

Heads swiveled in their direction, conversations stopped. Across the room, Michael looked up and their eyes locked. He grinned. She grinned. He was glad to see her. It would be alright.

# Epilogue

And it was alright. Not everything was easy, and some grievances took longer to resolve than others. It wasn't easy for Serena Elizabeth to hear that John had always known he was her birth father, but she could understand the need he felt to tell lies to protect the Augustus family name.

Minette lived another four years. She was healthy and wise and used her wisdom to smooth the path of truth that John and Serena followed to find contentment. Kala bonded with her great grandmother the very first night at the party, and the two grew close as Minette told Kala all the stories that Serena had forgotten or never known.

Michael was overwhelmed with happiness to know that she was alive and safe. He and Anne welcomed Serena and Kala with open arms. Gradually Michael and Serena grew close and spoke on the phone most every day.

While Michael and Anne only had one child, Sam and Helen's brood of four remaining children had all married and produced offspring. Kala was delighted to have even more cousins and often commented on the shock of going from no family to being a member of two big families in only a six month period.

Until Kala graduated from high school, Brian and Serena maintained a long distance relationship. Their relationship moved from accidental parenthood to friendship, to courtship and finally to marriage.

At their wedding, which took place at the Waldorf, of course, the full Augustus family met the full McGuiness family for the first time. They were completely different in almost every way and yet, their common love for the bride and groom, and their daughter, ensured that the wedding reception was a roaring success.

While dancing with his sister, at her wedding, Michael saw Valerie's ghost one last time. His step faltered, Serena looked to see what had caused him to stumble.

She saw the woman from the river and asked softly, "That's my mother, isn't it?" Michael nodded. Valerie smiled and they both heard her say, "Be happy." Then she was gone.

The family legacy of lies drew to a close as the younger generation swore to tell the truth, the whole truth and nothing but the truth.

Thank you for purchasing and reading

**FAMILY MYTHS by Tamara Merrill**


Reviews are greatly appreciated. Please tell
us your opinion on AMAZON, GoodReads,

HomeTown Reads,

or wherever you communicate with others.

# A Note About The Author

Tamara Merrill is an MBA turned writer or perhaps that should be a writer turned MBA turned fiction writer. She is a left brain/right brain woman. Her skills extend from writing fiction, to writing computer programs, and to tackling almost any DIY project. Tamara admits to reading excessively (she has what she calls "a book a day habit"). Tamara published her first short story at the age of nine in the official Girl Scout magazine; AMERICAN GIRL. She has published multiple short stories in the popular women's magazines and in anthologies. In addition to reading Tamara often teaches in the adult education system and enjoys walking on the beach, crafts, painting, dining with friends, and travel. She is available for book signings and appearances at book club meetings, either through Skype or in person.

Tamara currently resides in Coronado, CA.

She would love to hear from you.

Email: Tamara@TamaraMerrill.com

Facebook: @TamaraMerrillAuthor


Her website is, www.TamaraMerrill.com where she sometimes writes a blog titled BOOK A DAY HABIT, chronicling her reading and writing adventures.

An interview with the author and book club
discussion questions are available on line at

www.TamaraMerrill.com

www.ingramcontent.com/pod-product-compliance
Lightning Source LLC
Chambersburg PA
CBHW070319140726
47910CB00015B/267